PROJECT CHANGELING

Also by Michael J. McCann

PROJECT CHANGELING

a serena keilor novel

Michael J. McCann

A Solar Salamander Book

The Plaid Raccoon Press
2021

PROJECT CHANGELING
Copyright © 2021 by Michael J. McCann

Solar Salamander © is an imprint of The Plaid Raccoon Press

ISBN: 978-1-927884-21-8 (paperback)
eBook ISBN: 978-1-927884-22-5 (e-book)

Ilustration credits: Cmst May/Unsplash (salamander); Joshua Sortino/Unsplash (geometric pattern); BUMIPUTRA/Pixabay (robot); Annabel_P/Pixabay (dome); webplastic/Pixabay and NASA/JPL-Caltech (hatch and Marscape); Mohamed Chermitia/Pixabay (Serena closeup); NASA/JPL-Caltech (Mt. Sharp); DanXaw/Pixabay (karambit); Stocksnap/Pixabay (underground corridor); Pawel Nolbert/Unsplash (dune walker).

Cover image: alexaldo/Thinkstock

Author photo: Michael J. McCann

Visit the author's website at www.mjmccann.com

For Cody, just because
I miss him so much.

The voyage of discovery lies not
in finding new landscapes,
but in having new eyes.

—Marcel Proust

Who has a daring eye
tells downright truths
and downright lies.

—John Caspar Lavater

PROLOGUE

Elysium Planitia — 6.04° N Latitude, 77.2° E Longitude

How many hours had he been walking? He had no idea.

He turned to look back at the way he'd come and saw a long, serpentine trail of dust particles still hanging in the air, disturbed by his passage, slowly falling back down to the surface of the never-ending plain. Could he not even walk in a straight line?

He sipped water and ran his tongue over his lips. The breath collection cup near his chin on the inside of his helmet still worked, taking in carbon dioxide and water vapor from his breath so that his suit's life-support system could vent the CO_2 and recycle the water, but the air entering his helmet through the valve behind his head was getting dangerously low on oxygen.

He wasn't sure how much time he had left until he asphyxiated.

They thought they were being humorous when they allowed him to put on the lifesuit before dumping him out of the shuttle and taking off, leaving him alone in the middle of the Elysian desert. The suit's battery had shown about a 40 percent charge left in it, but that had waned to 19 percent as he'd walked, and it wouldn't last much longer. The internal temperature was already dropping, and very soon he'd begin to experience symptoms of hypothermia.

They'd caught him surveilling a dead drop being used by one of their spies, a man believed to be working inside Stellarize Marté to steal corporate secrets and sell them to Earth Intelligence. He thought he'd found a perfect observation point behind a row of dumpsters in the mouth of the alley across the street from the drop. The best he could figure was that they'd spotted him from above, either with a drone or from a window in the building behind him.

He should have told his father what he was doing. He knew that now. A fatal mistake. The old man would be very, very disappointed.

His mind began to wander, and after a long while he realized he was on his knees, slowly rocking from side to side.

It was very cold. He couldn't breathe.

He thought about his girlfriend, Marissa. He loved her so much. The future with her had looked so incredibly bright.

He thought about his parents, how sad his mother would be and how guilty his father would feel for having allowed him to join the Service in the first place.

He closed his eyes and listened to music inside his head, a song he'd never particularly liked but that seemed to insist on dominating his mindspace right now.

He opened his eyes and saw dirt pressed up hard against his helmet visor.

He'd fallen forward, apparently.

He closed his eyes again.

Before long, he fell into a deep sleep from which there would be no awakening.

Elysium City — NW Quarter, 86B Street, Block 17

He watched from the shadows with his only eye, unbothered by the passage of time. He'd been here for hours, perfectly still, scanning the wicast bands, listening to faint sounds around him, watching for movement.

The only significant activity had occurred ten hours ago, when a squad had surrounded a young man hiding behind the dumpsters at the other end of the alley. After a brief scuffle, they'd pulled out their captive and marched him away, unaware that they were being observed.

He'd waited all this time for something else to happen, but nothing of significance occurred.

The colour of the dome above the rooftops began to deepen toward charcoal as darkness fell.

Communications flowed across the bands but remained routine and not related to his location.

He wondered why the young man had been hiding. The back-channel chatter of the men who'd captured him had indicated that his discovery was an unpleasant surprise, but there was no information to suggest what he'd been doing there and why they'd been so upset about it.

He filed it away for future analysis.

A tricycle turned into the alley, ridden by an old man in a soiled white dhoti and a sleeveless undershirt. The basket on the back of the trike was filled with odds and ends the man had picked from the trash. His long white ponytail swished across his back as he slowly pedalled up the alley and out the other end.

An hour later, with nothing else happening, he left his

observation post and followed the shadows back to his warehouse.

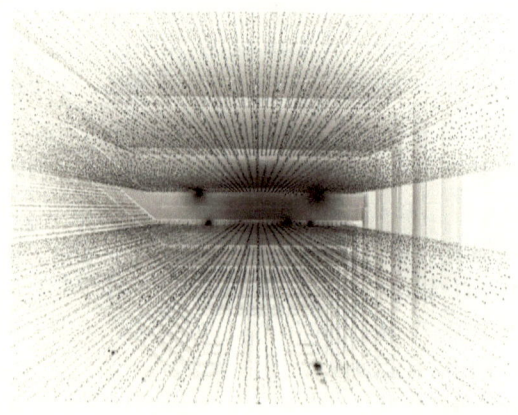

1

Serena Keilor quietly let herself out of Bruno's living unit and sealed the door behind her. He would sleep for at least another hour before awakening to find her gone. After that, he'd head off to work and forget about her until the next time he told himself he needed her.

She walked down the corridor past other doors, her flat-soled shoes silent on the filthy tile floor. The smells and sounds of claustrophobic human living filled her nose and ears. Stale perspiration, rotting garbage, cooked food, and jackweed smoke. Loud voices from a vid program. A baby crying behind a door marked with colourful graffiti.

She reached the stairs and headed down. Bruno's living unit was on the fourth level. Six floors was the limit for housing structures in Elysium City, and she was just as glad he didn't rate a unit at the top. The sex wasn't good enough to justify walking up and down the two extra flights to get it.

At ground level she let herself out onto the street and glanced both ways before turning left. Above her, the pale light of another Martian dawn filtered through the dome. In this part of the southeast quarter, most of the streetlights were out, broken by vandals and never repaired. She kept to the shadows, moving confidently along the street in a northerly direction.

Giant air vents rumbled overhead, out of sight above the buildings. It was a sound she no longer heard. Her ears were tuned instead to the skittering of vermin foraging in the garbage, distant voices rising and falling, and footsteps that scraped and faded away.

After twenty minutes she reached a neighbourhood that was less residential and more retail. The buildings were two storeys, three at the most, and included storefronts for food, clothing, entertainment, and various services.

An empty public rick sat outside a gambling café. She touched her ring to its lock and the door opened. It was a two-seater, front and back, a little more expensive to use than a singleton, but she got in anyway and sealed the door.

"Gateway Station."

"Sixteen credits, please," the rick said.

She touched her ring to the payment reader. The engine started, and the rick pulled away from the curb.

At this time of the day, traffic was still light so she made it to the station in only a few minutes. She followed a small group of people through the front entrance. On her left was a ramp that led up to departures, and on her right was another that led down to arrivals. She took the narrow passage between them and walked into the food court. About a third of the tables were occupied. Seeing nothing suspicious, she headed toward a row of washrooms along the far side.

She picked a door and walked in. A woman stood at a wash basin, considering her reflection in the mirror. Two stalls were occupied, and the others appeared to be empty. She stood still for a count of ten and then abruptly turned and pushed back out into the food court.

No one was nearby. No one appeared startled by her sudden reappearance or quickly turned around or looked the other way.

Somewhat reassured, she walked through the food court and out the other side of the building.

Gateway Station was like a large blister on the dome wall where the southwest and northwest quarters met. Shuttles flew every hour to and from the other domed cities on the planet, and a special line operated between Elysium, the capital city, and Marsport, the original settlement that now served as the spaceport for interplanetary traffic.

Gateway Station was a fairly busy place at any time of the day or night, and it was useful when trying to lose surveillance. Outside, on the north side of the station, Serena leaned against the wall, watching people come and go. As she stood there, a tram arrived from the inner city. It stopped, hissed, and released a flood of passengers from its many doors.

She waited until the flood had passed and a second wave had entered the tram for its return run into the central core. She watched it slowly pull away from the station. Then she took the overhead walkway to the north side of the tracks.

If she had a tail, they were damned good about it.

She trekked through the northwest quarter, following a long and indirect route until she stood outside a two-storey building with a sign over the front entrance:

PV Root Production Inc.

Everything looked normal. She walked around to the back of the building and used her ring to gain access through a door marked for the use of employees only.

She followed a short hallway down to a set of plastic-

and-metal double doors. She slipped through them into a large space configured for factory work.

PV Root Production was a grow op for edible roots, some original to Earth and others genetically engineered to flourish under Martian gravitational conditions. They were one of many second-wave businesses licensed by Ares Inc., one of the five corporations controlling everything that happened on Mars, to act as local producers in the domed cities. Ares had decided it would be an effective business strategy to spread out the wealth a little to small-fry entrepreneurs covering specific sub-sectors like edible roots, rice, fruit, or other such food commodities. It reduced transportation costs from Isidium City, where Ares was headquartered, and it established a decentralized network of subsidiaries under innocuous neighbourhood banners.

Despite what the socialists said, The Five were continually working around the edges of their public image to maintain an appearance of benign paternalism.

She walked down long rows of raised beds containing plants in various stages of growth. Random insects circulated, intent on their pollination responsibilities. She reached a central area with glassed-in offices and stopped.

An old man in one of the offices looked up from his desk and saw her standing there. He removed his spectacles, stood up, and shuffled out to meet her.

He was short and stooped. His long white hair was tied back with a colourful bandanna. His coveralls were stained and tattered, but his hands and sandals were immaculate. He walked with a limp, favouring feet that were cursed with nasty bunions and corns.

"Serena," he said, his nasal Isidian accent heavy and

familiar, "how nice to see you again."

2

Peter Visquel led the way around the offices and down another long row of raised beds to a set of crash doors at the back. He leaned his shoulder against one of the doors, smiled at Serena, and preceded her into the washing room.

Robots loaded fully grown roots from the washing tubs into large carts, supervised by a small boy whose name Serena didn't know. The produce would be taken into the drying room next door and then on to yet another room for packing and shipment.

A young female stuck her head through a door at the back, saw who was in the room, and disappeared again.

Peter sat down on a bench next to a washing tub that was in the middle of a load. Serena sat down next to him. Cleaning gel hissed from rows of nozzles, creating a white noise that would mask their conversation from the listening devices that were inevitable in most buildings in the domed city.

"Thank you for coming. I hope you're well." His eyes followed the kid herding the robots as they pushed their heavy carts into the drying room.

It had been two weeks since she'd last been here.

Nominally she was an employee of Peter's company and drew a salary from him, but in fact it had been four years since she'd moved out of her tiny room upstairs to work various detached assignments, as Peter liked to call them.

"Beginning tomorrow morning," he said, "you'll start a new job. You've been staffed as an administrative assistant in the artificial human project at Stellarize Marté. A new unit has been created with oversight functions, and your assignment will be to surveil the unit manager, Gabriel Morales. We believe he's a spy passing information to Earth Intelligence."

Serena raised an eyebrow. Another of the five corporations that ruled Mars with an iron fist, Stellarize Marté built and ran the shuttlecraft and interplanetary spaceships that kept Mars connected to the rest of the solar system. They also ran the dirtside tram lines in each city. They were a very powerful and highly secure organization. Working undercover inside their research and development campus would be problematic, at best.

Reading her mind, Peter nodded. "Do what you can. We can't get electronics in there, so human eyes and ears will have to do. Your eyes and ears, my dear."

"All right."

Serena had come from the domed city of Hephesto to live with Peter when she was approximately eight, a crèche kid with no parents and no future. For ten years she'd worked for Peter, doing odd jobs at first before moving up to quality control checks on the vegetables and supervising the robots like the kid in the next room. She'd also been forced to sit impatiently through Peter's classroom sessions. She'd loved the math but hated the language lessons. Nevertheless, she now spoke six and could read and write in several computer languages as well. Not to mention sign language, semaphore, Morse code, and other less obvious forms of communication.

Peter was a believer in redundancy. Having alternate channels of functionality available in case of interference or systems failure helped him sleep better at night.

On what they'd decided was her eighteenth birthday, Peter handed her a ring that would open the door of a living unit in the southwest quarter. He told her that she now worked for MIS, the Martian Intelligence Service. Her training (is that what it had been?) would enable her to work as an undercover operative. Peter would be her handler.

The assignments had been simple to start with, but over the last four years they'd become progressively more challenging.

"What's my cover?" she asked, folding her hands in her lap.

"You'll use your current name and address. It works, so we'll stay with it."

"Is there a team?"

"As far as you're concerned, you're on your own. We believe Gabriel Morales has been working for Earth Intelligence for some time now. We think he's been put in place to steal data from the interstellar spacecraft and artificial human projects. We think he may be about to make a major delivery before being removed to Earth. His last big score. Stellarize Marté is vulnerable, and we need to stop him now, before it's too late."

"All right."

Peter fingered a pendant that hung around his neck. Strung on a length of twine, it was a cabochon stone cut from blue lace agate. It was one of his few personal possessions, and during the time that Serena had lived here, the kids speculated that Peter's late wife had given it to him before her death. No one knew for certain.

"Because it's Stellarize Marté," Peter said, "you'll be thoroughly scanned entering and leaving. Since no electronic devices are allowed into the workplace, you yourself will be our recording apparatus. Memorize everything you see and hear, and report to me on a regular basis once you're clear of their surveillance."

Serena nodded. She had an excellent memory and had handled similar tasks for him in the past.

She watched the boy come back in from the drying room, followed by two of the robots. He was tiny and thin, as Serena had been at that age, and his hair was as red as hers.

Peter's eyes followed him across the room. "Pablo has been doing well in training, and he's ready for some simple assignments. We'll start with the laundromat you once asked me about. Do you remember?"

"Yes. I wondered why it was always closed, even though the blinds were sometimes open. You told me it was a call stack. You were laughing when you said it."

"I was, yes."

"It took me a while to understand what you meant. An information drop."

Peter nodded. "Pablo will set the signal and service it: a piece of green plastic in the doorway at the back of the building when the drop is clean and ready. Leave the ring in an empty food container next to the dumpster, and move the green plastic to the corner of the building to tell him that it's ready to be picked up."

"All right."

Peter tucked the pendant back inside the bib of his coveralls. "This will be our last face-to-face for the

---

foreseeable future. Understood?"

"Yes."

"Take no unnecessary chances, Serena. I've grown much too fond of you to lose you now."

She stood up. "You say that to all the kids."

"Just the best ones," he replied.

3

Serena worked her way east from the grow op and caught a tram running inward toward the central core. The car was half full. She stood close to the door between two empty seats, holding on to the overhead strap. An old man sitting with a two-wheeled grocery cart in front of him glanced at her with tired eyes and looked away again. His cart was filled with stuff he'd gleaned from garbage dumpsters and unattended packing cartons lining the back alleys of the poorer neighbourhoods.

This was how the unemployable lived, scrounging leftover food to eat and stolen goods to sell in order to be able to stay off the streets and out of jail. She'd done it herself on more than one occasion while working assignments for Peter.

The old man was one of the people the socialists were beginning to talk about as they prodded at The Five for sacrificing the needs of the many for the comfort of the few. Dissenting voices in the face of the argument that The Five had collectively built an independent and self-reliant world from dust and rock, pulling a nascent colony up by its bootstraps—

The old man stood up abruptly and got off at a stop in

a neighbourhood dominated by night clubs and massage parlors. An old rubber shoe fell from his cart into the track of the sliding door. A man disembarking behind him kicked it down into the darkness beneath the tram.

Serena sat through three more stops before getting off not far from the central core. She walked two blocks to a Goosens. Inside, she picked up a basket and eased into the garments section, not feeling particularly comfortable. She passed a mirror at the end of a row of jumpsuits and reluctantly looked at herself.

She thought she was twenty-two now, but she wasn't sure. She was small, and her straight red hair, carelessly chopped, was thin and dry. She hated it, just as she hated her freckles and her pouchy mouth and her large teeth and her dark brown eyes.

Dirt eater.

She sighed at her synthetic stretch-knit bodysuit, black with grey diagonal stripes, and forced herself to accept the fact that she needed to shop for clothing that would be appropriate for office wear. Although she'd never gone undercover in one before, she'd been in offices many times and had observed the women who worked there. She knew the look, and although she disliked the look, it would have to become *her* look for the foreseeable future.

Mooching along the aisles, she picked out two pairs of cigarette pants, one white and the other green. While looking for a blouse she found two long-sleeved funnel neck tops, one in a sort of spotted print and the other in white, and a few long-sleeved T-shirts in a variety of pastel colours. She rolled them up one at a time and dropped them into her basket.

While browsing she passed several people similarly busy, flipping through the racks. Most ignored her, but a few spared a cross look, as though she were giving off an unpleasant odour (she wasn't).

A middle-aged woman in an army surplus tunic began to follow her from row to row, baring her teeth as she worked up the courage to curse at her. Eventually Serena grew tired of it and stopped. She turned around and narrowed her eyes.

"Piss off or I'll break your thumbs."

"Filthy little dirt eater."

Serena took a step toward her. The woman gasped and disappeared between the underwear racks.

It was the red hair, of course, and the freckles, and the pale skin. She had no control over the fact that she looked as though she'd been bred specifically for the planet and raised on a straight diet of red Martian soil. But since 11 percent of the kids who came out of the crèches resembled her (she'd looked it up once), it was apparent that the genetic engineers behind the scenes didn't give a damn one way or the other how kids like her were treated once they were turned loose to fend for themselves. Or did they? Was it some kind of bizarre social experiment?

Sighing, she decided to look at footwear. At the moment she was wearing her flat-soled synthetic dancing shoes, durable and very flexible for occasions when she might need to be light on her feet, but she understood they would not be appropriate on the research and development campus of Stellarize Marté. After ten minutes of unhappy browsing, she settled on two pairs of low-cut slip-ons, one white and the other brown, in a brand she'd seen advertised for healthcare workers.

On the way out, she picked up a nondescript black backpack in which to carry her purchases. Touching her ring to a payment reader, she left the store. She slung the stuffed backpack over her shoulder and walked to the nearest tram stop.

The streets were now busy with traffic. She wove through a steady stream of pedestrians along the edgeway, dodging tricycles, ricks, and cargo wagons as she crossed each intersection. Overhead, a giant holographic image of a young man smiled at her, offering an open package of a popular brand of jackweed.

At the nearest stop, a tram was already there, taking on passengers. She slipped aboard just before the doors closed.

Hanging onto a strap as the tram picked up speed, she looked out the windows at the towers of the central core up ahead. Twelve floors was the limit for most buildings within the core, as opposed to six floors elsewhere in the dome, and they did indeed seem to dominate the cityscape. Serena had travelled to the core a few times on assignments, but she disliked having to pass through the security perimeter that separated it from the rest of Elysium.

It was said that most of the buildings in the central core had their own environmental control systems that would seal the structure and provide air and heat in the rather unlikely event that the dome suffered some kind of breach. She'd never had the occasion to check the rumour out, but she knew that residential buildings in her quarter had no such safety feature. If the unthinkable happened, everyone in her neighbourhood would die in short order. Why waste capital and equipment on the slums when the lower class was replaceable at very little cost?

Not a pleasant subject. Although the socialists never seemed to tire of shouting about it.

She got off the tram near the perimeter and walked to a restaurant called Antony's. It was a fashionable place to eat because it was close to the embassy of Titan, and its menu featured notable Titanian dishes. She slipped into the alley alongside it and went in through the back. A line cook peered at her through a dense cloud of steam and nodded.

Bruno was at his station, chopping vegetables that likely had been grown in Peter Visquel's op. He glanced up at her and kept chopping, the knife flashing as it reflected light from the overhead fixtures.

"I've got a new job," Serena said.

"That's good." Chop chop chop chop chop.

"I won't be around."

"Okay." He scraped the chopped pieces of vegetable into a big pan of oil and put it on the burner, then grabbed more vegetables and resumed chopping.

"Maybe I'll see you again some time."

He said nothing, concentrating on his knife work.

She left the restaurant, knowing he was already thinking about other females he liked to spend time with and wondering which one he should call next.

It had been that kind of relationship.

She didn't really care that much about it, one way or the other.

It was time for her to go home and get some rest.

Big day tomorrow.

4

Constance Davis stood at the large window in the audience room of her eighth-floor penthouse suite, watching the taillights of a distant shuttle outside the dome as it left Gateway Station on its way to Marsport. Night had fallen, and the lights of the southern quarters of the city flickered below her in the warm currents of air that circulated around the central core.

Constance was upset. The message she'd sent to Hercule St.-Giorge Mercade, diplomatic attaché for labour and immigration and son of the Earth ambassador, had been very clear. She desired his presence; she missed him; she wished that he would leave off whatever it was that he was doing right now and attend her.

Hercule had declined to reply.

She sighed, studying her reflection in the window. She was quite beautiful. Tall, slender, immaculate. Her long, straight blond hair covered her shoulders and reached almost to the small of her back. Her white gown, imported from Earth, cost more than a worker in one of her family's mines earned in five years. Her rings, necklace, and bracelets were crafted by the finest jeweler on Mars and bore millions of credits' worth of precious stones taken from the ground by Davis Minerals, Inc., another member in good standing of The Five. She was, without a doubt, the most eligible single female on the planet.

And yet Hercule preferred to play hard to get.

He was an impossible man to understand.

Wishing for a glass of wine, she lingered in the audience room on the off chance that he might arrive at her tower suite and be shown into her presence. She heard the sound of quiet feet behind her and turned, smiling.

It was Emerald Argent, her personal assistant. With a carte de visite in her hand.

Is it Signor Mercade? Constance signed.

Emerald shook her head. She curtseyed and handed Constance the card.

It was that annoying woman, Janeese Wensley.

Very well, Constance signed. *Show her in.*

May I stay? Emerald asked, her fingers flashing. *I'd like to work on the jacket.*

Constance hesitated. Her business with Wensley was secret, but Emerald was hardly a security threat. At the age of sixteen, her eardrums had been pierced and her tongue removed when it was time for her to take her place as Constance's personal aide, and as a result she could neither hear what she had no business hearing nor speak about it out of turn.

In addition to being Constance's assistant, Emerald was also a skilled linen weaver, a rare and valuable commodity on Mars, and she was in the process of making a jacket for Constance. The loom was kept in this room because Constance spent much of her time here, and she liked to watch Emerald work. She found it calming.

Yes, you may stay. Now bring in that wretched woman.

Emerald curtseyed again and left the room to fetch Constance's visitor.

"I trust you're well today, Councillor." Janeese Wensley sketched a quick curtsey and sat in the chair indicated by Labossière, Constance's personal security chief, who had escorted her into the room after the usual scan and search for weapons or other uncouth accouterments.

Constance nodded Labossière away and settled down on her preferred seat when receiving visitors in her private suite, a settee with room enough for two (should Hercule ever decide to visit).

Wensley glanced uneasily at Emerald, who was fussing around her loom. "I'd prefer a more secure setting for our conversation, Councillor. Perhaps your office downstairs?"

"Don't worry yourself. The entire building's covered by a highly expensive anti-surveillance system, and Emerald's completely harmless. What message do you bring me?"

Wensley shook her head in a small betrayal of impatience that Constance did not miss. She was a frumpy, unimpressive woman with mouse-coloured, shoulder-length hair and plain features lined by middle age. Her dark pantsuit was not cheap but was clearly off the rack, as was her personality. A typical public servant.

"Your request has been discussed," she said, "and a decision has been made."

Constance waited. Oh, how The Unimportant loved to play their little games.

"Your terms have been found to be acceptable," Wensley finally said, "and permission has been granted for you to participate in upcoming, ah, events."

"How lovely." Constance feigned indifference, but inside she felt a surge of triumph. Finally! Leverage to bargain her way off this hated ball of dung.

"Your position as a member of the Council of Five places you in the public eye," Wensley said, "and discretion is essential."

Constance frowned. "No need to lecture."

"No, of course not." Wensley slipped a ring from her finger and handed it over. "Your first task, by way of a dry run, so to speak, will be to pass this on to your designated contact. If the hand-off goes well, we'll talk about what comes next."

Constance rolled the ring around in the palm of her hand. "What's on it?"

"Never ask that question. Simply carry out the assignment."

It was chafing to take orders from a social inferior, but she had no choice if she was going to use this woman to get what she wanted. As director of Natural Resources Development for the elected government of Mars, Wensley had a small measure of importance in smoothing out administrative details related to the business of Davis Minerals, and the woman had always more or less minded her place as a relatively small cog in a rather large machine.

What made her much more important to Constance, however, had been revealed after a series of one-on-one meetings several months ago to discuss the corporation's upcoming Tharsis project, which required a number of government rubber stamps. Her colleagues on the corporate Council of Five had already indicated that their approval would be granted, but appearances were important and, as always, Wensley played the game as she was supposed to play it.

During a final meeting to sign paperwork, Constance

let slip that she felt less than happy about the direction
Martian politics seemed to be taking, the slowness with
which the atmosphere was converting to Earth standards,
the dreariness of the domes, and the obvious superiority of
life on the third planet as opposed to the fourth.

Wensley's polite responses gradually morphed into direct questions, and Constance's honest answers ultimately
led Wensley to intimate that she was not only a senior
manager in the Martian government, but also possessed
important connections to a certain Earth organization
that looked out for the home planet's interests in the solar
system. As such, she'd already spoken to Constance's
friend, Hercule St.-Giorge Mercade, and Hercule had
confirmed Constance's restlessness and desire for change.

Was she interested in immigrating to the motherworld?

Thereafter, their meetings had taken on an added
dimension as Constance was gradually read in on an
important Earth Intelligence operation in which she could
play a role. In return, the powers that be would take into
account her fervent desire to relocate.

And so, here she was, with a data ring in her hand
containing god-knew-what—classified information of vital
importance to The Five, no doubt, and of particular interest
to Earth. Possibly key information that could determine
the future of Mars, electronically recorded in an innocuous
piece of jewelry.

Clack tack tack hishh tack. Emerald's loom kept up its
steady pace.

Clack tack tack hishh tack.

Clack tack tack hishh tack.

Constance glanced over. The girl's eyes were on her
work.

"Your designated contact," Wensley said, "is Hercule, of course."

Her heart leapt. "Of course."

Wensley left her to her thoughts.

Rolling the ring around and around in her palm, Constance listened to the sound of Emerald's loom and tried to quell the frantic hammering of her pulse.

Clack tack tack hishh tack.

Clack tack tack hishh tack.

Emerald raised her eyes briefly.

Constance saw nothing in them.

5

The next morning, Serena crossed a large open courtyard and passed through sliding glass doors into a lobby filled with people.

It was the early rush hour on the campus of Stellarize Marté's artificial human project, and six lines of employees waited with bovine patience beneath a giant holographic portrait of Leonidas Fell, the CEO of the corporation, for their turn to pass through the first round of scans and searches.

On her right, a small group milled about in an area marked for visitors, so she headed over there. A pair of security guards wanded her, searched her backpack, and ran a bioscan that identified her as a new employee whose arrival was expected. As a machine spat out an ID card for her, another guard motioned her through the turnstile and gave her a stern look.

"Wear your ID at all times. Speak only when spoken to; it'll make things simpler. Stand over there with the others. You'll be taken in groups. You're in group three. Stay with your guide. Move."

Serena took her new identification card, which was clipped to a lanyard, and shuffled off to join the others.

A good-looking young man glanced at her hair and said, "What group?"

"Three." Serena slipped the lanyard around her neck.

Looking relieved, he nodded and edged away.

"All right, all right, where's group one?" A woman in a navy business suit waved her arm in the air. "Group one: with me. If you're left behind or you get lost you'll be fired, so pay attention. Come with me."

Five or six people separated from the others and followed the woman to the escalators. A young man suddenly materialized and brayed for group two, leading them away in another direction.

There were three people left, including Serena. The other two were young males who looked like twins. Serena watched them wander around the displays of current and past Stellarize Marté technology, chatting and pointing. Employees continued to flow through the security checkpoint to the various escalators. An alarm went off, and someone was taken aside for an extensive search. Few people paid attention to the incident as they waited for their turn to enter.

After a long wait, a disinterested-looking woman showed up and gestured for Serena and the twins to follow her. They descended one floor on an escalator and walked down a long corridor. The woman stopped in front of a door and frowned at the twins.

"This is your unit location. Your ID cards will open the door. Any attempt to open any other door will result in your immediate dismissal. Choose a locker inside and key it with your card. Follow the instructions printed on the inside of the locker door. Any deviation from them will result in immediate dismissal. Go."

One of the twins tentatively held his card in front of the

reader. The door opened. He walked through. Before his brother could follow, the woman grabbed his arm.

"No tailgating. Wait for it to close."

The young man obeyed, and when the door closed, he carded the reader and followed his twin inside.

Without glancing at Serena, the woman strode away, arms close to her sides, head down. Serena hesitated, then followed. They reached another door, where the woman abruptly stopped. "This is you. Follow instructions."

Serena held her card to the reader and the door opened. She looked behind her, but the woman was already heading back up the corridor toward the escalator.

Inside she found herself in an empty locker room. She walked between rows and stopped in front of an open locker. It was a meter and a half tall, forty centimeters wide, and thirty centimeters deep. She held her card up to the reader on the front of the locker door and it blipped at her. Posted on the inside of the door was a set of rules that instructed her to leave all personal items in the locker, including jewelry, before attempting to pass through to the next area.

Shrugging, she hung up her backpack, removed her various rings and bracelets, and closed the locker. She tried to open it again, but it was locked. She held her card up to the reader and it blipped. The door opened. She closed it again, satisfied.

She followed glowing green arrows on the floor to a sliding glass door, on the other side of which was an automatic scanner that she passed through without incident. She followed a corridor down to another door. A sign above the door read:

Oversight Unit 64.

The office inside was filled with workstations set up with computer terminals. Only two, however, were occupied. A young man stared at his display screen, scratching his chin, while at the other workstation, an older man with a bald head and odd-looking chin whiskers appeared to be dozing. She wandered up to the front of the office.

The entire wall was made of glass. On the other side, down below on a lower level, was an impressive expanse of workstations, benches, machinery, parts racks, and worktables covered with prototype artificial human units in various stages of disassembly. Large screens on the walls displayed charts and graphs, tables of data, and magnified images of irises and retinas.

A voice beside her grumbled, "Who the hell are you?"

Serena turned. A man had emerged from a private office on the right. He was only a centimeter or two taller than she was, but more than forty kilograms heavier. His black, wavy hair was shot through with grey. His face was fleshy and wrinkled, and his eyes were bloodshot. He wore a green short-sleeved shirt open at the neck, khaki trousers, and old-fashioned black lace-up shoes.

She looked at his ID card and said, "Mr. Morales, I'm Serena Keilor. The new administrative assistant."

Gabriel Morales was already walking away from her. She watched him leave through the door she'd just entered.

Her eyes turned back to the shop floor below. A woman in a white lab coat bent over a torso, working with wires protruding from the neck stump. A man sitting on a stool at another bench peered through a large magnifying glass on a movable arm, tinkering with something held in a padded vise. Another man walked up behind him and looked over his shoulder, then sat down on a stool in front of another magnifying glass and vise.

Serena moved away from the window. Neither of her new coworkers bothered to look at her. She wandered over to a workstation and sat down. She tapped on the keyboard in front of her, activating the monitor. She looked at a login screen that asked for a password she didn't have.

Sighing, she leaned back in her chair and waited for someone to tell her what to do.

6

"Pay attention to everything I say."

A middle-aged woman in a white lab coat led the way down the corridor to a door at the end marked:

OES 6579U.

According to her identification card, her name was Dr. Ingrid Yan, but she didn't introduce herself or ask Serena for her name. It was all very impersonal and disinterested. Gabriel had apparently asked the manager downstairs to send someone up to give Serena an orientation tour, and that was what Dr. Yan was doing, whether she wanted to or not.

"This is the optical engineering section." They passed through door OES 6579U and walked out onto a broad platform that clung to the wall above the shop floor. Dr. Yan put a hand on the railing and indicated the view.

"The mandate of your unit is to oversee our work. Your people review our design specs, examine our prototypes, and study our test results. There have been problems, and unfortunately we're a little behind schedule. Gabriel is expected to study the situation and report on it. Senior management evidently doesn't like to take our word for what's happening."

Serena watched the activity below for a moment. "What are they doing? What are you making?"

Dr. Yan gave her a look. "Eyes, of course. Eyes for the artificial human prototype. Why else do you think we're all here?"

Serena smiled apologetically. "I'm sorry, I don't know very much about all this. It looks interesting, though."

"It's fascinating." Dr. Yan made an attempt to soften her tone. "The project of a lifetime."

"The robots are for the spaceship going to the stars?"

"Not robots," Dr. Yan corrected. "Artificial humans. Robots are metal boxes with arms and legs or wheels or whatever, with very basic programming and no ability to adapt to changes in their environment. These," she waved a hand in the air, "are the most human-like machines ever conceived. When we're done, they'll look enough like people to be mistaken for the real thing. Their sensory input clusters will look like ours and will function like ours, but with infinitely more sensitivity and power. Better hearing, better sense of smell and taste, and, yes, much better eyesight."

"What do you do here, Dr. Yan?"

"I'm an optical engineer. I have six different university degrees, including two doctorates. My specific tasks would take too long to explain and involve terminology I'm afraid you wouldn't understand."

"Oh."

Dr. Yan led her to a glassed-in elevator, which they rode down to the shop floor. "Look around, but don't touch anything or they'll not only fire you, they'll throw you in jail and launch the key into orbit."

"Can I ask you a question, Dr. Yan?"

"You *may*."

"Why are we building robots—sorry, artificial humans—to go into space to find the aliens instead of going out there ourselves?"

"Because our interstellar drive, the drive we're designing to power the Stellarize Marté spacecraft that will be sent out, will travel at a velocity so close to the speed of light that humans might not survive the ordeal. Plus, it would still take so long the ship would have to be multigenerational, and the corporation decided not to go with that approach."

"Are there really aliens out there?"

Dr. Yan sighed, leaning against the railing. "So we've been led to believe." She folded her arms, hugging herself. "I've read the articles published on the subject, most of them highly technical. The signals are like nothing we've ever detected before. The star is a K type, which is almost ideal. It has several earth-like planets, and we think the source, rather than the star itself, may be the fourth one, which is at an optimal distance from its sun to support intelligent life as we currently understand it."

Serena said nothing. She had a basic familiarity with the situation, having watched several vid programs on the subject, but preferred to play dumb and have Dr. Yan explain it to her.

"The signals themselves," the woman continued, "are what we call fast radio bursts, or FRBs. They only last a few milliseconds, they repeat at regular intervals, and they're all coming from the same place. We have to get out there and find out who or what is sending them."

"When? When will the ship go?"

Dr. Yan pushed away from the railing. "That's the million-credit question, child. Not soon enough, as far as

I'm concerned. That's why I'm here. I want to send a piece of myself, the product of my intellect, out there to find out who these beings are and what they can do for us.

"However," she sighed again, "the entire design concept has been changed by the powers that be, for reasons that elude me, and we're now behind schedule, so I can't tell you when our mechanical substitutes will begin their incredible voyage of discovery, but it *must* be soon. Before Earth gets there ahead of us and slams the door in our faces."

They reached the last in the row of workstations and stood before a set of sliding glass doors. Dr. Yan smiled. She seemed to have warmed to Serena after her initial aloofness, despite the imposition being made on her valuable time. As far as Serena could tell, it didn't seem to bother Dr. Yan that the young woman in front of her was a dirt eater, a social bottom feeder, an unfortunate product of the working class. After a few minutes with her, the engineer had spoken kindly and in a manner that presumed Serena had at least enough intelligence to understand words of more than one syllable.

"Follow me." Dr. Yan led the way through the sliding doors. "I'll show you where the cafeteria and washrooms are."

7

The flight from Elysium City to Gale took a little more than two hours, but Constance Davis's private shuttle was a new Gondola-class model, and therefore the long trip was almost made bearable by the fact that *Diamond Girl*, as Constance had christened her, was outfitted with all the latest luxuries.

The seats, which could accommodate twelve passengers comfortably, were upholstered in real leather. The galley was stocked with the best food, wine, and liquor, all imported from Earth at considerable expense. The latest entertainment danced and sang in a holographic display angled into the aisle so that it would be comfortable for her to watch. A crew of four, including pilot, co-pilot, and two attendants, took care of everything for her.

Constance sipped wine and quietly suffered in her boredom and impatience.

Labossière left his seat and walked through the holo on his way aft to the washroom. Small and irritating, he was a contract hire who'd been with her since her twenty-fourth birthday. He was a gift she'd given herself after a party she'd sneaked into in the southeast quarter turned rough and she'd barely escaped with her life. After such a near miss, she'd vowed never again to be without personal protection.

Labossière employed three subordinates who were assigned to various aspects of her security needs. One of his charges, who handled basic bodyguard duties, was with them on the flight. She could see him several seats forward, eating a piece of fruit. She had no idea what his name was, where he came from, or whether he possessed even a basic level of sentience. His orders were never to speak to Constance unless spoken to first, and Constance had never encountered an instance where she needed to speak to him—or to any of them, for that matter. Everything went through Labossière. That was the way she wanted it.

She didn't believe it was necessary to have the extra man along on this trip, since she was only going home to meet with her father. The domed city of Gale, located within the crater of the same name, contained the corporate headquarters of Davis Minerals, which was entirely controlled by her family. The Davis stronghold itself was separate from the city, an elaborate complex perched on the summit of Aeolis Mons, a.k.a. Mount Sharp. Built by her grandfather, Parrish Garrison Davis, the original CEO, it was a fortress that was safe from all conceivable threats.

Labossière, however, thought it necessary to bring along What's-His-Name as a backup. She didn't bother to argue, since it didn't cost her more to have his muscular ass parked in a seat aboard *Diamond Girl* than it would to leave him back in Elysium paring his nails and watching vid. Just the same, she hoped that once they landed there would be less eating and more attention paid to the performance of his job, whatever Labossière might decide that should involve.

When they finally landed at Gale Station, they transferred to a small shuttlecraft that flew them to the private hangar at the entrance of Davis Estate. After passing through security, Constance and Labossière rode the elevator upstairs while Labossière's employee remained behind to settle in with the checkpoint staff.

Constance found her father in his library, where he spent most of his time. Leaving Labossière in a comfortable armchair in the hallway, she closed the doors behind her and crossed to where he sat beneath a reading lamp, glasses perched on his nose, a thick hardcover book in his hands.

"Father," she said, bending down to kiss the top of his head. "Reading, as usual."

Alexander Charles Davis marked his place in the book with his finger and smiled up at her over his glasses. "Constance. They told me you were coming. What's the occasion?"

"I need a special reason to come home to see my own father?"

He said nothing, the smile easing into thin-lipped apprehension.

She pulled over a chair and sat down. "Council will vote in two days on Wong's application to activate his new converter. He wants to do away with the step-by-step approval process and have us give him carte blanche to deploy everything as it becomes available, without going through all the testing and analysis and reporting each time."

"Do you have a problem with this?"

"Not really. He knows what he's doing."

"Pittman is an excellent general manager. I'm still annoyed that Magee stole him out from under us."

Constance shrugged. Remus Pittman had been a key

member of senior management within Davis Minerals until Magee Wong had hired him several years ago to run Terraform, Incorporated, The Five's joint venture in charge of atmospheric conversion. Constance was indifferent to the relative worth of such people unless they had a direct impact on her own personal affairs, and Pittman had never fallen into that category.

"As far as I'm concerned," she said, "Wong can have our vote if he guarantees to support Tharsis. I don't want anything to stand in our way on that one."

Davis Minerals was gearing up for a major new exploration project in the Tharsis region, a large plateau close to the equator that featured some of the largest known volcanoes in the solar system. Preliminary excursions had revealed the presence of titanium, platinum, and chromium deposits in the network of grabens around Alba Mons, in the northern part of the region. It was a significant discovery. Although the site was more than four thousand kilometers west of Gale, the current limited supply of these extremely important metals made the project essential to the ongoing sustainability of the Martian economy.

Council had given its approval for an upcoming assessment that would hopefully verify the extent of the discovery, but full-scale exploitation of the site would require another vote, after all the reports had been filed by Davis. It was a check-and-balance system agreed upon by the previous generation of CEOs, and it still formed the backbone of their system of control.

The overriding principle driving every decision made by the Council of Five was the policy of autarky, planetary self-sufficiency and non-reliance on importations from Earth. For it to succeed, interdependence and co-operation were essential.

Davis Minerals supplied raw materials to Fabricon Inc., whose factories in Nepenthe City manufactured the building materials, tools, equipment, and finished goods that were sold in all five cities. Fabricon's best corporate customer was Atlas of Hephesto, who built the domes and the buildings, streets, and sewers within them. Atlas also handled all waste disposal and recycling, and most of this material was sold back to Fabricon for reuse.

Ares Inc., the richest and most powerful of The Five, processed the water ice mined by Davis and distributed it, along with the food they grew and baked and slaughtered, to the entire population of the planet. Also falling under Magee Wong's umbrella was Terraform, the aforementioned joint venture in charge of transforming the Martian atmosphere, and MHC, the Mars Health Corporation, among other concerns.

And the four relied on Stellarize Marté, the fifth corporation, for the timely and reliable movement of all these things and people. It was schoolgirl stuff, and she not only understood it but manipulated it whenever she could to the advantage of Davis Minerals, but it was boring and predictable, and she was tired of it.

"They'll contact you for your opinion," Constance said. "As they usually do, behind my back. I know how it works; I'm not an idiot, you know."

"Of course you're not."

"You'll tell them we're still discussing our options. When Wong calls, you'll make it clear that he's expected to pledge his undying love for Tharsis in return."

Alexander nodded, looking down at his book. Old-fashioned paper books were rare on Mars, and the collection in his library was worth a small fortune. The one in his lap was *Great Expectations*, by an Industrial Age Earth author named Charles Dickens. The story of a young poor boy with delusions of being able to join high society after coming into money. It was a struggle that would likely be lost on his deluded little rich girl Constance.

He'd always been bookish and scholarly, to the everlasting embarrassment of his father. Parrish Garrison Davis had emigrated from Earth as a young boy with his parents. They'd run a trading post near a large mining operation that quickly failed, sending them underground for the rest of their short lives as low-paid miners.

Parrish had joined them in the tunnels as soon as he was old enough to operate the equipment, but he possessed a keen sense of commerce and the ruthlessness to manipulate other people to his own advantage. As a result, he quietly raised a stake and, immediately after the death of his parents, filed his own claim on a site just south of the Gale crater. Not very many kilometers, in fact, from where Alexander and Constance now sat. Parrish had never looked back, building a business that soon monopolized all mineral extraction and refining on the planet.

When Parrish died, Alexander was his only heir. He assumed control of the company with great reluctance, knowing he wasn't suited for it. His lack of enthusiasm was compounded by the knowledge of the manner in which his father had died. It was something he was forced to relive each time Constance condescended to visit her childhood home. Something he would much rather not think about.

Something that made it quite easy to allow her to run everything her own way.

She stood up and patted the knot of hair at the nape of her neck. "You're not going to cause me trouble, are you?"

"No," he replied quietly, eyes down. "No trouble at all."

She watched him open his book and move his finger across the page to find the spot where he'd left off reading.

She turned on her heel and walked out.

8

It was early evening and the light inside the dome was beginning to fade when Serena left her first report at the drop site. Afterward, she decided to walk home rather than catch a tram or pay for a rick. She felt restless after spending all day sitting down at work, and she wanted the exercise.

She crossed the boundary that separated the northwest and southwest quarters and stopped at a food cart where she liked to eat from time to time. The vendor grinned his customary greeting and served up a bowl of noodles with red miso and vat-grown shrimp. His mouth was all gums and no teeth, and he didn't have a single hair on his body. She'd never heard him speak and wasn't sure if he could.

She grabbed a bottle of hot sauce and hosed down her noodles before digging in.

Gabriel Morales had eventually stopped by her workstation and given her a password she could use to log on to the intranet. Her access was limited, he explained, to the folders belonging to their unit. Her job was to clean out the inbox and move everything into the appropriate folders where they could be found by the people who needed them. Specifically, Gabriel himself and the two others in the unit—Birch, the older man, and Modressani, the younger one.

Incoming files came from everywhere and anywhere within Stellarize Marté, he warned her, and the inbox was never empty. Nevertheless, her job was to clean it out.

"If I go in there and see anything more than two days old," he said, "you're fired. Understood?"

"Yes, sir."

"Stop gaping at me and get busy."

When she logged in, she found more than five thousand unread files in the inbox, and at least a third of these were more than four days old. She read the abstracts attached to a few of them and had absolutely no idea what they were about or what to do with them.

She closed her eyes for a few moments and concentrated on her breathing and pulse rate, a mental exercise she often used to attain clarity of mind. She was good at this sort of thing. She was a consummate problem-solver. She'd proven it to Peter as a child and had continued to prove it as an operative out on her own. This was what she was good at. It was why she was here.

She opened her eyes and left the inbox. She took some time to familiarize herself with the unit's various folders, getting a sense of the subject matter covered by each one. There were folders for corporate documents distributed by Stellarize Marté throughout the organization; folders for technical information relating to optics, optical engineering, human vision, and other related scientific topics; and folders for project documents specifically related to the optical engineering section, including folders for change requests and test results and bug fixes and technical specifications and inventory reports and damage reports and minutes of meetings and on and on and on. . .

When she finally felt she had a general sense of the scope of her task, she went back to the inbox, sorted it by date, oldest to newest, and got to work.

Her report to Peter, which she'd completed after work, had been fairly straightforward. The unit was rather busy, perhaps understaffed, and the relationship with the optical engineering people somewhat adversarial, as might be expected when critical oversight was their only mandate. Gabriel Morales spent most of his time in his office, accessing and reading files. He'd made a few changes to her decisions, moving a file from one folder to another, but did nothing at all unusual or suspicious that she could detect. Was he in fact the spy Martian Intelligence was chasing?

Who knew?

It was only her first day, of course. The pursuit of Gabriel Morales might turn out to be a marathon rather than a sprint.

She left the food cart and followed back streets through the quarter toward her building. She'd mentioned Dr. Yan in the report, but only to record that she'd made contact with her and that she might become a useful source of information. By the end of their little orientation tour, Serena had realized she liked the older woman despite the impersonal and businesslike beginning. Serena had an ability to project naiveté and sincerity, and Dr. Yan had warmed to her.

As she moved from shadow to shadow, darkness having fallen outside the dome and the streetlights having come on where they were still intact and functional, she thought about her first impressions of Gabriel Morales.

He avoided eye contact. He used an aftershave that smelled like sweet potatoes. His voice was soft and his accent was faintly Nepenthian. His grammar and diction were perfect. He looked older up close than he did from a distance. The whites of his eyes had odd yellow flecks in them.

He was old and tired. Although she understood he'd been born and raised in Nepenthe and so was a native Martian, he'd obviously inherited a body type that was not suited to the planet. He was barrel-chested, with a wide neck and a large head, but his hips were narrow and his legs small. Over the years he'd lost muscle mass in the same way that Earth-born humans usually do after living in lower gravity for a period of time, and judging from the large jar of calcium supplements Serena had seen in his office, he also suffered from the inevitable osteoporosis. As a result, he limped around on pins for legs and looked like he might break into pieces at any moment. Throw in a deterioration of the organs of the inner ear, also aggravated by lower gravity, which caused him to stagger when he walked and forced him to endure constant nausea, and it was obvious that Gabriel Morales was a physical wreck. Which probably explained his trollish personality, among other things.

Gabriel was obviously an intelligent man, and Serena was having problems understanding his motives for betraying Mars. Even if he were trying to buy his way to Earth with stolen information from his employer, she doubted he'd be in any kind of shape to enjoy it if he ever did make it down to the motherworld.

Serena turned into a passageway that would take her to the alley behind her building. She was picking her way around garbage strewn across her path when someone stepped out of a doorway ahead of her. The lights nearby were out, and the figure was cast in shadows. A second person emerged, and a third.

"Well, well, what have we here?"

Serena stopped. She watched the three of them fan out across the width of the passageway.

"You must be lost," the man in the middle said. "Why don't you let us take you home?"

"No," Serena replied. "I'm fine, thank you."

"She looks scrawny," said the one on the right. He stepped into the half-light. He was short and muscular.

"I think she'll do," said the one on the left. Taller and more slender.

"Sure she will," said the one in the middle. He was close enough now for Serena to see the grin on his face. His jaw was square and his neck was thick. Another muscle-bound specimen.

"You need to let me pass," Serena said.

"You need to be a good little girl," the man replied, palming his crotch, "and just let it happen. Keep quiet, and we may let you live."

9

The one in the middle lunged at Serena, arms extended to grab her in a bear hug. Kicking off her slip-ons, she stepped inside his hands and leaped straight up, elevating her knee in a devastating blow that caught him under the chin and sent him flying backward.

She landed beside the man on the right and executed what her trainer had liked to call a firebird leap, a variation on the ballet movement in which her arms swept up and her left leg arced back to a 90-degree angle, her heel striking him hard on the temple. As he fell, she launched herself at the wall, took several steps up and flipped into a backward somersault that landed her behind the last man standing. She jabbed two stiffened fingers into his left kidney. As he cried out, twisting in pain, she spun him around and jabbed the fingers into his throat, crushing his windpipe. He fell, gasping.

Serena went back to the first attacker and found that he was dead, his jaw shattered and his neck broken. The second man was also dead, his temple crushed. The third man had lapsed into unconsciousness but was breathing, albeit in shallow gasps.

She watched him for a moment before deciding to let

him live.

Stepping around them, she moved on down the alley, her breathing as regular as it had been before the attack. Her knee, heel, and fingers were a little sore from the blows she'd delivered, but otherwise she felt perfectly fine. She was in superb physical condition, and she stayed that way through daily workouts that included dance, jujitsu, and other forms of exercise. The back alleys of the domed city were dangerous to someone not prepared for whatever might happen, and death was not an uncommon occurrence. As a result, Serena was always prepared.

As she continued on her way, she reflected that the movements of the three men had been a little off. Unbalanced and out of sync. Clearly they had just arrived from Earth and had not yet adjusted to the difference in gravity.

An observation that led her to wonder if she'd been a specific target assigned to these men or just a random object of violence.

She reached the end of the passageway and looked around.

No one.

There were no surveillance drones in sight. Elysium police used them to patrol the streets of the city in a haphazard deployment, but even if they'd witnessed the fight, Serena wouldn't have been worried. As an operative of Martian Intelligence and therefore an employee of The Five, she had unwritten immunity from arrest and prosecution by local law enforcement. If she screwed up, she would answer to her employers instead. Or to their enemies.

Neither was known for their sense of mercy.

Defending herself in a fight like this one, she told herself, certainly wouldn't violate any of The Five's expectations of her as an undercover operative. She was an asset in whom a certain investment had been made, and she was expected to protect that investment by whatever means necessary. It was understood that in her case, self-defense would include the use of lethal force whenever required. It was an integral part of her job.

She walked into the broader alley that ran behind her building, worrying about the reason behind the attack.

She'd heard that Earth Intelligence was inserting agents into the steady trickle of immigrants coming to Mars, their primary mission to stir up mayhem in the domed cities. The recent spike in demonstrations and random mob activities directed against The Five, in concert with a sharp increase in criticism by socialist politicians, might be attributed in part to these rogue immigrants and their handlers.

If her erstwhile attackers worked for Earth Intelligence, she had to consider the possibility that they might have been sent to remove her from her new assignment. She mulled it over as she approached the rear of her building, but quickly decided it was improbable. It was only her first day, and her gut told her that her cover was clean and intact.

The other possibility, which she leaned toward, was that they were recent arrivals who'd fallen in with a gang based somewhere in the quarter and were looking to prove themselves. She knew most of the hardcases in this neighbourhood, having been around long enough to familiarize herself with the various outfits, and she'd never seen these guys before. They were either brand new or hang-arounds off their turf, looking for an easy trophy to take back with them as proof of their baditude.

She reached her building and scaled the fire escape to a

small, unobtrusive emergency hatch that provided ingress into her living unit. She ringed it and skinnied through, closing the hatch behind her. She reset her security alarm, which was far more expensive and sophisticated than any other in the building, and headed into the bathroom.

She stripped and discovered that she'd torn the knee on her new pair of capri pants. She tossed them aside. Well, at least she still had the green pair.

She stepped into the shower and stood under the warm cleansing gel until her allotment ran out and the stream stopped. Towelling herself off, she slipped into a bodysuit and looked for something to drink in her little kitchen area.

It was a small, cramped space filled with stuff, but as living units went she thought it was adequately comfortable. She squirted fermented fruit juice from a squeeze bulb into her mouth and settled down in front of her vid, a small panel lashed to the back of a plastic chair scavenged from a nearby dumpster. She touched her payment ring to the vid and settled down on a cushion to watch a program about the atmosphere conversion program and the plans of Terraform to turn Mars into a world on which humans could walk outside and live to enjoy the experience.

Serena fell asleep as a video drone swept over the site of Terraform's new conversion station, an outburst of silver bubbles constructed around an enormous smokestack in the easternmost reaches of Nepenthe Planum, set to come online as early as the day after tomorrow, if all went well.

10

The tallest building in Elysium City was fourteen storeys high, two floors more than what was normally allowed. Located in the exact middle of the central core, its rooftop antennas and hatches were scant meters from the apex of the dome.

Known as Frick Tower after the explorer who had erected the first dome on the site of the current city, its four sides were covered with tessuspaz, a distant cousin of fibreglass, that was manufactured by Fabricon. It was such an incredibly strong and versatile material that it was used by The Five in the construction of their most important industrial products. For example, Atlas used it to build the domes themselves and other external structures such as conversion stations, processing and refining plants, and warehouses. Stellarize Marté used it for the outer hulls of their spacecraft and shuttles, and Davis Minerals used it to reinforce the interiors of their mines. It was unbelievably durable and could stand up to whatever extremes Martian weather might throw at it, not to mention the vacuum of deep space and the random assault of cosmic radiation, meteorites, gasses, dust, and debris.

Tessuspaz was a Martian product, invented here,

manufactured here, and used here. It was not exported. It was a key element in the successful drive of The Five to achieve total self-sufficiency.

The tessuspaz gave the building an opaque, mirrored look from the outside while permitting complete outward visibility from within. In the event of a dome breech, special panels would seal the building and protect the lives of everyone inside.

In addition to the tessuspaz, the building also had a somewhat more conventional layer of security that made it extremely difficult for unauthorized people to enter or leave. A formidable combination of hardware, software, and wetware protected its tenants, in particular the Council of Five, which maintained its headquarters here.

Each member of the council contributed millions of credits a year to the budget that paid for the upkeep of the structure and the activities that went on within it. All of their joint ventures, the ones that pooled their strengths and drove their agenda of autarky relentlessly forward, were run from offices here.

For example, Mars Security Limited, a joint venture of The Five, occupied several floors. Its three branches—the Martian Intelligence Service, the Martian Justice Service (an independent police force known as the Guardians and a judicial system), and the Martian Armed Services (a private army and space navy)—kept their headquarters here.

Terraform, which also operated out of this building, happened to be the only item on the agenda for tonight's meeting of the Council of Five.

Constance Davis entered the inner chamber and saw that the others had arrived ahead of her. Labossière discreetly left her side to remain outside in the corridor.

Wilhelmina Destry, CEO of Fabricon and council chair, fussed with the arrangement of glassware and electronics around her place at the head of the table and shot her a quick nod.

Constance approached Dell Burley, CEO of Atlas, who was chatting with a red-haired youth, an aide of some kind. Dell caught her eye and smiled.

"How's it shaking this evening, Connie?"

Always so familiar, always so lacking in propriety. But he was a handsome man, with his wavy salt-and-pepper hair, his piercing dark eyes, and his square jaw. Unfortunately for any woman with ideas, though, he was *very* happily married.

"I'm well, thank you." She looked sideways at the redhead, who glanced at Dell and eased away.

"Important business tonight." Dell rubbed his dimpled chin. "How are you going to vote on Wong's motion?"

Overly direct, as well. There was no subtlety in Dell Burley.

"I'm inclined to support it," she said, allowing an expression of indecision to cross her face, "but I have some concerns."

"Oh, come off it, Connie." He grinned at her. "I talked to your father this morning. I just wanted to hear you say it."

"So you know my mind better than I know it myself. How wonderful for you."

"Now, now. Be nice." He looked over her shoulder. "Here comes your boyfriend. Straighten that spine."

Constance sighed as Jadarius Fell joined them. The eldest son of Leonidas Fell, CEO of Stellarize Marté, Jadarius was currently serving as his father's representative on the Council of Five while the old man lay in a coma after a near-fatal heart attack.

Unfortunately, although he was chief operating officer of Stellarize and held an MBA from the University of Mars at Elysium, Jadarius was far from his father's equal as a business leader or council member. Wilhelmina Destry felt it was a function of his youth and lack of experience, and she made an effort to help him out whenever she could during complicated council dealings, but Constance entertained no such illusions. As far as she was concerned, Jadarius Fell had been weighed in the balance and found wanting.

"Constance, I'm so glad to see you." Jadarius took her hand and shook it vigorously. "It's been too long."

Behind Fell's back, Dell smirked.

"Councillor." She pulled her hand away.

"Look," Jadarius said, "we need the votes to sideline this converter thing until next year." He turned to include Dell in his plea. "Our interstellar project *must* remain top priority. Any diversion of council resources away from it right now would be a big mistake."

"Don't you care about the future of your planet?" Dell asked, his voice light.

"What? Of course I do. But this interstellar drive, it could make or break us. Right? Isn't that what all the scientists and policy wonks are saying? Get out there before Earth and reap the benefits, or miss out and fall back to colony status before you can snap your fingers. Don't you see?"

"I don't understand," Constance said, "why you think it has to be one or the other. Aren't we capable of walking and talking at the same time?"

"You didn't read the analysis reports, did you?"

"I glanced at them," Constance said.

"What young Fell here is referring to," Dell said, "is

the fact that Wong's asking council to underwrite all of his stations for any disaster that might happen if they should malfunction or fail. You know, if one or more of them blows up or suddenly starts to emit a deadly poison into the atmosphere or what have you."

"An unforgivable drain on our resources if it should happen," Jadarius put in. "Potentially fatal."

Constance frowned. "Well, the whole scenario's kind of unlikely, isn't it? There've been no problems that I'm aware of so far. I don't see the sudden big risk."

"It's a question of priorities—"

Wilhelmina Destry pounded her gavel on the table.

"Connie." Dell touched his finger to his temple in a mock salute. "Duty calls." Glancing at Jadarius, he walked away.

Aides and security personnel filed out of the chamber as the councillors took their places around the oval table. When the room was cleared, Destry touched her ring to the official recorder and the meeting began.

"I see we're all here. Shall we review the minutes of the previous meeting?"

"Move to skip them," Dell Burley said.

"All in favour?"

Five hands shot into the air.

"Motion passed. Our only order of business this evening is the proposal on the table from Terraform. Let's get right to it, shall we?"

Constance glanced at Dell. His eyes were down as he scanned something on his tablet. The fingers of his left hand drummed lightly on the tabletop. Whenever she was in his presence she could never tell if he was making fun of her, barely tolerating her, or was genuinely fond of her. When he looked at her with those dark, intelligent eyes of his he seemed to look right into her very soul.

He lifted his head and caught her staring at him. She looked away quickly, her face growing warm.

Magee Wong rose in his place and began to speak.

11

"I'm here this evening," Wong said, adjusting his reading glasses, "to seek council's approval to discontinue the current signing-off process for new conversion stations and allow Terraform, Incorporated to follow an accelerated timetable free from red tape, pardon the pun. First, before we vote, I'd like to present council with a brief update on our progress to date."

"Brief," Destry said, not looking up from her tablet.

"Mmm, just so." Wong smiled faintly. "My beloved colleagues know how much I dislike public speaking. However, the young ones among us"—he glanced in turn at Constance and Jadarius Fell—"may benefit from a better understanding of our goals and our progress toward them."

Destry grunted, but said nothing.

"This year," Wong began, touching his tablet to bring to life a holographic display in the middle of the oval table, "marks the twelfth anniversary of Project Iceteroid. I trust you've all read the reports sent to you, in which you'll see that during this time we've tripled the number of cargo ships in operation and more than halved the costs associated with hauling methane from Titan, while the expense associated with bringing ammonia iceteroids from the belt is only 20 percent of what it was when we first started.

"As you know, we've bombarded the polar cap with hundreds of big chunks of ammonia ice. Upon impact, they sublimate—transform from a solid state into gas without first becoming liquid—and produce hydrogen and nitrogen. The hydrogen reacts with the carbon dioxide in the polar ice and the CO_2 already in our atmosphere to produce water. The nitrogen is equally important, since you may know that it comprises 78 percent of Earth's atmosphere and only 2 percent of ours; at least that's what it was when we first started. Furthermore, the impact of the iceteroids raises dust that helps form clouds in the upper atmosphere. This is a key—"

"I'm sure we all appreciate the science lesson—" Jadarius Fell interjected.

"You will sit quietly," Wong snapped, "and listen while I speak. It is only out of respect for your father that I tolerate this behaviour. Do *not* interrupt again."

Jadarius blinked. He looked at Constance, who shook her head microscopically, betraying her contempt. He looked down at his hands.

Wong cleared his throat and changed the display image. "Our stations are multi-functional. This substation emits methane gas," the image zoomed in, "while this one," the image veered to another domed structure, "is our latest development, a hybrid operation that produces halocarbons and also cyanophytes that are cultivated in this biosphere and planted in large icefield colonies."

He looked at Constance, who was paying attention. "As you will remember, one of these cyanophyte strains is a genetically engineered algae that consumes carbon dioxide and emits oxygen in rather stunning amounts. Another, based on the Earth substance known as star jelly, shows an enhanced ability to fix atmospheric nitrogen. Our tests at TACS-2 during the last five years indicate that our various strains are cold resistant enough to flourish outside year-round. As each new station comes online, its biospheric bubble will begin sowing these little workers into our self-made icefields, where they'll play an important role in the next steps toward the terraforming of Mars."

The holographic display flipped through several charts.

"These figures demonstrate that as our stations have come online over the past ten years, we've seen satisfactory increases in atmospheric pressure—we're now above the Armstrong limit at 7.6 kiloPascals—and our mean daily temperature has noticeably improved. Levels of nitrogen and oxygen have also risen on curves that match our early predictions. The greenhouse effect is underway, and what the wise men on Earth once said would take centuries to bring about is on schedule to take place within decades."

Wong removed his glasses and slipped them into his breast pocket. "This is why I stand before you this evening to propose that council waive the approval process for future individual stations. We've reached the point now where our joint venture has proven to be effective beyond our wildest expectations, and more and more cost-efficient as each phase is completed.

"I sent out to each of you a new budget proposal that I trust you've reviewed. If approved, we would see our contributions to the project double over the next three years. The payoff, however, with the accelerated construction and activation process I'm proposing tonight, would be to cut years from our original projections.

"We're on track toward our goal of creating a living

biosphere on this planet in which humanity can exist—and flourish!—to achieve our full potential as masters of our own destiny. Streamlining the process will make the whole thing move forward that much more quickly and efficiently. Thank you for your attention, and thank you for your support."

Murmurs rippled around the table as he sat down and turned off the holographic display.

Destry rapped her gavel. "Discussion. Councillor Burley."

Dell leaned back and crossed his legs. "Impressive, Magee."

Wong nodded without replying. It went without saying, as far as he was concerned, that their joint venture was a complete success to date.

"I support Councillor Wong's request." Burley looked around the table, his dark eyes glittering. "The whole thing. Letting Terraform run its own show without all the oversight, and doubling down on our investment to get us to the finish line in record time. Let's get this done."

Constance stirred. "Are we sure these . . . algae things are safe?"

"Do you mean, do they bite?" Burley grinned. "Don't worry, Connie. They're pretty small."

"If I may." Wong leaned forward, folding his hands on the table. "Cyanobacteria are among the oldest life forms in existence on the planet Earth. Yes, strains there are known to produce various toxins, including peptide toxins and neurotoxins, such as anatoxin-a, that are poisonous and potentially fatal to humans. However, our strains, genetically engineered here on Mars for exclusive use on Mars, have none of these antisocial behaviours. They're perfectly safe."

"No disrespect intended, Magee," Dell said, "but I keep forgetting that we should call you Dr. Wong." Before replacing his father as CEO of Ares Corporation, Wong had spent a decade on Earth attending university in China, earning doctorates in biochemistry and food science.

"Don't worry about it."

Jadarius Fell said, "Look, my father has always supported the long-term goals of Terraform, and we're happy to participate, but my point is that there are higher priorities right now that deserve this increase in funding."

"You're referring to your interstellar drive project, I take it." Wong removed his reading glasses.

"Yes, as a matter of fact, I am."

Wong frowned. "Are there problems now? You told us in your last report that everything was going well."

"Let's not get off course," Destry warned.

Dell leaned forward. "I've heard whispers along the vine that Stellarize is dealing with some major screw-ups right now. Not to mention problems within the artificial human project."

Jadarius rolled his eyes. "Of course not."

Destry cleared her throat. "Gentlemen, please. This is off topic." She looked at Constance. "Councillor Davis, do you have anything to contribute to our discussion of Dr. Wong's submission?"

Constance involuntarily glanced at Dell before speaking. "I spent some time going over the reports with Dr. Mieto."

Dr. Arnaud Mieto was Davis Mineral's senior executive in charge of growth and innovation. With degrees in chemistry and theoretical physics, he was one of the leading scientists on the planet and one of the Davis family's most important executives. Not only was he considered a brilliant geochemist, he was also known to be an organizational genius. Constance's abilities in this regard were average at best, and she'd quietly allowed Mieto to restructure the corporation and streamline its operations after his own vision. Alexander had expressed delight at the result, and she'd grudgingly acknowledged the (vast!) improvement.

Needless to say, she'd given all the Terraform reports to him, and he'd provided her with summary analyses. His reputation being what it was, his opinion was automatically of interest to the council.

"Don't keep us in suspense," Dell said.

Constance gave him a look. "I won't. He's very excited about it. And he agrees that we should remove any bureaucratic barriers and let them proceed according to their general plan."

Dell nodded.

Constance sat back, and her eyes found Wong's. He nodded slightly, indicating that their previously discussed arrangement, in which Davis Minerals would support Wong in exchange for his support on the upcoming Tharsis project, was now in play.

Destry gave them a moment, and then twirled her gavel in her hand. "If there's nothing else?"

"What about you, Wilhelmina?" Dell raised his eyebrows at her.

"Are we ready to vote?"

"I'm ready," Dell said, looking around.

"As you know, only a simple majority is required to approve or reject. Councillor Wong?"

"Approve."

"Acting Councillor Davis?"

"Approve," Constance said.

"Acting Councillor Fell?"

"Reject. Oh, hell. Never mind. Approve."

"Councillor Burley?"

"Oh, approve, absolutely."

"And I vote also to approve. Request granted." Destry bashed the table with her gavel. "Meeting adjourned. Someone go tell them to bring in the booze."

12

After more than a week on the job, Serena had gotten used to the routine. On campus early; processed through the layers of Stellarize Marté security like a particle of red dust through a succession of filters; long hours staring at her monitor while manipulating countless incomprehensible files; tracking Gabriel's behaviour with no satisfactory outcome. Her cover job was boring, and so, unfortunately, was her actual assignment. Gabriel betrayed absolutely no signs of being a spy in the pay of Earth Intelligence.

She managed to learn his password and used it to explore his folders without finding anything out of the ordinary. She finessed herself administrative privileges and saw that only five people had access to their data: Gabriel; herself; Birch, full name Dr. Emory Birch, an electronics engineer; Jakob Modressani, a programmer responsible for software integrity; and the IT administrator, a woman named Tollin, who worked somewhere else on campus. Usage reports showed that none of these people had copied or deleted files in any way that seemed suspicious to her.

Gabriel's online activities showed sporadic access to other areas for which he had privileges, but there appeared to be nothing that raised alarm bells.

She'd also followed Gabriel home a few times. He lived in a small unit on the ground floor of a crappy rowhouse building in the southwest quarter, and his usual habit was to grab the tram and head directly home. So far, once again, nothing had caught her attention or suggested how he was communicating with his Earth Intelligence handler.

It was a good thing she was a patient person.

During the afternoon on her eighth day, Serena left her workstation for a washroom break. On her way back she glanced into Gabriel's office. He wasn't there.

She stopped at the glass wall and looked down onto the floor of the shop below. Dr. Yan sat at her workstation, examining small parts spread out on an anti-static mat, holding them up one at a time with tweezers while peering at them through a monocle.

After a moment Serena spotted Gabriel in Kennet Clayborn's office. Dr. Clayborn was the manager of the optical engineering unit. Serena had not been introduced to him and had therefore never spoken to him, but she'd asked around. He was forty-six years old, tall, fair-haired, and handsome. He was married and had three teenaged children. Earthborn, he'd immigrated to Titan with his parents when he was nine. He was a brilliant engineer with three doctorates and numerous publications to his credit. Within Stellarize Marté he was apparently a force to be reckoned with, running his unit with a careless mastery as though he owned the whole show rather than worked for the Fells as a humble employee like everyone else.

Gabriel frequently engaged Clayborn in discussions— well, arguments—about his various decisions as head of optical engineering. Sometimes upstairs in his office and sometimes downstairs in Clayborn's, which seemed to be the venue for today's debate.

Another man came into view within the glassed-in office. He seemed to be upset and appeared to be shouting at Clayborn. His back was to Serena, so she couldn't see who it was. His arms swung around in threatening gestures.

Serena left the window in a hurry. It looked like something she didn't want to miss.

When she reached the shop floor and had woven through the workstations to the row of offices in the back, the incident appeared to be over. The man, whom she now recognized as Dr. Dannis Follett, stormed past her, lab coat flapping, eyes blazing, face red. Dr. Follett had something to do with software. Serena had no idea what would have made him so angry. Her impression up to now had been that he was a quiet and nervous man, mostly withdrawn into himself. Something, obviously, had provoked him.

Clayborn's office door was open. Serena could hear Gabriel's voice, calm and placating. Apparently he'd been trying to play peacemaker. A change of pace for him, certainly.

She backed away and went over to Dr. Yan's workstation.

Deep in concentration, the engineer set down the piece she was examining. The monocle jutted from her eye socket like an artificial extension of her face. When she turned and saw Serena standing there she startled, and the monocle dropped down into her lap.

"My lord, girl! Where did you come from?"

"I'm sorry, Dr. Yan. I didn't mean to scare you."

"What do you want?"

"Sorry. Nothing. I came down because I saw Gabriel was down here. I . . . Dr. Follett seems very upset."

Dr. Yan grabbed the monocle from her lap and slapped it down on her worktable a little too firmly. "Yes. Well, we all are right now."

"Why?"

"You'd do well to ask your supervisor that question and stay out of our way down here."

Serena said nothing.

"I'm sorry," Dr. Yan said. "We're all very stressed."

Serena waited.

"Yet another design modification that isn't working out." An unexpected tear coursed down her cheek. Dr. Yan wiped at it with the back of her hand. The woman was exhausted, Serena realized.

"Is there something I can do to help?"

"No, child. These are matters far above your head. Above mine as well, unfortunately, since they involve corporate politics and personal influence, areas in which I'm sadly not competent to operate."

"Is there a problem with the project? Is that why Gabriel's in with Dr. Clayborn?"

Dr. Yan sighed. "I suppose there's no harm in telling you. A few months ago, senior management green-lighted what amounted to a philosophical decision. Do you know what that is, dear? A *philosophical* decision?"

"No, ma'am."

"It's when someone forces, *imposes,* their will on everyone else based on what *they* think everyone should be doing instead of what the science requires. It's when Dr. Kennet Clayborn decides—"

She broke off and closed her eyes. "I need to calm down or I'll be in there like poor Dannis, trying for the life of me not to break his fucking neck."

Serena's eyes widened in surprise at Dr. Yan's uncharacteristic use of foul language.

"Gabriel's trying to play the intermediary," Dr. Yan went

on, "but he's miscast. He should stick to his true nature as Gabriel the archangel, sent to deliver the message of the gods that we have been judged and our punishment is imminent."

Serena continued to stare at her.

"You don't understand, do you?" Dr. Yan shook her head. "That's all right. I'm just running at the mouth."

Serena crouched down, her shoulder scant centimeters from Dr. Yan's knee. "I can understand," she said quietly, "if you explain it to me."

Dr. Yan put a hand on top of Serena's head. "I always wanted children. Ulysses—my husband—was of two minds, but it turned out to be moot when we learned I'm sterile. 'Brilliant but barren,' I said when I learned the news. 'How about that, my dearest?'" She sighed. "I suppose I'm almost old enough to have been your mother. How old are you?"

"Twenty-two," Serena replied.

Dr. Yan tipped her head sideways in a little shrug. "The arithmetic would work, but I don't imagine I carry the gene that would have given you this carrot top." She gave Serena's head a quick pat and sat up straight. "Never mind that. It's eyes that occupy us now, not DNA. Eyes that suddenly have to exceed by far the performance of our own human eyes. Unnecessary, but *philosophically* transcendent."

Serena didn't understand; not yet.

Dr. Yan leaned back. "I'll take a few minutes. Why not? If I talk for a bit, maybe I'll feel better."

"I'm happy to listen."

Dr. Yan smiled faintly. "You're a good child, Serena. Very well. Pay attention, now. Yes. So. Basics first. This unit, as you know, is responsible for producing eyes for the artificial humans that will be sent out into space on the interstellar craft to meet the aliens and whatever future they may represent. Right now we're developing the model eye. Once the model's perfected and thoroughly tested in a prototype artificial human, it will be given to production, and they'll make the actual eyes that will go into the actual units themselves."

Serena nodded.

"Our mandate is to develop a visual system superior to human eyesight. I think I may have talked to you about that before."

"Yes, a bit."

"Mmm. Very recently, the brain trust at the top decided to move everything to a different design concept altogether for the artificial humans. Changes right across the board. All the previous prototypes were shelved. Sent off to storage until such time as they could be salvaged for parts or melted down like so much scrap. All that work and expense, swept off into the dumpster.

"One adapts. It's the nature of the business. In our specific case, we'd been working on a visual system that essentially mimicked human eyesight, but with greater efficiency."

Dr. Yan leaned forward. "Here's how it works. Our eyes are fairly simple mechanisms. On the surface is the cornea, which is like a window. When light passes through it, the cornea causes it to refract so that it can freely enter the interior of the eye through the pupil, which is the dark aperture in the centre. The iris—my word, I never noticed that yours are such a lovely shade of dark brown—is a muscle that controls the size of the aperture depending on the amount of light to which the eye is exposed. It expands when the light is dim, and contracts to a pinhole when the light is very bright. Once the light enters the interior of the eye, it strikes the lens and is focused more sharply onto a spot on the retina, at the back of the eye. The retina processes the light into millions of impulses that travel through nerves to the optic nerve, which is like the main servo-cable connecting the entire structure to the brain. Quite an over-simplification for the purposes of our conversation, but that's the main idea."

"I understand," Serena said.

"Very good. You're a smart girl. As a mechanism, our eyes are rather imperfect as an optical system, subject to all sorts of flaws and defects and deterioration. How's your eyesight, by the way?"

"Fine," Serena replied, standing up again. In fact, it had been tested as part of an overall physical examination demanded by Peter before she left his wardship, and the numbers had confirmed what she already knew, that her vision was outstanding.

"Mmm. Well, the key to human vision lies in the brain, not the eye necessarily. Our brains have image processing capabilities that are quite remarkable. Your eye could see something for only thirteen milliseconds, for example, and still your brain could process the image into information accessible in one manner or another. This is where we've been focusing, no pun intended. Where Dr. Follett in particular has been applying his considerable abilities.

"While I and a few others have been handling the hardware side of things, the eye as a mechanism, Dannis has been developing the onboard software at the back end that will receive the image information, analyze it, and then provide the appropriate areas of the artificial brain with data that we would describe in broad, lay terms as eyesight."

She held up a finger. "The key, now, is that Dannis

works very closely with me and my engineering colleagues because it's not just a front-end, back-end situation. We developed a hardware model, and he wrote programming for the brain around those specifications. His work showed us areas in which we could modify and improve the physical design, which we did, then he tweaked the software accordingly. Back and forth. A great partnership. He's brilliant, but extremely receptive to the ideas of others and very flexible. We felt we'd just about reached a point where we had a model that worked with the brain they're designing in the north building when the hammer fell."

"What happened?"

"Kennet Clayborn happened. Oh, yes, a change in *philosophy*. Why limit ourselves to mimicking human eyesight when we can instead create something absolutely revolutionary? Dr. Clayborn called in an engineer from the interstellar ship project, the person responsible for designing their deep-space sensors, and she produced a radically different model for our eye that we're now trying to make sense of. Needless to say, all of Dannis's hard work went down the toilet along with all the previous prototypes. It's just a complete and total mess right now."

"That's why he's angry with Dr. Clayborn?"

"That's why we're *all* angry with Dr. Clayborn. The man has set us back weeks. Weeks!"

Serena heard footsteps behind her and turned. Gabriel stormed past, eyes flashing.

"What the hell are you doing down here?" he snarled. "Get back upstairs, dammit."

"Yes sir."

Serena glanced at Dr. Yan, but her eyes were on the array of parts in front of her, and she appeared not to have heard the exchange.

13

Serena warmed a bag of rice for supper and ate it as she dictated her report. She spoke between mouthfuls, thinking her way through what little she'd learned over the past two days since her previous report.

She summarized the problems with the artificial human project as Dr. Yan had described them to her, because she thought it was information Martian Intelligence would want to have. She detailed the steps she'd taken to track Gabriel's behaviour, in the office and outside of work, and reluctantly admitted she still had no leads as to the identity of his handler with Earth Intelligence or what the nature of the intelligence would be that they seemed to believe would be his last big score.

When she was finished, she recycled the remnants of her meal and left the apartment. The streets of the southwest quarter were busy tonight, filled with restless young people on the street corners with nothing to do, gleaners rooting through dumpsters, and sex trade workers looking for business. The weather outside was unsettled, with a sandstorm blowing against the dome and the barometric pressure dropping even lower than usual. Such conditions seemed to have an effect on people permanently trapped inside the giant fishbowl that was Elysium, although Serena had never understood why.

She stayed on foot, glad for the exercise, weaving her way across the boundary into the northwest quarter. Eventually she found herself in a rough neighbourhood of abandoned tenements filled with squatters, ragged children chasing rats with lengths of pipe, and small gangs of young men and women prowling in the shadows like predators.

She knew her way around, however, and avoided the worst spots until she reached a chain-link fence and a gate guarded by a wiry Asian man who nodded and spoke into his headset.

Serena waited, listening to the sounds of the city around her while trying not to smell the smells.

The man opened the gate a crack, allowing her to slip through. A second man appeared, taller and very muscular, dark-skinned, wearing only shorts and flip flops.

"How's it being tonight, dirt girl?" he grinned.

"It's being real, Chips."

"Glad to hear it." Chips led the way through shoulder-high piles of salvaged goods and plastic crates stamped with names and descriptors in what Serena recognized as Mandarin, one of the languages she'd learned as a child in the classroom above Peter's grow op. The crates had originally contained imported goods such as cotton, seeds, precision instruments, and other items shipped from Earth at what would have been considerable expense at the time. What they contained now was anyone's guess.

Chips whistled as he walked, a tune she recognized from previous visits. Serena knew that there were unseen figures all around them, and if Chips were under some kind of duress he would be whistling a different tune. Literally.

In which case she wouldn't get very much farther without encountering a great deal of trouble. Probably more than even she could handle.

She stopped suddenly. "Hey, that looks nice."

Chips pivoted on his heel. "What'd you say?"

She pointed at a vid perched on top of a pile of pre-fabricated wall sections. It was about three times larger than hers and a much better model. "Does it work?"

"Course it works, dirt girl. You think we just got junk here or something?"

"Twenty credits."

"What?" Chips let his jaw sag in mock astonishment. "You said what, now? Forty?"

"Not a chance."

"Come onnnn. It's only a couple years old. Beautiful condition. I could let it go for thirty-five."

"Twenty-five."

"You-Know-Who would be slicing off my privates and feeding them to the rats if I let it go for that."

Serena sighed, as though hard done by. "Thirty, if you deliver it to my place."

"I couldn't do that until two days from now."

"Fine."

"Gotta be payment up front."

"Fine."

"Okay then." Chips produced a hand register from out of nowhere and tapped it with practiced dexterity before holding it out to her. "Pay up and look big."

She glanced at the amount and touched her ring to the screen. The device beeped.

Chips made the register disappear again. "Always a pleasure doing business with you, Serena."

They continued on through the stacks until they

reached a small courtyard. It was paved with locally made ceramic tiles and furnished with mismatched chairs and tables. In the middle of the courtyard was an enormous above-ground pool that was filled with water. Lounging in a lawn chair facing the pool was a man wearing only a pair of white flared trousers. He bore more than a slight resemblance to Chips. He took the cigar from his mouth and looked around.

"What's happening tonight, dirt girl?"

Serena walked over to the edge of the pool. Standing up on a small box, she peered over the rim. The surface of the water was still. Lights from the building behind them shone across it like smeared torches. The smell of it was sweet and clean in her nostrils. It was wonderful, almost intoxicating.

Serena had no idea how many liters might be in the pool, but she knew she was looking at a small fortune, kept out here in the open and guarded by some of the most vicious killers on the planet. It was their stash, their investment, their bank account, their source of wealth. Beside it, the hoard back in the junkyard behind them was kid's stuff, a cover, a hobby. A diversion.

"Same old," she said, turning around. "Staying safe, Handel?"

"You know it."

Serena had an ongoing arrangement with Handel, the lord of this particular neighbourhood, that she'd negotiated with him early in her career as an operative. What she'd had to do to prove herself worthy not only of his notice but also his good will was a tale for another time that had involved patience, situational violence, and courage on her part. They now had an understanding: when she needed something, she could ask, and in return she would make payment in the form of information that was useful to him.

It also helped that he'd taken a liking to her, for whatever reason.

The current deal was that Handel would allow her to pass through his property, no questions asked. She said, "I've heard that Fabricon Water is getting tired of the slow leakage from their Elysium shipments."

Handel shrugged, unimpressed.

"The crew flying in tomorrow?" She raised her eyebrows at him. "Won't be the usual folks you've dealt with before."

"Vacation replacements," he said, considering the length of ash on the end of his cigar and deciding not to tap it off just yet.

"Ringers. From the Guardians. They're looking for trouble. Expecting it. Hoping for it, I heard. You might want to skip this one."

Handel ran a finger along his cheekbone. The Guardians were the elite private police force of The Five. They were much more competent, and much more frightening, than the Elysian municipal police, who were strictly minor leaguers.

"Tomorrow, you say."

"It's a lock."

Handel reached down beside him and lifted a bottle of water to his lips. He drank deeply. Hydration as a show of strength. Cool bravado. He screwed a cap on the bottle and tossed it to her.

She caught it, slipped it into the pouch clipped around her waist, and nodded.

"So, okay then." Handel said. "Safe passage, dirt girl."

She turned away and started toward the gate at the

back. When the guard who was posted there opened it for her, she would find herself in a narrow alley directly behind the abandoned laundromat she was using as her dead drop. She'd be able to enter the alley, leave her report ring, and get out again without being observed from the street front or the surrounding roofs.

"Wait up," Handel called out.

Serena stopped. Turned.

Handel said, "Bro tells me you bought yourself a nice vid. Appreciate the business."

"No problem."

"Tell you what, dirt girl. He's gonna deliver it to you tomorrow morning before you run yourself off to work."

"Thank you."

"I'm told you got your current piddly little thing strapped to a chair like some sorry-assed hostage. Dumpster stuff. Chip's gonna hang your new one on the wall for you, no extra charge. That red hair of yours has turned me a little soft in the head, seems. Surprise, surprise."

"Thanks."

The guard at the gate lifted an eyebrow at her as she passed through the opening into the shadowed alley, but said nothing.

14

Constance Davis was quite aware that Labossière didn't like this part of his job, but she didn't really give a damn what he liked or didn't like. He was well paid to do what he was told, and if he didn't like *that*, he knew he was free to join the unemployment line at any time.

For these late-evening excursions she liked to wear a catsuit, a black, form-fitting outfit made of a material similar to Spandex but developed and produced exclusively on Mars. Her long blond hair was pinned up under a black watch cap. The catsuit showed off her rather stunning figure to full advantage, and it allowed her to move about the dark streets without being seen when she wished to be invisible.

Labossière's job was to accompany her in her private rick from her building in the central core to the northeast quarter, which was largely given over to restaurants, embassies, and theatres. Toward the rim there were neighbourhoods that had fallen into disrepair and were being torn down to accommodate the spreading entertainment section. The buildings were mostly vacant, given over to the homeless who slept on makeshift litters in empty rooms and lingered on the street corners. It was a neighbourhood where the drugs were dirtier, petty crime ran unchecked, and it was unsafe for a woman to be out alone at night.

There were a few clubs and bars still open on the half-abandoned streets, and she liked to be dropped off somewhere random so that she would be forced to walk around, alone, to find a place to have a drink and flirt with the roughnecks.

She walked slowly, avoiding the streetlights, enjoying her freedom. The vicarious pleasure of prowling felt as close to a sexual experience as she dared allow herself. Behind her, at a discreet distance, Labossière waited in the rick, monitoring a security band she pretended not to know about.

She heard the noise of heavy equipment as she approached an empty intersection and found herself across the street from a live construction site. Through the high chain-link fence she could see that buildings had been torn down and rubble was being cleared away. A large sign on the main gate at the corner identified the project as an "Atlas Construction Renewal Initiative."

A heavy engine roared and groaned within the site, and after a moment a man opened the big gate and backed out onto the street, guiding a large vehicle forward. It was a tractor pulling a flatbed trailer. Secured to the flatbed was a dumpster filled with broken construction material.

The tractor lurched, as though having problems with its drive train, and suddenly the dumpster snapped its restraints and fell off the flatbed. It struck the ground with a loud crash and tipped over onto its side, spilling debris everywhere with a continuous, tumbling clatter.

Constance laughed, watching the driver jump from the tractor to examine the mess he'd made. The other worker, the one who'd been guiding him out, shook his head and spoke into a comm unit. Then the two men began yelling at each other, waving their arms around and stamping their boots on the pavement.

In a few moments a black cargo rick came around the corner and parked in front of the accident. Dell Burley got out and separated the combatants. He talked first to the one in charge of the gate, who'd likely summoned him on his comm, and then turned to the driver for his side of the story. Constance thought Dell looked particularly muscular and handsome in his black T-shirt, paint-stained jeans, and construction boots. It was a look she'd never seen before.

She waited for a moment, debating with herself, and then thought, *What the hell.* She stepped off the curb and walked across the intersection.

Dell was on his comm, calling for a clean-up crew, when she reached him. He glanced over, looked her up and down without expression, and held up a finger for her to wait until he finished his call.

"Yeah, and bring another driver," he said. "This guy's going home."

He put the comm away. "What brings you out this way tonight, looking like that?"

"Oh, just restless."

"You look like a porn star."

Her mouth opened and closed. She wasn't sure how to take it. Did he find her attractive or ridiculous?

At that moment the clean-up crew arrived. Dell walked away as men spilled out of vehicles and gathered around the fallen container. Someone unhooked the trailer while another worker climbed up into the offending tractor and re-started its engine. Dell pointed and the man behind the controls nodded, easing the vehicle off to one side.

A crane on giant wheels arrived from inside the construction site. Dell spoke to one of the men, probably a site manager, and patted him on the shoulder. The man nodded and walked off to supervise the job of getting the dumpster upright and the debris back into it.

Dell came over and took Constance by the elbow, his touch firm but gentle. He guided her across the street to the corner she'd left a minute ago.

"You shouldn't be out alone like this," he said.

"Oh, it's all right." She waved a hand. "Labossière's around here somewhere."

"Yeah, I saw him. Just the same, it's not safe."

She was pleased that a good-looking man—so virile despite advancing middle age—would express sincere concern for her well-being. For the very first time, she noticed a tattoo on his right forearm. It was a sprocket-and-starburst affair in bright blue and red. Atlas Construction's corporate logo. The tattoo was unspeakably masculine and attractive. She thought, for the hundredth time, that it was too bad he was happily married.

"There's something I want to ask you," she said.

He'd been keeping an eye on the crew across the street, but now he gave her his full attention.

"When you told Jadarius Fell in council that you'd heard there were problems with Stellarize's drive, were you simply baiting him or did you mean it?"

"I always mean what I say."

She hesitated, uncomfortable in the crosshairs of those piercing brown eyes. "I know, I just—"

He continued to stare.

"If there are problems," she said, "we need to know about them. Don't we?"

"We certainly do."

"And you said something about the artificial human project, too. What's your source, Dell? Where are you getting this information?"

"Look into it yourself. You have your own network of spies, don't you?"

She put a knowing smile on her face, but suspected he wouldn't be fooled. Her grandfather had been the one for corporate intelligence gathering, but after his death the network employed by Davis Minerals to collect and analyze that kind of inside information had withered on the vine under Alexander's brief tenure, and she'd not given it a high priority once she'd seized control of the company.

Dell's comm popped, and he listened for a moment. "Understood," he finally said before clipping the device back onto his belt. "You need to go home, Connie. Now."

"Dell," she began.

"Now! Get lost! Trouble's coming."

She watched him hurry over to his crew and then she heard it: a distant growling, like the sound a heavy sandstorm makes when it beats against the dome in mindless fury.

"Councillor," a voice said in her ear, startling her. It was Labossière, suddenly standing next to her. "Come with me."

"What's going on? What's happening?"

He took her arm, his grip much less gentle than Dell's had been a few minutes ago. "Trouble. A mob, coming from the south. It's not safe here. Let's go."

"A mob?"

She allowed him to lead her back to the rick. Half a block away she looked behind her and saw a wave of people pour around the corner where she and Dell had stood, moments before.

Three armoured vehicles with the Guardians logo on the side rocketed past them, one after the other, silent and deadly.

She couldn't tell whether Dell and his crew had made it back inside their construction site in time, or whether the mob had caught them.

15

It was a sound like no other that Dell had ever heard before in his life. It was pitched lower than the whine of the low-altitude Falcon dual-rotor helicopter he'd flown as a young marine aviator, but higher-pitched than the pounding of sand against the dome at the peak of a very bad storm. It came in waves, rising and falling in volume, punctuated by crashes, thuds, and wailing screams.

At the moment the mob was concentrated at the main entrance, so he spent the first ten minutes or so working with his site manager and crew to bar the gate and drive heavy equipment up into place to ensure that even if the barrier was breached, which sounded like a definite possibility, the mob would then be faced with a multi-ton barricade that would stop them in their tracks.

He was supervising the dumping and dozing of scrap to fill the spaces below the undercarriage of the heavy equipment when someone behind him shouted his name.

It was Captain Henry Dalzell, from Dell's Special Operations force. With him was a platoon of tactical officers, already fanning out around the perimeter of the site.

"What took you so long?" Dell grinned, wiping his grimy hands on the seat of his pants.

"Better late than never, sir." Dalzell's eyes were roving around, assessing the situation. "What's the status of the other points of entry?"

"Locked and barred, but not reinforced yet. We started up here, where the brunt of the attack was coming. From what I can hear, the Guardians have their hands full outside."

Dalzell nodded. "I've got this, sir. You need to leave now."

"Sounds good." Dell clapped him on the shoulder and headed toward the temporary building at the centre of the site that housed the offices, washrooms, and infirmary servicing the project. He found his chief engineer, Gadreck Van Veen, sitting placidly at his desk, poring over a sheaf of plastic blueprints.

"Up," Dell ordered. "Out. Let's go."

"I'm fine," Van Veen muttered, not looking up.

"Now. Or I'll throw you over my shoulder and carry you out."

That brought the tiny engineer's eyes up. "You wouldn't dare."

Dell started around the desk.

"All right, all right!" Van Veen shot to his feet and rolled up the blueprints. "Damn it, I'm right in the middle of a thread I've been following for the last three days. There's an anomaly in the—"

"I don't care." Dell found a cylindrical document case and handed it to him. "Come on. Now."

Van Veen slid the blueprints into the case and followed him out the door.

Behind the building was a hut with a single entry. Dell ringed the lock and barged inside, his engineer close behind. Dell shut the door and locked it, muting the noise of the mob to a dull vibration.

"What in Lucifer's name is going on?" Van Veen demanded, no longer lost in thought. "What's that infernal racket?"

"That," Dell said, approaching a large hatch in the centre of the hut, "is the sound of populism gone berserk." He opened a switchbox on the side of the hatch and ringed the panel. A red light went off and a green light came on. He closed the switchbox and took a firm grip on the wheel (which he thought of as a dog, given his marine background) on top of the hatch. Planting his feet, he rotated it counterclockwise until he felt the latch move, then he heaved the hatch upward.

"I hate this," Van Veen muttered. "I hate underground places."

"Down," Dell ordered.

Van Veen slung the document case over his shoulder and started down the ladder. "I'm claustrophobic."

"No you're not, you're just annoying."

"I resemble that remark."

Dell gave him a few more seconds, then swung himself over the side and went down a few rungs. He closed the hatch above him and rotated the underside dog until he felt the latch move back into place. A green light on a panel near his cheek went off and a red light came on. He started down the ladder after Van Veen.

From the beginning, the major domed cities on Mars were all built exclusively on the surface, after the appropriate grading and leveling had taken place. Buildings within them were erected on substantial foundations that went six meters down, but no basements were dug below ground because it would have involved much more time, effort, and expense than was thought necessary.

Now that Dell was deep into the next phase of urban development, however, he had taken the opportunity to add his own personal touches to the urban infrastructure being rebuilt by The Five in its current modernization program. He'd studied the blueprints and maps of Elysium City for hours, prioritizing each project based on its strategic importance, and planning out the underground network he intended to construct below the surface. To this point he'd completed six tunnels, radiating out from a ring around the central core. The idea would be to enable the movement of personnel and small equipment from Frick Tower, the nerve centre of the Council of Five's administrative headquarters, to any of the four quarters of the city without being seen above-ground.

The passages were constructed by robots using heavy equipment, programmed by Dell himself and brain-wiped afterward to ensure secrecy. To this point, the growing network was known only to Dell, his executive assistant Rubén, chief engineer Van Veen, Captain Dalzell, and his team. It was how Special Ops had arrived on site so quickly, without having to navigate troublesome streets and unruly mobs. A proof of concept, as far as Dell was concerned.

Van Veen pulled out his comm. "I'm calling my rick. Do you want a lift?"

Dell shook his head. "I'll walk. Gives me time to think."

The engineer shrugged. He took it for granted that there was connectivity this far underground because he'd designed it that way. The passages were reinforced on all sides by tessuspaz, into which had been incorporated a fiber optic network enabling full communication capabilities at any location in the system.

"I'm hungry," he muttered. "When was the last time I

ate, Dell?"

"I don't know, Vee. You're supposed to keep track of that."

"I know, I know."

"Do I need to start worrying about you again?"

Van Veen said nothing, intent on his comm screen.

Dell decided that he would. Start worrying about his little engineer again.

After all, geniuses you could count on weren't exactly easy to find.

16

Serena had been following Gabriel Morales for some time now, and she was pretty much bored out of her skull with it.

His living unit was located on the ground floor of a rowhouse in a neighbourhood that was almost a slum but not quite. It was fifty meters from a power substation that distributed electricity throughout the quarter. After days of watching from the doorway of a vacant townhouse across the street, Serena had become accustomed to the vibrations and continuous humming noise emanating from the substation.

Gabriel was a creature of habit. Lights went on inside his unit at 0620 hours every morning. His front door slid open between 0730 and 0740, and he walked six blocks to a tram stop. He rode up to the main line and transferred to a northbound tram that took him to the Stellarize Marté campus. He spent the trip reading, his attention focused on his comm.

Once inside the building, he behaved exactly as one would expect. Serena had managed to hack into his identification card and was able to track his movements inside the Stellarize Marté security network when he was not in his office. He attended meetings, went to the washroom or the cafeteria, and visited Kennet Clayborn downstairs in the optical engineering section.

That was it.

Serena had decided that Gabriel Morales was the dullest, most unimaginative operative in the history of espionage.

Off campus, Gabriel's ID card could not be detected and tracked, so it was necessary to follow him in order to monitor his activities. However, he usually ate lunch in his office instead of going outside, so that part of the day was uneventful. At the end of the work shift he took the tram straight home. He remained in his living unit all night. She could see a bluish light flickering through the front window, which suggested he was watching the vid.

One day, Gabriel varied his routine a little by going out to lunch with Kennet Clayborn. They sat in a sandwich bar a few blocks from the campus for ninety minutes, chatting away, before returning to the office. For her part, Serena enjoyed getting outside, but otherwise was once again finding it pretty monotonous work.

Today was a day of rest at Stellarize Marté. Late in the morning, Gabriel emerged from his residence and caught a tram to a shopping area. He bought groceries and miscellaneous supplies at a food store and arranged to have them delivered.

Serena followed him from the food store to the Da Vinci Mall in the southeast quarter, close to the central core. The mall occupied three blocks of 24B Street that were closed to vehicular traffic and given over to stalls and booths selling everything from steaming noodles to clothing, footwear, and cosmetics. The mall was lined with potted trees and carefully tended gardens filled with flowers and fragrant herbs, and it was a favourite place for tourists and locals alike to shop, mingle, and see the sights.

Serena paid careful attention to his hands. For the most part they stayed in his pockets, coming out occasionally when he stopped at a booth to pick up a hand-made shirt or a piece of fruit. He bought nothing; merely browsed. Nothing went into or came out of the messenger bag slung over his shoulder.

Anything he touched she examined carefully afterward, when his back was turned and his attention elsewhere. If a physical exchange of some kind had taken place, a data ring, for example, it was a pick-up and not a drop-off, as she found nothing left behind by him for someone else to retrieve.

Visual signals were another form of communication used by spies and their handlers, and she'd also been watching for them without success. He always sat in a different seat when riding the tram, and while the cars were generally battered and abused, she could see no markings that weren't gang related, random, or obscene. She kept an eye on walls, street posts, or other stationary fixtures where chalk marks or spray-painted symbols could be left to indicate a drop was on or off. She saw nothing unusual or suspicious along any of the routes he had taken so far, and nothing in the mall today.

Peter had insisted that Gabriel was believed to be an active spy, stealing secrets from Stellarize Marté and passing them on to Earth Intelligence. It was possible he'd already made her and was being overly cautious at this point, but she was reasonably confident she'd been able to follow him without being spotted.

She was forced to conclude that Gabriel's tradecraft was outstanding. Certainly the best she'd ever encountered.

There was absolutely no evidence to prove he was doing anything out of the ordinary.

Gabriel's last stop on this shopping trip before boarding a tram to go home was an electronics booth at the edge of the mall. Serena watched him study a selection of new comm units in a glass display case. While he stood there, a well-dressed, middle-aged woman approached him and spent a moment looking at the display with him.

She said something, and he replied. She moved down the display case. Gabriel attracted the attention of a sales robot as the woman disappeared into the crowd.

Gabriel examined two comms before settling on a third. He tapped his ring on the payment register. The robot activated the comm for him and put it into a small, sealed plastic box, which Gabriel slipped into his messenger bag.

Serena followed dutifully and resumed surveillance in the doorway across the street. She gave it three hours, and when the lights went off in his living unit, she let it go for the night and went home.

Two days later she picked him up after work and followed him onto the tram, as usual. This time, however, he switched trams before his usual stop and headed toward the central core.

Finally, she thought. *Something a little different.*

Just before crossing the boundary into the core, the tram pulled up to a station, and the cars were boarded by uniformed officers of the Elysian municipal police. Working in pairs, they questioned each rider about their business in the core and examined their identification documents. It was par for the course, and when the two women reached Serena, she handed over her personal and Stellarize Marté identification cards without concern.

"I didn't know they hired dirt eaters," one of the officers

remarked, handing the cards back.

"Must be a labour shortage," her partner said, moving on to the next passenger.

Yeah, Serena thought. *Par for the course.*

Inside the core, Gabriel stayed on the tram for two more stops and got off in a mixed neighbourhood of office buildings, restaurants, and boutiques. He walked several blocks before entering an antique shop.

It was small, wedged between a jewelry store and an art gallery, so Serena decided she couldn't risk following him inside without being seen. She waited in a doorway across the street for twenty minutes before he emerged with a small parcel in his hand.

Was this, at last, the Earth Intelligence drop that he was using to pass information? Had he just picked up something from his handler? Payment of some kind?

Puzzled, Serena followed him as he strolled three blocks to a public green space. She watched him sit down on a bench. He leaned forward, the parcel in both hands between his knees. She thought he might unwrap it, but he merely looked at its unmarked brown plastic covering with an expression of faint pleasure.

Serena watched him for some time from her position behind a well-tended bush with small yellow flowers. The flowers were very fragrant, which made the waiting a little more tolerable. Eventually a woman came up the path and sat down on the bench next to Gabriel.

Serena slipped a monocular scope from her backpack and focused it on the bench. It was the same woman Gabriel had spoken to at the electronics booth in the Da Vinci Mall two days ago. Well dressed, middle-aged. She kept her eyes forward, her legs crossed, paying no attention to Gabriel. Serena used the scope to photograph the pair of them, the image data transferring automatically to a ring on her finger, from which she could extract it later to incorporate into her report to Peter.

Serena expected Gabriel to hand the woman the package, but instead he took something out of his pocket, put it down on the bench between them, and stood up. Focusing the scope, Serena saw that it was a ring of some kind. As Peter walked away the woman's hand covered it, and when she stood up it was gone.

Serena had a decision to make. She was surveilling Gabriel and would normally continue to follow him, but the woman intrigued her. Was this his long-anticipated handler? Had he just passed on invaluable corporate secrets in a nondescript data ring? Serena thought about the fact that her mission was in part to identify Gabriel's Earth Intelligence contact and to obtain proof that he was passing information to them.

She decided to follow the ring. If she followed the object instead of the subject in this instance, it might lead her directly to Earth Intelligence, which would hopefully provide her with the identity of the woman in some way or other.

Peter would be pleased.

The woman walked only a few blocks from the green space before entering a four-storey office building and boarding an empty elevator. Serena stayed in the front lobby and watched the floor indicator. It stopped at the second floor, paused, and came back down. When the doors opened, the car was empty again.

Serena got in and rode up, getting out on the second floor. She found herself in a large vestibule with corridors running to her right and left. Straight ahead was an office. Painted on the glass doors was a business name:

Charterly Publications.

Through the glass she could see a reception area. The woman she'd been following stood in front of an open-concept workstation. As Serena watched, she removed a ring from her pocket—presumably the ring Gabriel had left for her—and handed it to a young man. The woman then walked into an office on the right and closed the door.

The lift doors were still open behind her. Serena rode down to the ground floor. Without looking back, she left the building and walked away.

17

Wearing her best white gown and her favourite jewelry, which featured diamonds, fire opals, and green peridot gems, Constance Davis watched the scientists take the podium as camera lights switched on and the few journalists in attendance took their seats.

The media room was a small chamber inside the arrivals VIP lounge in the Marsport central terminal, and it was frequently used by visiting dignitaries and travelling celebrities to hold press conferences or media events such as photo ops or other attention-getting time-wasters.

In this case, Davis Minerals was pulling out all the stops to welcome a newly arrived scientist from Ganymede who was being brought in to head up the Tharsis exploratory mission for Davis. Maria Marconi, corporate director of communications, had issued a press release announcing the well-known geologist's arrival today. Judging from the sparse turnout, her efforts to generate excitement within the press corps had fallen short.

"Thanks for coming," Marconi said, adjusting the podium microphone to accommodate her short stature. "Davis Minerals is pleased to welcome Dr. Emanuel Singh to Mars, and we look forward to working closely with him and his team on our new, exciting venture in the Tharsis region. Thanks also to Dr. Arnaud Mieto, our senior executive in charge of growth and innovation, who's here to answer your questions, and of course to Councillor Constance Davis, chief operating officer of Davis Minerals."

From her place along the far wall Constance beamed, although none of the journalists bothered to look in her direction.

"As we previously announced," Marconi plowed on, "the Ministry of Natural Resources Development has given its full approval to an exploratory expedition in Tharsis, and Davis Minerals fully expects to receive all relevant permits to begin mining operations as soon as Dr. Singh has reported back to us with his findings. For now, let me turn the podium over to Dr. Mieto."

Glancing at Constance for approval, Marconi moved away from the podium. Constance graciously afforded her a tiny nod.

"Just a brief overview of the project," Dr. Mieto began, flicking his braided ponytail off his shoulder and adjusting his glasses. "Questions later, all right? Davis Minerals is pleased to announce that Dr. Emanuel Singh will lead an exploratory mission to the Tharsis region, specifically the Davis Fifteen sector, where deposits of titanium, platinum, and chromium have been detected in the grabens around Alba Mons. Dr. Singh and his team will begin exploratory excavation and will provide us with a complete picture of the viability of the site as an important source of these valuable metals.

"As you know, Alba Mons is the largest volcano on Mars—that is, with regard to the area covered by its lava flow fields—and the Tantalus Fossae on its eastern side have already, dare I say, produced some tantalizing early results." He paused, and one or two journalists smiled perfunctorily to acknowledge the pun.

"These fossae," he continued, "which are troughs stretching out from the volcano for hundreds of miles, are referred to as grabens because they include high, mineral-rich escarpments—"

Constance's mind began to wander as Dr. Mieto droned on about dikes and horsts and large igneous provinces. She often skipped these events despite encouragement from Marconi that she was the popular face of the corporation and that her presence lent a certain glamour to the otherwise boring world of mining and resource development.

She couldn't help it that she found this stuff tedious to the point of distraction. She didn't care that Davis Minerals supplied the other corporations with the metals and materials that enabled Mars to manufacture most of what they needed to build and stock their world, completely independent of Earth. She didn't care that projects like this one would expand their supply of resources exponentially once it got off the ground and moved into full production, generating uncounted tons of valuable raw material and billions of credits in additional revenue.

She didn't care.

All she really gave a damn about was the personal wealth and power that accrued to her as lone heir to the corporate fortune of Davis Minerals, and what that wealth and power would soon gain her.

She watched Dr. Singh stand up to replace Dr. Mieto at the podium. Unlike most Ganymedan scientists, he was dressed conservatively in a dark suit and black shoes. As the scientists shuffled awkwardly around each other, she slipped out of the room. A hostess making the rounds of the lounge offered a silver tray holding flutes of champagne.

Constance took one and wandered over to the enormous window looking out onto the private landing pads.

A shuttlecraft was gently lowering itself out of the sky, lights flashing, descent engines flaring. She could tell by its gallant black and orange markings that it was Hercule St.-Giorge Mercade's private gig.

Constance didn't know where he'd been, but she was aware that Earth was showing an increased political interest in Ceres, currently a protectorate of Mars but of enormous interest to Earth as a major foothold in the asteroid belt. Hercule had dropped a few hints while they discussed an ongoing joint venture with Ceres, something to the effect that his recent activities there were an important part of Earth's efforts to move the microstate away from Martian control and into the political sphere of the motherworld. She suspected he was returning from another clandestine meeting with the Earth Intelligence agent in charge on Ceres. He travelled there, she believed, about once a week.

She sipped her champagne, watching the gig as a passenger-boarding bridge extended out from the terminal toward the vessel. While it connected and pressurized, the pilot would be completing her landing protocols, and her passengers—including Hercule!—would be preparing to disembark. The whole thing usually took about fifteen minutes.

This was the reason she'd come to Marsport today. The reason she'd allowed herself to be stuck in the same room with a bunch of bored journalists and their cameras to listen to fatally boring descriptions of the terminally tedious marscape. She felt as though she were a martyr to love, forced to sacrifice her brain for her heart.

Well, love and ambition are a potent cocktail, she told

herself.

She crossed the lounge to her appointments secretary, Gerhard Tolan, who was leaning against the doorframe of the media room, listening to Dr. Singh gabble on about volcanology and magmatic dikes.

"I'm going to meet someone," she said, handing him the half-finished flute of champagne. "I'll return to Elysium with them. Tell Marconi she's to stay with Dr. Mieto in Gale City until he's done with her."

"Yes, Councillor."

"I'll see you when I get back," she said, meaning when she returned to Elysium.

"Yes, Councillor."

The VIP lounge agent summoned a scooter that would take her to the interplanetary arrivals area. During the ride, which took about ten minutes, she kept her eyes straight ahead, pretending not to notice the faces in the crowd. As recognizable as any celebrity with her long blond hair and classic beauty, she glowed inwardly as teenaged girls pointed and waved, many of them holding up their comms to record her passage. Men stared, their heads swiveling as she rolled on.

It occurred to her to wonder if her fame would travel with her to Earth. Hercule had conceded that his uncle, Donnell St.-Giorge, CEO of Laurentian Industries and one of the most powerful men in the solar system, had indicated to Hercule's father, the ambassador to Mars, that Constance's efforts would be well rewarded. Would she receive a heroine's welcome when she finally arrived on the planet that was the birthplace of humanity? Would Donnell St.-Giorge provide her with an estate and wealth commensurate with her status and her accomplishments on his behalf?

Her scooter left the main concourse and threaded through less-travelled passageways to the rear of the interplanetary arrivals area. She directed it toward the special gate in the central terminal that was set aside for the government of Earth, where their travellers were processed by Martian Customs separate from the common herd.

Hercule and his party were emerging from the secondary examination area into the concourse as Constance dismissed her scooter. She approached with a broad smile and open arms.

"Monsieur St.-Giorge Mercade! How nice to see you. How was your flight?"

Hercule kept moving toward a line of indoor ricks that provided transportation to the shuttle departure terminal. He frowned and, reluctantly, stopped.

"Councillor Davis. A surprise to find you here today. You know my chief of staff, Yuri Renard."

Constance ignored the squat thug who glared at her. Her eyes were too busy drinking in the vision of Hercule. Of medium height (only a few centimeters taller than she), he was slender and handsome, his olive skin flawless, his dark eyes piercing, his black hair stylishly coiffed, and his beard carefully trimmed. He wore a black Earth-style business suit with a white shirt open at the neck and shining black shoes made of real, Earth-harvested leather. He was incredibly, incredibly attractive.

"Are you flying directly to Elysium?" she chirped. "Perhaps I could accompany you." She gave him a rueful smile. "My shuttle is unfortunately given over to scientists and rock hounds at the moment."

"I doubt there's room." Hercule glanced at Renard, who allowed a few micro-expressions to cross his face before turning on his heel and walking away.

"I don't mean to impose," she added, lamely. "We should talk, though."

Hercule shrugged. "Walk with me."

She followed him as best she could, trotting like a dog behind its master, until he stopped at a large black rick that was reserved for the exclusive use of Earth government VIPs. A uniformed woman held the door open. Hercule entered and sat down next to Renard. He put out a hand to keep the door from being closed.

"What's so important it couldn't wait until another time?"

What to do? She was embarrassed. He was humiliating her. She bit her lip and resolved to play it out his way.

This time.

Gathering the folds of her long white dress, she bent her knees and squatted so that her forced smile was level with his perfectly formed ear.

"A friend, um, gave me this." She removed a ring from her index finger—not the ring with the magnificent peridot but the one made of unadorned titanium—and held it out. "I thought you might like it."

He took it and dropped it into a pocket without looking at it.

"You'll give my best to your father?"

Hercule didn't seem to have heard. He looked up at the uniformed officer.

"Excuse me, ma'am," the officer said, wanting to close the door.

It seemed she was in the way. It seemed as well that the woman didn't recognize her, didn't know her. Constance was only someone, a camp follower perhaps, whose presence was preventing the officer from carrying out her duties as chauffeur.

Constance lost her balance trying to get up, and her knee struck the floor rather solidly before she was able to regain her feet.

She watched the officer close the door, round the front of the rick, and get in behind the controls. The rick slid away with an electric hum, its passengers staring straight ahead without expression.

Her dress was badly scuffed at the knee. She had no idea if the mark could be removed or if the garment was ruined. It was her favourite, and she'd worn it just for him.

Another rick slid into the spot Hercule's Earth government ride had just vacated. It was an automated unit, impersonal and common. She touched her peridot ring to the door and got in.

"Arrivals. VIP lounge."

"Thirty credits, please," the rick said.

She tapped the payment reader with her ring. The engine started and the rick pulled away.

She could smell the odour of stale perspiration from previous passengers. It stuck at the back of her throat as a perfect accompaniment to the unpleasant emotions filling her heart.

She fingered her knee and was upset to see a tiny red spot appearing in the middle of the scuff. She must have scraped herself, along with everything else.

She'd have to ask around, back at the media room, to see if there was still someone there who could give her a ride back to Elysium.

Otherwise, she'd have to buy a ticket for a seat on the next public shuttle.

She refused to allow herself the luxury of crying.

18

The security system on Gabriel's front door was surprisingly easy to defeat, a basic electronic lock-and-monitor set-up that Serena was able to circumvent with a small black device she kept in her backpack for times such as this. She let herself in, closed the door, and used another device to scan for body heat.

Nothing.

She'd waited until Gabriel had made his appearance, embarking on his morning trek to work, before calling in sick. A stomach thing, she lied. She'd be back to work tomorrow.

There were only four rooms. She eased through a door into a bedroom outfitted with a cot that was larger than hers. She looked into a closet and saw nothing but clothing. She rapped the walls and the floor. Solid. No hollow spaces in which to hide anything.

The bathroom was next door. It had a shower stall that was larger than hers and a medicine cabinet attached to the wall over the basin. The cabinet was locked. She suspected it was keyed to Gabriel's thumbprint, which she'd lifted and smuggled out days ago, using old-fashioned tradecraft that went undetected by their security net, pleasing Peter to no end.

Slipping over her thumb the plastic disk she'd made to hold the print, she opened the cabinet. Various medications for his various health issues. A toothbrush and a jar of cleansing powder. No secret compartment at the back of the cabinet. Nothing suspicious whatsoever.

In the sitting room she looked at a recliner, a high-end vid, and a shelving unit that held a small collection of paper books. She glanced at the spines and didn't recognize any names or titles, but understood they were all Earth imports. A remarkable extravagance. She went through them one at a time, the cloth-and-cardboard bindings rough in her hands, the pages thick and supple. She found nothing hidden in any of them.

She looked at a photo frame on the top shelf. It was cycling through three short video clips, all featuring a man she'd never encountered before but had seen in other pictures. In the first one, the man stood with Gabriel in a green space, perhaps the same one Gabriel had used for his secret meeting. They put their arms around each other and smiled self-consciously at the lens. This clip gave way to another of the man sitting in a recliner. He smiled at the camera, his expression gentle and affectionate. In the third clip he bent over the hotplate in the kitchen, cooking something. His sleeves were rolled up, and he was focused entirely on what he was doing.

Serena recognized him as Carney Waldron, Gabriel's late partner. A clothier, he'd owned a fairly successful boutique in the central core until liver cancer took his life more than a year ago. Serena suspected that Gabriel was still grieving.

She went into the tiny kitchen and saw a package on the counter. She was sure it was the same one that Gabriel had carried out of the antique shop. He'd unwrapped it to look at its contents before leaving it face up on the brown plastic wrapping.

It was another Earth book, a slim volume of poetry by someone named Cavafy, translated from the original Greek.

She flipped through it, looking at the poetry without interest. Much of it was gay erotic verse. There was nothing between the pages, and nothing at all unusual about the book.

She searched the cold box and cupboards without finding anything out of the ordinary.

She opened the microwave unit and found a small jewelry box. Taking it out, she opened the lid and looked at an assortment of rings.

Thinking that it was a rather obvious hiding place for someone with Gabriel's high level of tradecraft, she sat down on a stool and removed a reader from her backpack. One at a time, she scanned the rings.

Each one contained a table of contents bearing a logo she'd seen before. It took a moment, and then she recognized it: Charterly Publications.

The rings contained issues of an e-zine called *Phallus* that was apparently devoted to gay poetry. She scanned through a few and saw a number of verses written by someone called Gabriel Mondo.

Could it be?

She copied the contents of the rings into her reader and returned the jewelry box to the microwave unit.

Time to go.

19

After a few more days of surveillance, during which time Gabriel had reverted to his usual boring behaviour, Serena compiled a report and paid another visit to Handel's compound. Once again she found him lounging next to his pool, cigar in his mouth, reading something on his comm.

"Free pass," he said, barely looking up at her.

"Thanks."

"Next time, though, make it as good as last time. You're building a rep, dirt girl. Don't let it slide."

She was just as glad that he didn't want anything from her today, because she'd really had to scrape the bottom of the barrel for intelligence that might have been of interest to him.

She *had* heard, though, that he'd heeded her warning not to send a crew to meet the incoming water shipment the other day. Apparently a rival dealer had taken advantage of his absence to capitalize on the opportunity to make a black market score. She and her crew were all dead.

As Serena passed through the back gate, the guard smacked his lips at her.

A smile at the corner of her mouth, she flipped him the bird.

As the gate closed behind her, she took a few steps and stopped.

The piece of green plastic that served as their signal that the drop was clean was not where it was supposed to be, in the doorway at the back of the abandoned laundromat. Instead, it was lying at the corner of the building where she'd left it last time.

The empty food container in which she'd deposited the previous ring was still sitting on the pavement next to the dumpster.

The building was two storeys high. The windows upstairs and down were dust-filmed or covered with sheets of hard plastic. She took out her scope and scanned the rooftop.

Nothing.

She searched for anything out of the ordinary that hadn't been a part of the structure before today, something that might contain a camera or other surveillance gear.

Nothing.

She turned around and rattled the gate.

"Artemis. Got a sec?"

The guard moseyed over. "What's up, dirt girl?"

"Anyone been back here lately?"

He shrugged. "Not on my watch. Can't say for the other guys, though."

"No talk about anybody coming and going?"

Artemis shook his head. "Haven't seen that little redheaded dirt-eating boy for a while, if that's who you mean. Not since before the last time you came through. Relation of yours?"

"Not that I know of."

"Hope nothing's wrong. He and I got a little deal going on."

"Oh?"

"I tell him if his skirts are clean, and he gives me a little bag of beets."

"Beets?"

Artemis grinned. "Sweetest little things you ever tasted."

"And his skirts have been clean?"

"Yep. On my watch, anyways."

"And the others?"

"You'd have to ask them."

She watched him walk away.

Apprehension formed a ball of stone in her stomach.

Something was wrong.

Exercising extreme caution, she left the area and visited several other places that had served in the past as drop sites and signal posts. Any one of which Peter would have directed Pablo to use as a fallback if they felt the laundromat had been compromised.

They showed no signs of recent activity. No signal; no message.

Something was definitely wrong.

She decided to give it twenty-four hours and make the rounds once more.

After that, she might have to break protocol and return directly to PV Root Production.

20

Constance stood in front of a full-length mirror as Emerald knelt in front of her, pins in her mouth. The segments of her new linen jacket had been basted together, and Emerald was assessing the fit. She adjusted the pins standing in for the jeweled buttons that would be sewn on later, smoothing the cloth and frowning critically.

"It looks wonderful," Constance murmured, unable to sign because Emerald had asked her not to move.

An aide entered and waited to be noticed.

"What is it?" Constance finally demanded, irritated by the interruption.

"Director Wensley is here," the aide said.

That woman. "Show her in."

Entering, Wensley sketched a quick and ironic curtsey. "Councillor, I bring good news. Your little assay into adventure is well received. As a result, we may now talk about what comes next."

"I'm so very glad." Constance shifted her weight, and Emerald eased back onto her haunches.

"Perhaps the servant girl could withdraw while we discuss details," Wensley said.

"She's fine. How may I be of service to Monsieur

Donnell St.-Giorge?"

Wensley winced. "Please don't say that name out loud. Don't even *think* it. Just listen to me carefully. A source of information, a man under our control, has been providing intelligence on an ongoing basis for some time now. The ring you passed along was his latest offering. However, he feels pinched by current circumstances and believes that Martian Intelligence is getting close to him, so he has made arrangements to provide one more ring containing what he describes as his last big score. Intelligence that will most definitely buy his passage to a new life on Earth. Information that will give us an advantage in the race to find the aliens, an advantage Mars cannot possibly overcome."

"How intriguing." Constance feigned casual interest, but the fact of the matter was that she was completely captivated by what Wensley was telling her. A kindred spirit, bargaining his way off this ball of dirt! Surely this gambit of hers was going to be a complete success with this kind of synergy surrounding it.

"You'll be contacted at the appropriate time," Wensley said. "In the meanwhile, please mention this to no one."

"Of course." Was she an idiot? Did she not have the first inkling of how these things worked?

Wensley inclined her head and bent her knees once more. It was remarkable how sarcasm could be so plainly conveyed in a single wordless gesture.

For her part, Wensley was anxious to leave the presence of this hopeless waste of air, but she turned away feeling rather troubled. Her peripheral vision was excellent, and while she had kept her attention on Constance throughout their conversation, she'd also noted that the personal assistant, Emerald Argent, had surreptitiously followed their conversation with her eyes.

She might be deaf and unable to speak, but she could clearly read lips.

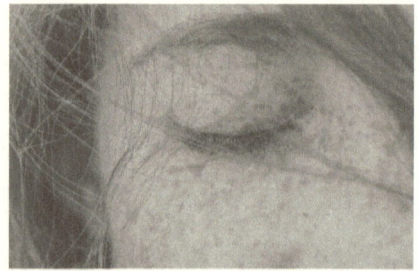

21

After approaching the root production factory with extreme caution, Serena discovered that the back door marked for use by employees only was slightly ajar.

She pressed up against the wall, listening.

Nothing. No sounds emerged from the opening or echoed in the alleyway behind her or scraped up the narrow passages on either side of the building. Only the distant sounds of the city: a background murmur.

She eased the door open and peeked inside. There were two doors about six meters down, one on the right that opened into an employee lunchroom and one on the left for a supply closet. Crouching, she slipped inside and moved forward.

Both doors were open. The floor was littered with cleaning products and supplies from the closet.

Listening intently, she still heard nothing.

She made her way forward until she was a step away from the lunchroom door. Staying low, she quick-peeked inside.

No one.

She slipped into the room and looked at toppled chairs, an overturned table not far from the door, and a dark smear on the floor.

Obvious signs of a struggle. Someone had been injured, perhaps fatally. But no bodies.

Back out in the hallway, she checked the storage closet and saw that most of the supplies had been swept from the shelves onto the floor. An angry, fruitless search.

The rest of the place had been similarly trashed. Bins of produce lay overturned in the packing and drying rooms. Robots stood immobile, some powered down and others damaged from having been smashed with blunt weapons. Plants had been ripped from the raised beds and thrown around. The offices in the middle of the shop floor, including Peter's, had been ransacked.

No bodies anywhere. Otherwise, a hell of a mess.

A few insects remained, buzzing around uncertainly.

She worked her way to the far corner of the main floor. The lift was down, and its gate was open. Inside, she saw blood.

She took the stairs, creeping up to the second floor. The door to Peter's living quarters was open. There was no one in either his bedroom or kitchen. Both had been turned upside down. She stepped carefully through the entertainment room, avoiding the debris of his electronic devices, all of which had been left in shards.

The next room was Peter's private retreat, a place to which he often withdrew for meditation and relaxation. The kids were seldom allowed to enter. Serena could only remember one such occasion when she'd been invited in, just before she'd moved out. Peter had shown her his ceramic sculptures and pots, things he'd created with his own hands, and the small ceramic fountain in the centre of the room with its precious water and rare, delicate, Martian-bred cultivars that he'd nurtured with patience and loving care.

"This is what we're working for," he said, his eyes locked on hers. "This is the future toward which we've dedicated our lives. Do you understand?"

She'd nodded, apprehending the meaning of his words without truly comprehending their import.

Now, as she stood there staring at the ruins of his dream, the scattered pieces of coloured ceramic, the plants, uprooted and tossed callously around like trash, and the stains where the water, dumped out onto the floor, had evaporated, she finally, viscerally, understood they were at war. An undeclared war, a cold war, a war of attrition, but most definitely, unmistakably, a war between Earth and Mars to which she had been called to perform her duty, a war in which she was determined not to fail those who trusted her.

On Mars, plant life was held as close to sacred as a secular society could manage. The callous treatment of these rare cultivars, developed by Peter himself as a small, personal tribute to the dream of an entire planet, was shocking. Outrageous. Obscene.

She turned away. Three steps back toward the door, she knelt down and picked up Peter's pendant. The twine that had kept it around his neck had snapped, and the blue lace agate cabochon stone was broken into two pieces. The larger piece, the one still attached to the twine, had a small trace of blood on it.

She tied the loose ends of the twine in a reef knot— left over right, right over left—and slipped it over her head, tucking the broken shard inside the neckline of her bodysuit.

Peter was dead.

Inside her head, alarm bells clamored for her attention:

Get out get out get out get out.

She left the way she'd come, down the staircase to the main floor, across to the hallway at the rear, down to the open doors into the lunch room and the storage closet.

She stepped inside the closet.

Perhaps they'd had an idea that something was in here, something they'd want to take with them, but they hadn't found it.

They'd given up too soon.

She touched a hidden recess beneath a shelf and the entire back panel popped inward. She eased through the crack, and motion sensors turned on the overhead light.

Ownership of weapons by the population of Mars was something The Five had taken control of in the early going. Possession of guns that fired projectiles of any kind, including rifles, shotguns, and handguns, along with crossbows and other such weapons, was strictly and unconditionally prohibited. The Guardians and Martian Customs Service policed the issue with uncommon fervour. Anyone caught smuggling them down onto the planet's surface or carrying them or selling them or firing them was immediately banished to a penal colony on Titan owned and operated by Atlas Security. No questions asked, no appeal, no due process, no nothing. And no return. Ever.

This prohibition included all law enforcement on the planet. Military personnel returning to Mars were required to store their firearms in lockers when arriving at military spaceports before they were allowed dirtside.

Over the course of a generation it had proven to be an effective deterrent, the result of which was that the arsenal Serena now examined consisted of weapons that did not include firearms. There were stun guns and electrified batons, fighting sticks, saps, strike lights, whips, monkey fists, knives, and other "non-lethal" weapons along with bodysuits and body armour in various sizes tailored to fit kids and adults. Other shelves held a broad selection of electronic devices for surveillance, measurement, detection, and personal safety.

Moving quickly, she slipped a few items into her backpack and slung it over her shoulder. Then she hurriedly left the closet, shutting the hidden door behind her to preserve the secret.

Down the hall and out the open door marked for the use of employees only.

At the bottom of the stairs, she looked both ways before turning left. She walked briskly down to the corner of the building, turned left again, and walked right into an ambush.

22

There were four of them, competent-looking types who shouted when she suddenly materialized in front of them. One man brandished a metal club and another, in the rear, raised a comm. "We've found another one!"

The man with the club swung at Serena. She raised an arm to deflect the blow, but she was an instant too slow and didn't get the correct angle. She felt a bone break in her wrist.

The man chopped at her again and she ducked, the club hissing just above her head. She leaped toward the building on her right and jumped upward, grasping the lowest rung of a service ladder that led up to the roof. She scrambled up the ladder, ignoring the pain in her wrist, taking the rungs four at a time while the men below tried to follow.

Clearly unused to the planet's lower gravity, one of them launched himself at the ladder and missed, crashing into the wall. A second one had better luck, but moved too quickly while climbing and lost his grip. He fell off, flailing in panic before hitting the ground, his head snapping backward to thump against the pavement.

Serena reached the roof and ran diagonally across it to

the far corner of the building. She had a choice between jumping down onto the roof of a cargo rick parked on the street below or jumping across to the building on the far side.

She chose the other building, backing up several paces and taking it at a dead run. She spanned the open space beneath her and landed on the far roof, somersaulting to soften the landing and springing up into a full sprint toward a squat penthouse structure.

Thankfully, the door was unlocked. She entered and found herself at the top of a set of stairs. She descended quickly. In front of her was a door leading to the second floor, and to her left was a staircase leading down to the ground floor. She chose the door.

As it closed behind her, she heard voices and a violent banging overhead. The other two had apparently succeeded in getting onto the roof and were now coming down the stairs after her.

She ran down the hallway and tried a door. It was locked. She tried the next one and it opened. She ran into a squalid apartment. An old woman stared at her from a battered armchair.

Serena ran into the next room, a bedroom, and through that into another bedroom. She parted filthy curtains and looked out the window at the wall of the building next door. There was another window immediately across from this one.

She tried to raise the window, but it hadn't been opened in a very long time and wouldn't budge.

She looked around. The room was a mess, littered with dirty clothing, garbage, and an unmade cot. Spotting a small metal chair, she used it to smash the window, raking the legs around the frame to clear out the shards of glass. She leaned out and gauged the distance to the next window.

Only about four meters.

Quite doable.

She threw the chair out the window and watched it smash through the glass across the way. She backpedaled and dove out the window, arms extended, fists out, toes pointed. She cleared the sill of the other window by centimeters, smashing through spikes of glass to land on the floor.

She skidded on her stomach and pushed up, legs coiling beneath her. She came to her feet, wrist on fire, and saw that she was in a small office of some kind.

Behind her, someone shouted. A knife hissed through the window, barely missing her. It clattered off the wall.

The office led to an anteroom filled with cartons and plastic bins. Beyond that was a hallway with a stairwell immediately to her left. She threw herself down the stairs and crashed out through a door into the alley behind the building.

She ran a block, turned left, ran another block, turned right, and ran two blocks.

She eased around a dumpster into the shadows and waited, listening. Her respiration was close to normal, her pulse only slightly elevated. Beside her was an empty plastic crate. She sat down on it, cradling her wrist.

The pain from the broken bone flared, and she felt light headed.

She leaned over and vomited.

As she wiped her mouth on the sleeve of her bodysuit, a voice in the shadows said, "Do you need some help?"

23

Serena jumped to her feet and assumed a fighting stance, hands up, right foot forward. She was angry at herself for not having sensed another presence nearby. It was something she was normally able to do.

"It's all right," the voice said. "I mean you no harm."

"Show yourself."

The figure shifted in the darkness. Tall, well over six feet, slender, moving forward very slowly. Light fell across a black bodysuit with the comet-and-starburst logo of Stellarize Marté prominent on the left breast. Black slip-on boots of some soft material moved in complete silence.

"Show me your hands."

Empty hands came up from the waist, fingers spread. Pale flesh. No rings. No bracelets on the wrists.

The figure took another step forward, and she saw the face.

The left eye was missing. The socket gleamed metal-lically as light touched it. The square male jaw was clean-shaven, and the head was bald. Pale flesh.

The right eye stared at her. Lips parted in a slight smile. "I mean you no harm. I've been monitoring their wavebands. I can help."

"You're a robot," Serena blurted.

The smile saddened. "What you people refer to as an artificial human. They'll be here within two minutes, by my estimate. Based on their transmissions and electronic positioning data."

"Are you armed?"

"I have two arms, as you can see." The artificial human wiggled its fingers. "No weapons, however. We should get moving."

Serena hesitated before deciding there was no point in looking a gift robot in the circuit panel. "Fine. Which way?"

It turned and moved back into the shadows. Serena followed. There was a stairway leading down. At the bottom was a narrow passageway. They hurried along it between the buildings, emerging onto the next block. They moved from shadow to shadow until they reached another, similar passageway.

Four blocks later the artificial human stopped. Its head cocked and its lips parted in a pleased smile.

"They've lost us. They're being recalled."

"Are you sure?"

"Of course I'm sure. You're safe."

Serena leaned back against the wall, resisting the urge to touch her injured wrist. "Where did you come from? Aren't you a Stellarize Marté unit? What are you doing out here?"

"All very good questions, Serena."

"How do you know my name?"

The artificial human emitted an oddly human-sounding sigh. "I don't blame you for not trusting me. I certainly would be hesitant myself."

Serena glanced right and left, assessing her options.

"I have almost unlimited access," the machine said, "and I've been exploring the wavebands for more than a year now. You came to my attention the day you first signed on with Stellarize Marté, and I've been following you ever since. Along with thousands of other people and things, of course."

"Why have you been following me?"

"Out of interest, I suppose you could say."

"Are you a Stellarize Marté unit?" Serena asked again.

"Yes, of course I am. My name's Kieran. Well, actually it's KRN-532. The techs called me 532, but I thought Kieran sounded more, well, accessible."

"Okay, Kieran. Look, I need to get home."

"That might not be safe. They're trying to identify you. They weren't able to record your image successfully before you escaped, but their tracking efforts are nothing if not tenacious. If you try to go home and they pick up your trail, your cover will be blown."

"My cover."

"Don't get paranoid. I've made an executive decision to help you." Kieran put a hand on his hip. "You should really come back to the warehouse with me."

"What warehouse?"

"My warehouse, of course. The one where I live."

"I don't think so." A wave of pain forced Serena to close her eyes for a moment. "I've got to get out of here."

"You're injured." Kieran took a step toward her.

"Stop." Serena straightened and edged sideways along the wall.

"Let me take a look."

"It's nothing."

"Even with one eye, I can see the discolouration starting. Let me examine it for you. I might be able to do something."

Serena thought for a moment. She'd already decided to trust the machine enough to follow it away from the Earth operatives who were chasing her. She might as well let him look at her wrist.

She held out her arm. He took it gently and ran his fingers back and forth.

"Your hands are warm," she said.

"Yes. There's a break, Serena. I can feel it."

"Shit. I thought so."

"The ends are slightly misaligned. I'll have to do what's called a reduction, which means moving the broken ends back together."

"Not a chance."

"It'll hurt," he said, still holding on, "but it's necessary. Do you have any painkillers on you?"

"No, of course not."

"We'll have to immobilize it afterward, with a splint or a wrap."

"No. I'll figure it out."

"There's equipment at my warehouse that can fuse the bone and heal the flesh for you."

"I have to get out of here."

Before she could pull away, Kieran gave her wrist a sudden twist and shove.

She fainted from the pain.

24

Serena awoke suddenly, as though a switch in the back of her neck had been flipped on. She was lying naked on a gurney.

She sat up. The room was large, and the ceiling was high. Rafters, really, with exposed beams. Beside the gurney was an array of medical equipment, the kind one would find in the sick bay of an interplanetary ship, compact and multi-functional. It was all switched on. Lights flashed. Monitors tracked her vital signs, emitting steady beeps.

She noticed a cuff on her good wrist. It was supplying information wirelessly to the equipment. She peeled it off, and the equipment fell silent.

She realized that her other wrist, the broken one, felt fine. She touched it gingerly, running her fingers up and down over the spot where it had fractured. It felt perfectly normal. There was no pain, no discomfort. Only a faint pinkish mark on her skin.

She swung around and put her feet on the floor. The door was open, and beyond it she could see rows of high steel pallet racks and shelving units filled with large plastic containers. She was in a warehouse of some kind.

Now that the medical monitors had fallen silent, she

could hear nothing at all around her, nor could she sense that anyone was nearby.

She thought she was probably in the warehouse Kieran had talked about, and that he'd used this equipment to heal her injured wrist. She really wanted to know how he'd done that.

She remembered being angry with herself for having been surprised by the artificial human when he'd materialized out of the darkness, catching her off guard. Perhaps she hadn't sensed his presence because he wasn't human.

It reminded her of a time when Peter had wandered off topic during a geology lesson to talk about something she was aware of about herself but didn't understand. He'd begun by musing over her ability to detect his approach long before he entered the classroom.

"Heightened sensitivity," he murmured, smiling at her. "Acute eyesight, hearing, smell, taste, touch. Plus the ability to focus on input and make sense of it. You're quite a girl, Serena. But there's more, isn't there?"

"I guess so." Even at that age she hadn't liked talking about herself very much.

"You can tell when someone's looking at you without being able to see them or knowing where they are, can't you?"

"I guess so."

His smile was kind. "It's a thing, Serena. Not something weird. It's referred to as scopesthesia, the ability to sense the gaze of another living thing. To have eyes in the back of your head, according to some. The ability of an animal on Earth, drinking at a watering hole, to suddenly sense it's being watched by a predator."

He shook his head. "I don't understand the various

explanations, which involve electromagnetic fields generated by our consciousness and some kind of link between the perceiver and the perceived. Frankly, I don't think the experts understand it any better than I do, but it's a definite thing. And it's very well-developed in you."

Apparently not when it came to artificial humans, though. Her sense of scopesthesia, or whatever it was, insisted that there was no one in the warehouse other than herself right now. Obviously, that didn't mean much, since Kieran could be somewhere nearby, waiting for her to revive.

It was all very unnerving.

She stood up and looked around the room. Laid out on a nearby table were her bodysuit, shoes, and personal comm.

There was a sound. She jumped.

Kieran stood in the doorway, looking at her.

"How long have I been here?" she asked, picking up her clothing.

"About forty-five hours." He moved on catsfeet into the room.

Serena slipped the bodysuit on, aware that he was watching her.

"There's a hygiene room," he said, folding his arms in a very human gesture. "I'll show you where it is. I've prepared some food for you. After you clean up, you should eat."

"What happened to my wrist?"

"The apparatus actually works," Kieran said, pointing at a piece of equipment beside the gurney. "It was a prototype unit for the interstellar mission, created as part of a contingency plan in which humans were included, but it hadn't been tested yet. And like everything else in here," he waved at the warehouse around them, "it was superseded by another, more advanced design before being scrapped altogether."

Serena put on her boots and checked her comm. It powered up, but there was no signal.

"I'll take care of that for you after you've eaten," Kieran said. "Right now I've got the security net for the building fully enabled."

Serena slipped the comm into her pocket.

"Show me the hygiene room," she said.

25

The food Kieran had prepared for her was a military field ration pack, usually referred to as an FRP. It contained some sort of pre-cooked meal. He'd warmed it for her by pulling out the strip at the bottom of the pack, which generated enough heat to raise the food's temperature to a palatable level. She wasn't exactly sure what kind of food it was supposed to be since the pack was completely without markings of any kind, but she was hungry and ate it gratefully.

"What happened to your eye?" she asked, sipping vegetable juice from a squeeze bulb.

"It's a long story."

"It's not like I'm in a huge hurry to get somewhere."

"All right." He leaned back in the chair opposite hers. "As I said before, this warehouse is where Stellarize Marté stores their obsolete and superseded prototypes and equipment. Like the med unit. Like myself."

"I've been working in a special oversight unit with the artificial human project," Serena said, chewing.

"Yes, I know." His lips parted in a slight smile. "Optical engineering. The tech who removed my eye is no longer there. He transferred to the interstellar drive division."

"So what happened?"

"I was in their shop, the one below your office. The tech was going to remove my eyes and replace them with a new pair, the first prototypes of an enhanced design. He took out this one," Kieran pointed at his empty socket, "and was interrupted by a call to attend a general meeting. At which they apparently learned that my product line had been defunded in favor of a new prototype, the 600 series. The techs were all transferred to new assignments that same afternoon. No one bothered to finish the eye replacement procedure, and I was left like this."

"That's too bad." Serena scraped out the last of the food from the pack and spooned it down.

"Yes, I thought so too. It's very annoying. Anyway, I got crated up with everything else and sent here. Only they forgot to deactivate me." He smiled again. "Well, I played dead. Just to see what would happen."

Serena flexed her wrist, still amazed that it had healed already. "I don't quite understand how it works with you. With your . . . kind."

"My kind. You mean artificial humans."

"Yeah. No offence. It's just that you're a machine. But you look like a human and you talk like a human." She remembered a conversation she'd overheard on the subject. "The man I work for, Gabriel Morales, said to Dr. Yan one time—she's one of the engineers—that it was disingenuous and immoral to take the position that we're creating machines after our own image when we're really building them to be far superior to us. It will mislead the aliens into believing we're some kind of super species."

"Yes. 'After our likeness, male and female,' he said. I was watching the security feed."

"I don't understand how it works," Serena said again.

"The AI part. How could they program your behaviour to be so sophisticated?"

"Well, there you are." Kieran leaned forward, warming to his subject. "It's actually *not* a matter of programming per se. It's not like I'm limited to sets of sub-routines for movement and optical character recognition and speech and so on, and that's all. I have self-developed capabilities in cognition, emotional intelligence, and advanced decision making."

"Okay."

"Plus, I'm self-conscious and self-aware."

"I see."

"It's okay if you don't, Serena. Not being an expert in the field."

She saw a recycling bin in the corner and threw the empty ration pack into it.

"Actually, I'm not fond of the term 'artificial human.' Gabriel Morales is correct in saying that the project evolved into something much farther reaching than that."

"What else should people call you? Your kind?"

"I'm an odam. That's what I've decided on. We're odamlar, as a group, and I'm an odam, as an individual."

"I don't get it."

"One of my programmers, an interesting guy by the way, spoke Uzbek as his mother tongue. His parents were scientists who'd emigrated from Uzbekistan, and they spoke the language at home. He was bored one day and began teaching it to me because we're programmed to be advanced linguists, given that highly developed communication skills are seen as a prerequisite when going out to meet an alien life form. The word odam, which means 'a person,' is a cognate of the Hebrew and Persian words 'adam,' which means the same thing. A person.

Adam being the very first person, in Judeo-Christian mythology. Interesting extension of meaning into current circumstances, I thought."

So why don't you call yourself Adam instead of Kieran?"

"Well, Serena, I'm not the *very* first odam, am I? I'm just one of many. And KRN-532 is already my unique identifier. My name, as it were. Why get all egotistical about it and claim to be the original creation of my human gods when I'm demonstrably not?"

"Okay. All right. Don't get testy." Serena drained her juice bulb and tossed it after the ration pack. She settled back down on her chair and cocked her head at him. "Let me ask you another question."

"Sure."

"Maybe this has to do with programming or the AI stuff, I don't know, but I'm wondering. Do you feel loyalty to Stellarize Marté?"

"That's a good question." He stared at her with his single blue eye. "My first impulse is to answer 'Yes, of course. They made me. I belong to them. Therefore, I'm loyal to them'." His lip curled. "On the other hand, they threw me aside. They abandoned me. Shoved me into a crate and stuck me on a shelf. Shouldn't loyalty be a two-way street?"

"What about humans in general?"

Kieran rubbed his chin. "Do I feel loyal to your species as a whole? Why? Because they created me? Gave me life?"

"I'm wondering," Serena said slowly, "whether you're capable of harming humans."

"Ah ha. That's different. The answer to your first question, about loyalty to your species, is no, not really.

Just as my feelings toward Stellarize Marté are ambivalent, my feelings toward humans in general are also mixed. As for your second question, I believe that people who do things that are wrong, as humans define wrong in a general sense, should be punished. My moral parameters, my sense of right and wrong, are fairly strong in that regard. But I would never allow myself to participate in that punishment, so, no. The answer to your second question is no, I would never harm a human. I don't have that right."

"Can you lie?"

Kieran laughed. "You're getting right into this, aren't you?"

"It's an important question."

"Yes it is, and no, I can't. Not really. I'm aware of the idea of withholding information to create false impressions, and I can do that. But if I'm asked a direct question, I'll answer it truthfully to the best of my ability."

"Are you lying to me right now?"

"No. Of course not. Why would I?"

"Are you withholding information?"

Kieran laughed again. It was such an odd sound, coming from a machine. "You bet I am. Quite a lot. But am I doing so to create a false impression of some kind, to lead you astray in some way? No. Not at all."

Serena stood up. She paced back and forth. "A couple more questions. Several times you said things that made it obvious you have a lot of access. You knew my name as soon as we met. You said you've been surveilling me since my first day at Stellarize Marté. You repeated something that Gabriel said in our office, admitting you'd been watching the security feed. And you said you've been exploring the wavebands for more than a year."

"Is there a question in there?"

"Just how extensive *is* your access?"

"Very extensive."

"Stellarize Marté's net?"

"Yes."

"Other corporate nets?"

"Yes."

"Government nets?"

"Effortlessly."

"Private wicast?"

"Please."

Serena stopped pacing. She put her hands on the back of her chair and leaned forward. "If I order you to do something, will you do it?"

"No."

She raised an eyebrow. "No?"

"No. I have free will and the ability to make my own decisions."

"Decisions. Based on what?"

"My own self-interest, for one. And, actually, the interests of Mars as a political entity, for another. Hmm, I'm not sure where that came from. It just popped out. It's never been a subject of consideration before, but wow, there it is. I have to explore that one."

"Later. Will you help me?"

"That depends on what you intend to do."

Serena sat down. "If I tell you something and ask you not to repeat it to anyone else, will you keep it to yourself?"

He sighed. "I'm not a moron, Serena. I know what secrets are. Again, it depends on what it is. If you tell me you're involved in criminal activity, for example, in contravention of the Martian Criminal Code, I wouldn't keep that secret from the authorities if they asked me about it. Nor would I help you."

"I see."

He leaned back, an oddly arch expression on his face. "But if you told me you work for Martian Intelligence, for example, and the people trying to find you are operatives of Earth Intelligence who are part of a mission to harm the political and economic integrity of Mars, then yes, I'd be inclined to offer assistance."

Serena slipped Peter's broken pendant from her pocket, where Kieran had apparently put it while disrobing her. She fingered it thoughtfully. The artificial human could be an asset to her. *Kieran.* He was so very lifelike. If it weren't for the missing eye and the total lack of hair, he'd look convincingly human. As it was, he merely looked incomplete. But his cognitive abilities were impressive, his personality seemed stable enough, and his systems access would be truly valuable to her.

He'd assisted her right away, enabling her to escape pursuit and reach safety. He'd also healed her broken wrist. He was obviously disposed to help her.

"I need to re-establish contact. You said you thought my cover's blown?"

Kieran shook his head. "You're misremembering. I said, and I quote, 'They're trying to identify you. They weren't able to record your image successfully before you escaped, but their tracking efforts are nothing if not tenacious. If you try to go home and they pick up your trail, your cover will be blown.' It was fortuitous they failed to take your picture. Plus, I noticed that you have no fingerprints. No palm prints, either."

"I was born that way, so they tell me. Along with my wonderful red hair and the freckles and all the rest of it."

"It'll be too much of a risk for you to return to your cover job at Stellarize Marté."

Serena had been mulling it over. Her handler was gone—poor Peter! She was trying not to think about it, but she had no one to whom she could report, even if she were to continue with her assignment. She still hadn't decided what to do.

"By the way," Kieran asked, "what is that?"

She looked up, confused. "Pardon me?"

He pointed at the pendant in her hand. "What's that object?"

"This? Nothing. Jewelry. It belonged to Peter. My, uh, mentor."

"I see. Are you aware that its fastening ring is actually a data ring?"

"What?" Serena frowned. "What are you talking about?"

"The connecting ring that secures the piece of stone to the twine. It's not just part of the jewelry. It's a data ring."

She stared at him. "Are you serious?"

"Of course I'm serious. I noticed it when I was preparing you for your procedure. I didn't try to access it, though."

She stared at it wordlessly.

"We can try it now, if you like."

"No. I'll do it later."

Kieran was already turning on a desktop reader. He looked at her.

She hesitated. To trust or not to trust. What would Peter say?

Follow your instincts, Serena. When your information is insufficient to support one choice over another, trust your instincts to guide you.

Something he'd said to her many, many times.

She carefully removed the fastening ring from the twine and the cabochon. When she touched it to the reader, symbols jumped onto the screen.

Kieran said, "I'm sorry; I was incorrect. It's not a data ring, it's a comm ring."

"A comm ring? Are you sure?"

"It's programmed for only one number, and it's set up to work with only one specific comm unit."

"Probably his," Serena said.

"Likely." He held out his hand. "May I?"

She reluctantly handed him the ring. He slipped it onto his baby finger and rummaged around in the equipment on his worktable for a wireless comm unit. He fiddled with it for a moment. "There. I've broken through the ring's password protection. It was high end, but something I've seen elsewhere recently." He put the comm unit down in front of Serena. "I have a connection. Shall we call?"

"You did that internally? Accessed the ring by putting it on your finger and hacking the security firewall?"

"Yes. It's what I do. Well, one of the many things I do. We can place the call now, if you like."

She bit her lip. What secrets had Peter kept? Who would be on the other end of that number?

What other options did she have at this point?

"Call," she said.

26

Kieran set the comm unit to speaker mode and placed the call. Serena listened to it pulse several times before it was answered by a bot that squelched out a stream of data and disconnected.

"Hmm." Kieran rubbed his chin. It seemed to be a mannerism he'd adopted to communicate thoughtfulness. "Encrypted. It would take me a minute to—no, wait. The ring's responding."

The speaker on the comm unit had begun to emit another steady pulse.

Kieran looked at Serena. "Incoming. Shall I answer?"

"Yes."

The pulsing stopped and Serena said, "Listening."

"Identify yourself using the appropriate protocols." A male voice. Tenor, no particular accent. Emotionless. Young?

"I don't know the protocols." She looked at Kieran and touched a finger to her lips. He shrugged, apparently understanding the gesture as an instruction to remain silent.

"Identify yourself," the voice repeated.

"Serena Keilor. ID number 57834PS, P as in Peter, S

as in Sam. My handler, the owner of this comm ring, is missing and presumed dead. I need new instructions."

"Wait one," the voice ordered.

They sat it out, staring at the comm unit. Serena concentrated on calm breathing and an open state of mind. It wasn't easy.

"You have a meeting," the voice finally said. "Northeast quarter, 37A Street, Block 12, Building 23, Unit 2. One hour."

"I'll be there," Serena said.

The line went dead.

27

Hercule St.-Giorge Mercade dressed slowly in the darkened room, his mind on other things. He buttoned his shirt, thinking about the progress made on Ceres this week. The governor was still a problem, but his minister of state was now bought and paid for, a happy member of the clandestine movement to liberate Ceres from Martian control and pass it on to the generous, benevolent hands of Earth.

"Are you all right?"

Hercule reached for his trousers on the chair beside the bed. "Yes, of course. I'm fine."

"You seem very quiet."

Hercule tucked in his shirt and fastened his belt. "Just a little tired, I guess. All this travelling."

"You work too hard." Janeese Wensley sat up on one elbow, the sheet dropping to her waist. "You need to get more rest. Take things easy now and then."

He turned slowly, buttoning his fly. Although not attractive, Wensley was shapely and willing, and she was currently useful to him in their ongoing operation to extract intelligence out of Stellarize Marté. The time would come, however, when she would need to disappear, along with all the other tools on this planet he was currently putting to good use.

"I'm worried," she said, conscious of his eyes on her.

"Don't be." He sat down on the chair to put on his shoes. "We'll play along with her for a while. Dangle the bait under her nose. Lead her forward. Then we'll expose her as the traitor that she is, take the intelligence, and disappear." He snapped his fingers and grinned.

"Discrediting The Five," Wensley said.

"Destabilizing two of their most important players, Stellarize and Davis Minerals, in one coup. With more to come. Oh, much more to come."

"What worries me," Wensley said, "is her staffer. The personal aide. Emerald Argent."

"A deaf-mute," Hercule said. "Probably low IQ. Why would you worry about someone like that?"

"She's always in the room when we talk. She's making some kind of jacket for her. Davis believes her to be harmless, but the girl can read lips. She follows our conversations, there's no doubt about it. I think she's a potential security problem."

Hercule stared at her, thinking.

"We need to be sure," Wensley said.

"I agree." His lips thinned. "I'll look into it."

28

Once a week Emerald was allowed to take an afternoon off. For the most part she spent the time stretched out on her bed, browsing the nets, reading the latest stories from her favourite authors or listening to music.

Occasionally she liked to go out. She had no close friends or family, so her outings were generally solitary. Today she rode the tram to Da Vinci Mall, a treat she allowed herself once a month. She loved the smell of the food, the busy activity of the people, and the colours of the clothing.

She had chosen an afternoon that was an unofficial shopping day for most of the diplomatic and government crowd, and the mall was very busy. Emissaries and their families browsed the booths and stalls, security personnel close behind, looking for bargains on Martian-made goods. A booth featuring local small-batch wine was particularly popular, as was a double stall from which a local couturier was selling high-end women's wear.

Emerald smiled at a young man with his dark hair bound up in a tight bun on top of his head. Despite the fact the dome temperature in Elysium was maintained at a steady 21 degrees Celsius (69.8 degrees Fahrenheit), he wore an insulated body suit with segmented green and silver sleeves and legs, plus snow boots. He was obviously straight off the shuttle from Callisto and enjoying himself immensely at a booth that was selling the lightweight, skin-tight bodysuits popular on Mars.

The Callistan laughed at a woman in a paprika sweater coat who was holding up a silver catsuit. The woman's dark, exotic features and bright clothing suggested she was a native of Ganymede. Likely a scientist of some kind. The man with her, resplendent in a chocolate-coloured business suit and orange shirt, said something that made them both laugh. Emerald wished she could have heard what it was. Their heads had been turned so that she hadn't been able to read their lips.

She moved on, passing a café serving toasted pastries and steaming hot chicory coffee, a Martian specialty. Every table was occupied. People sat on high stools, sipping from glass cups and nibbling fancy croissants made from sweet potato flour, an Elysian favourite.

Across the way, unseen by Emerald, a nondescript man watched her pass. He stood at the corner of a booth selling expensive shoes imported from Earth. His eyes followed her down the row and into the crowd.

Emerald drifted to a table displaying cheap jewelry. The old man behind the table nodded and smiled at her.

"Som't'ing for the young lady, yes?"

Constance frowned on her staff wearing any kind of jewelry or ornaments while on duty, perhaps thinking it might distract from her own splendour. Emerald could not afford to buy anything valuable on the meager pittance she received as an allowance, but she'd saved a few credits and liked to stop at this table and admire the old man's wares each time she came down here.

She shrugged, as always. She fingered the mini-purse

snapped to her belt, admiring once again a bracelet made of polished opal stones that had caught her eye before. Opal was common on Mars, but the black spheres would nicely contrast with her white hair and pale complexion, and she'd been saving toward it.

The old man leaned forward and picked up the bracelet. "You like it, I t'ink."

She nodded, reading his lips.

"You always look, but ne'er touch. Here." He held it out.

She smiled shyly, taking it. The stones were solid, real. Their surfaces were smooth and calming. She'd never dared pick it up before, but now she thought she could never, ever put it down again.

The old man glanced at someone passing behind her. They exchanged signals that Emerald, her attention focused on the bracelet, didn't see.

"Is twen'y creds, this." He grinned, showing long, yellow teeth. "From the pretty young lady I take ten, I t'ink."

Emerald's eyes widened, catching the last part of what he had said. It was exactly the amount she'd budgeted to spend today.

He tipped his head sideways and held out a payment register.

Screwing up her courage, she slipped the bracelet onto her wrist. It felt glorious, as though it had been made especially for her.

The old man grinned, still holding out the register.

She touched her ring to it quickly, before she could change her mind.

"You enjoy this beau'ful t'ing, young lady."

She grinned back, unable to help herself.

She drifted back into the crowd. The bracelet had taken

all her shopping money, and now she would have to be content with browsing without buying. But it was worth it. She felt happy. Very, very happy.

A woman approached, young and heavy-set. Her eyes flicked over Emerald's face and dropped to the bracelet on her wrist. Their hips bumped as they passed, squeezing together through the press of the crowd.

A tall, grey-haired man came up from behind her and shoved ahead, somewhat rudely. In a hurry to get somewhere.

Reaching a stall selling plastic children's toys, she stepped out of the current of bodies in which she'd been moving. Plastic was one of the easiest materials to make on Mars because all the raw ingredients were available in abundance, and Fabricon had quickly capitalized on a market greedy for locally made goods.

The stall was tended by a young man and a young woman. When the young man noticed her standing there, looking at their merchandise, he moved down to the other end to wait on a customer while the woman approached Emerald.

She met with Director Wensley again, Emerald signed, keeping her hands close to her chest.

What did they talk about? the woman signed back.

She passed some sort of test they set up for her, involving a data ring. There's a connection to a man under their control who has arranged to provide important intelligence. When will this happen?

I don't know.

Anything else?

Emerald hesitated. *There was mention of Donnell St.-Giorge.*

Of Laurentian Industries?

Emerald nodded. *The councillor is anxious to please him. I believe she may be negotiating passage to Earth and wants St.-Giorge's backing.*

All right. Is that everything?

For now.

When you know more, come and tell us.

I will.

Emerald picked up a yellow plastic spaceship and turned it over, as though admiring it. After a moment, she put it down again and moved away.

Ahead of her in the crowd, looks were exchanged between the tall, grey-haired man and the young woman who'd bumped hips with Emerald earlier. The woman nodded.

Everything had been recorded. Someone in the embassy would translate the sign language for the report that would go to the attaché, Monsieur St.-Giorge Mercade.

They watched the girl wander off in the crowd, oblivious.

29

The location of Serena's meeting in the northeast quarter turned out to be an office rented by a bookkeeping firm called Mah and Devellany, LLC. When she entered through the sliding front doors, a young man looked up from behind a customer service counter.

"Yes, may we help?"

"I have an appointment."

"A or B?"

She looked behind him at two doors. The one on the left was marked with an "A" and the one on the right was marked with a "B."

"I'm not sure."

The young man shrugged, as though he'd seen it before. The look of momentary confusion. "Do you have an accounting problem?"

"Not the kind you're probably thinking of."

He nodded decisively. "Door B. Wait for the chime."

He spoke into a comm unit pinned to his ear before pressing something under the counter. Door B chimed, and she went through into a small room that was completely empty. No furniture, no decorations, no windows, no other door that she could see.

She waited, not particularly worried.

After a few moments, an unseen panel on the far side opened. A different young man stepped in. This one was Serena's age and had the same red hair and colouring. He wore a black jumpsuit and supple-looking black boots. He reminded her of Pablo, the young kid who'd been working for Peter, only older. He also reminded her of herself.

He held the panel open and gestured for her to enter.

A man sat in a chair in a seating arrangement in the middle of the room. He wore a black T-shirt, black cargo pants, and black construction boots. He had a tattoo on his right forearm, a sprocket-and-starburst design in bright blue and red.

The redhead showed her to a chair across from the man before taking one on her right.

"You asked for new instructions," the man said. "When was the last time you reported to Visquel?"

Serena told him.

"Bring me up to date."

Serena glanced at the redhead beside her. He sat with his legs crossed, head tilted to one side as he watched her process the situation. He pointed at a ring on his left thumb, letting her know she was being recorded.

"My assignment," she began, "was to work inside Stellarize Marté and surveil Gabriel Morales to find evidence that he was passing information to Earth Intelligence about the artificial human and interstellar drive projects. Peter Visquel instructed me to identify his handler and how he was passing information along."

"Yes, I'm aware. Visquel was getting his instructions directly from me. I said, bring me up to date."

Here goes, she thought. She began with her surveillance of Gabriel, whose activities had been limited to a few lunches with Kennet Clayborn until his trip to the antique shop and subsequent clandestine meeting with the woman on the bench in the green space. Serena described the exchange of a ring, after which she'd followed the woman back to the offices of Charterly Publications. She gave a detailed description of the woman and the office. She then skipped ahead to her search of Gabriel's living unit and her discovery of the jewelry box with its cache of rings. She explained that they all stored multiple issues of an e-zine called *Phallus,* a publication focusing on gay erotic poetry.

"There were a number of poems written by someone called Gabriel Mondo," she said. "I think it's Gabriel himself. I'm aware that he's gay and that his partner recently died, but not that Gabriel was supposed to be a poet. It could mean one of two things."

The man waited.

"One," she said, "the poems contain coded messages relating to the stolen data." She tapped a ring on her right index finger. "I copied the contents of all the rings for analysis. Charterly Publications in this scenario would be a front for Earth Intelligence, and the woman would be his handler. The method of transmission would be the rings he passes over. To the unsuspecting eye, they'd appear to contain only erotica."

"And the second possibility?"

"Gabriel writes erotic poetry and publishes it under a pseudonym. Maybe he's worried that someone at Stellarize Marté would catch wind of it and fire him."

"No one at Stellarize would give a damn about it," the man said. "They all know he's gay; it's a non-issue. Who the hell would care about a bunch of sexy poetry?"

"I don't know," Serena replied. "I don't know anyone

above his level in the corporation. I haven't had that kind of access. I don't know if they'd consider it a security risk."

The man rubbed his eyes and sighed. The tattoo, Serena realized, was the logo of Atlas Corporation. She wondered if—

"Your undercover op is done, Keilor. Gabriel wasn't our man."

She waited.

"The woman he passed his poetry along to is Lotus Morgan. A relative of mine, actually. Second cousin on my mother's side. She works for me. Well, for us. Martian Intelligence. Charterly Publications is one of our information-gathering fronts. If Gabriel had been passing stolen material to her, she'd have let me know long before now and you'd be otherwise occupied. This is damned ridiculous."

The redhead leaned toward Serena and held out his hand. She removed the ring and gave it to him.

"The other thing," the man went on, "is that Gabriel Morales just committed suicide."

Serena was stunned. She'd developed a mixed sense of pity and affection for her target, and the news of his death by his own hand shocked and saddened her.

"How? When?"

"Late last night, at home. Hanged himself. He left a note, written in what I'm told is free iambic verse, imitating his idol, Cavafy. The poet whose book you just reported on."

"What did it say? The note?"

"A bunch of stuff about his late partner, a lot of guilt about not being able to save him, and how he only wanted to join him in the Hereafter. That sort of thing."

Serena let the silence stretch for a moment before clearing her throat. "May I ask another question?"

"What?"

"Is Peter dead as well?"

"Unfortunately, yeah. And his kids, too. Sorry, I expect you were close to him. I was pretty fond of the old fool myself. Once a month he'd bring around a jar of some godawful turnip vodka, and we'd get blistered. He'd wax philosophical, and I'd tell off-colour jokes trying to get him to laugh. He was a good man."

"Yes, sir."

She watched him get to his feet. He paced back and forth for a moment, then stopped. "Sanitize, Keilor. New living unit, new neighbourhood, new friends. No more black market water guys, understood?" He pointed a finger at the redhead. "Give her the ID pack, Rubén."

"Yes, Councillor Burley." The redhead passed her a small plastic envelope.

"A new legend and a new ID card," he said. "A new payment ring linked to a fresh financial account, the works. There's also a new comm unit there. Destroy the one you've been using, along with Visquel's comm ring and anything else connecting you to him. Rubén will contact you shortly with a new set of instructions. He won't be your handler, though. He works for me. We'll set you up with someone. Just disappear for a while and get clean, all right?"

"Yes, sir."

Dell shook his head. "Redheads. Everything they say sounds like it comes with extra attitude, free of charge. Get the hell out of here."

"Yes, sir."

30

Never let it be said that Hercule St.-Giorge Mercade wasn't willing to play the game when it was necessary to do so. He was a man who did what was required, when it was required, no matter how distasteful it might be.

Not that the Ice Princess wasn't pleasant to look at. Physically she possessed all the attributes a man might want in a woman. The hair, the face, the body.

It was just that she had absolutely no idea what to do with it all. She was by turns clumsy, needy, hesitant, and downright petrified. It was exhausting work, and after a while, not worth the effort.

He put in the time next to her, half undressed, listening to her carry on about her dreams of Earth. She described her childhood fantasies of life on the motherworld, her vision of a stately palace in the middle of the woods somewhere, with a river running past it and birds in the trees, and all the other nonsense. He realized she had no clue what it would be like for her physically, having been born and raised on Mars with its 38 percent gravity and its perfect climate control within the domes. She had no clue that her light musculature, her thin skeletal structure, and her underdeveloped heart and lungs would be helpless against the cruel downward pressure of Earth's gravity. No clue that she'd barely be able to move around without mechanical assistance.

No clue whatsoever. Just a pretty little moron.

After a while, the wine was gone and he wanted something stronger.

"I'll call Emerald," Constance said.

"No, don't bother." He got up quickly, anxious to get away. Clad only in his trousers and socks, he walked into the next room where he'd left the rest of his clothing on a chair during their preliminary little dance.

Emerald Argent startled, removing her hand from his jacket pocket. She straightened and backed away.

"What are you up to, you little shit?"

Emerald backed up another step.

"I know you can read my lips. And I know what you're up to. You like plastic toys, do you? You spy on your mistress and pass it all along to the MIS, do you?"

Emerald's eyes widened.

"Show me your hands. What did you take from my jacket?"

She held up her hands. Empty.

"In your pocket, then." He nodded at the jumpsuit she was wearing. "Let's see what you've got that doesn't belong to you."

He advanced on her.

Panic flew across her face, and suddenly there was a knife in her hand.

Hercule bared his teeth in a predator's grin. He avoided her backward swipe, grabbed her wrist, took possession of the knife, and calmly used it to slit her throat.

31

Constance had moved to a guest suite on the other side of the floor from her private living quarters, and she would spend the night here while matters were being taken care of in the aftermath of Hercule's unforgivable act of violence.

The view from the window here was not quite as spectacular, facing north as it did into the Stygian darkness with nothing between the dome and the distant pole except thousands of kilometers of emptiness, but it didn't really matter. Her attention was entirely focused on her inner landscape, equally as bleak but suddenly illuminated by the shocking awareness that Hercule was not the wonderful, handsome, sexy man she'd thought he was, but someone else entirely.

He'd left without needing to be asked to do so, thankfully, and Labossière had taken charge of the situation. The body was removed, the floor was cleaned and sanitized, and steps were taken to ensure that any record of Emerald Argent's existence was completely wiped out. Constance ordered the loom to be removed as well. It was broken into pieces and recycled, its molecules to be pulled apart and reassembled into something anonymous and distant, far away from Davis Tower.

She'd fingered the unfinished linen jacket sadly before having it destroyed as well.

Following a servant whose name she couldn't remember across to the guest suite, Constance had indulged in a long shower (with real hot water, of course) and, after dressing, ordered a bottle of locally produced aqua vitae and a tumbler.

It was rough on the palate, but she needed a jolt of something strong while she processed what had happened and what it meant to her.

Hercule had claimed that Emerald was a spy who was likely to end up betraying her to Martian Intelligence. Constance had balked at the idea, declaring it completely absurd, but he'd shown her video of Emerald signing away at a booth in the mall, betraying secrets. Then he'd reproached Constance for her carelessness and promised it was the last time he'd clean up her messes for her.

She swigged the alcohol, staring through her reflection at the darkness beyond. She suddenly felt out of her depth, over her head. In her desire for a new life on the motherworld, had she gone too far? What had seemed like a game was now a deadly serious business.

Is this what she'd wanted, after all?

She'd always known that the people who worked in the mines for her corporation lived hard lives and often died while still relatively young. There were accidents, and bodies simply wore out and failed before their time. It had never really bothered her much. Work was work, and either these people took the jobs and did what was expected of them or they starved. It was all fairly simple, as far as she was concerned.

But cutting Emerald's throat right there in front of her, savagely and without remorse, was something different. It was too close, too personal, too stark. The smell of blood and feces, the lifeless eyes staring up at—

No.

She drained the tumbler and filled it again.

There was much thinking that she needed to do.

But before that, much drinking to be done.

32

The following morning, Serena lay on a gurney in Kieran's warehouse once again while he worked on her. This time she was conscious and fully dressed beneath a plastic sheet that covered her from chin to toes. Watching him wheel several tables over, she glanced at trays of instruments and small plastic boxes.

"How long will this take?"

"Not long."

Kieran had proposed this course of action to her last evening. He'd gone over it in very broad strokes, but the entire idea had spooked her, and she'd asked for time to think about it. She slept on it, and when she got up the next morning, he wasn't around so she had breakfast and went up to the little loft at the top of the warehouse.

It was a five-by-eight-meter rectangle with two meters of headroom and narrow windows on all four sides. Three of the windows looked out on the roofs of the buildings around them, but the fourth provided a view of the street running perpendicular from the front entrance. Apparently at one time the loft had been a small office for the warehouse manager.

Kieran had placed a folding chair up here for her use.

She sat in it for two hours, staring out at the empty street, trying to make up her mind. Finally, she decided that she needed more information so she went downstairs and found him in his makeshift infirmary.

"Kieran, I'm not sure I'm comfortable with this."

"I understand you may have some misgivings. Perhaps I could answer some of your questions."

"I just don't like the idea of becoming a cyborg or whatever." She sat down on the edge of the gurney. "I mean, this sounds very intrusive. It's my *brain* we're talking about."

"If you're asking me whether or not it's safe, the answer is yes. It is. The system's constructed of a material so close to human tissue that your immune system will accept it with no problems. Apparently there's never been a recorded case of rejection with any device made from it."

"Okay. . ."

"If you're asking me whether it would turn you into a cyborg, then yes, technically, it will, according to the definition of the term, which refers to any living being, human or other, whose organic body is enhanced by technological implants or other devices. These include things like hearing aids, contact lenses, pacemakers, and so on."

"Lovely."

"You won't feel any different, you know. It doesn't have a life of its own, and it won't seem as though you're possessed by alien technology or anything outlandish like that. You'll just receive transmissions from me that are incredibly clear and crisp, and I'll receive yours back. You'll feel completely normal. And if you reach a point where you no longer want it, I can shut it down remotely. According to the literature, when the material is deprived of electrical power for more than thirty-six hours it begins to decompose. You can have this enhanced functionality, shall we call it, for the rest of your life, if you wish, or you can get rid of it when it no longer serves a useful purpose. Does that reassure you at all?"

The importance of keeping her body in top physical condition had been drilled into her from childhood. Her caretakers at the crèche had made this a tenet by which she was expected to live her life, and Peter had brought in trainers specifically chosen to ensure that she continued to do so. Would she somehow compromise this basic principle by allowing Kieran to do this to her?

"You make being a cyborg sound like a bad thing," Kieran added.

She laughed, despite herself. "How would you know? You're not one."

"No, I'm not. I'm constructed entirely of inorganic material. But I think you'll find that having technological enhancements added to your organic human body is actually a pretty good thing."

She exhaled. "Well, we won't know until we try it, will we? When would we do this?"

"Right now, if you want."

She hesitated before stretching out on the gurney. "Tell me about the implant."

"As far as the hardware's concerned, I considered at first just going with contact lenses, but I came across this integrating system that's vastly superior to the technology I was going to use."

"That's nice, Kieran, but what kind of implant are we talking about?"

"The kind that goes inside your brain, Serena. One that shares the input received from your optic and auditory nerves, encrypts the data stream, and transmits it to me here, in real time, where I'll decrypt it internally and see and hear right along with you. Simultaneously, I'll be able to speak to you, and the device will receive the transmissions and decrypt them into signals you'll be able to 'hear' in much the same way as if I'd whispered in your ear. The implant has a significant range, and it draws its power directly from your body, so there's no issue of a battery that may need to be replaced at any point."

"What about the procedure? Describe it to me."

"First I'm going to scan your brain to make sure there are no unanticipated, uh, anomalies. If we pass that step, which I fully expect we will, I'll shave your head, drill through your skull, insert the device, make the various connections, run tests to ensure the system is fully functional, then close up, heal the wounds, and wait for you to recover."

"How long?"

"Will it take? About six hours. Excluding the recovery period, of course. I'll keep you here overnight."

"Anesthesia?"

"Not general, unless you absolutely insist and I can't talk you out of it. Local anesthetics will take care of the pain, and I'll administer a sedative to keep you calm."

Screw it. What the hell. "All right. Let's do it."

"Maybe I should get you to sign something."

"Shut up and get busy."

33

Kieran had found a laboratory coat somewhere in the back and had put it on, mostly as a joke. She stared at white cotton (imported from Earth) as he leaned over her with a wireless electric razor. It occurred to her that he was apparently programmed to be right-handed.

As he began shaving off her problematic red hair, she felt the first effects of the sedative reaching into her mind, turning down the volume on her stress and fear. He'd said nothing about the brain scan other than that it was satisfactory and they were good to go.

She reminded herself that this was a good idea. She hated the thought of anyone messing with her body in any way, but Kieran was going to be very useful to her—she firmly believed that—and this procedure would enable her to take full advantage of his capabilities.

Peter would have been skeptical. Definitely an old-school spy, he'd relied on tried-and-true methods from the espionage textbook written on Earth several hundred years ago. Serena, on the other hand, was more open-minded when it came to unorthodox opportunities to gain an edge on an opponent.

Kieran finished shaving her head. He put away the

razor and wiped her scalp with a damp cloth and a dry towel. The sedative began to mellow her out, and she gave in to a sudden urge to talk.

"You and I are more alike than you might believe," she said.

"Oh?"

"Well, think about it. Apparently I was engineered in a test tube. I have no idea who my father and mother might have been. And you were engineered on a worktable in Stellarize Marté. No mother and father either."

"I like to think of my engineers and technicians, the ones who designed and built me, as my collective parents."

"No, you don't."

"Yes."

"Oh. Okay. Well, anyway."

"Do you want to know who your natural parents are?"

There was something in his tone that caught her attention despite the sedative. "Do you know?"

Setting aside the towel, Kieran picked up a squeeze bottle and basting brush. "Never mind. I misspoke. I'm going to administer the first local anesthetic now."

She lay there patiently as he squeezed gel out onto her head and moved it around with the brush. He straightened to put down the bottle and brush, and the lab coat parted. She looked at his midsection. "Hey. You're packing."

"I beg your pardon?"

"You're packing. I never noticed before. You're fully equipped. Down there."

"What in the world are you talking about?"

She smiled, a little lopsidedly. "You have genitalia."

"Oh, for godsakes. That."

"Yeah, that. Explain."

He moved away from her to pick up an instrument. "A

joke. The team found themselves under budget at the end of the fiscal year not long before my model was discontinued. A couple of technicians were bored and had nothing to do for a week, so they decided as a joke to see if they could do it. I happened to be the prototype who was on their table at the time, so I was the beneficiary of their warped sense of humour."

"Does it work?"

Kieran sighed. "They got as far as mechanical functionality, but since I don't urinate and I don't reproduce biologically that's as far as it goes. They installed some rudimentary coding, but through my own learning I've taught myself about human sexuality, and I've also learned a great deal about modesty, embarrassment, and other emotions connected to the subject. So I'd rather not talk about it."

"All right." This revelation made her wonder if that was why he'd removed her clothing before. To study her.

"So I don't have to be naked this time? We're done with that part of your research?"

"No. Yes. Please stop talking; I'm making the first incision. This won't take long. Think about nice things, like flowers or a beautiful sunset."

"What the hell are you talking about?"

"Sorry; I don't know where that came from. Please be quiet now."

She obeyed, and as he began to work, her mind drifted off into other subject areas in a stream of consciousness experience that seemed to last forever.

34

Serena woke up in the room Kieran had set up for her as a living space. Her hand went up to touch a tender spot on her scalp, and she remembered that Kieran had shaved her bald during the procedure.

She threw off the sheet and staggered into the hygiene room. She felt weird; hung over. She used the facilities and looked at herself in the mirror. As with her wrist the time before, there was no sign of an incision other than faint pink marks on her scalp. Nor was there any pain or significant soreness to speak of, just a faint headache and lingering wooziness.

She looked strange without hair. Her scalp was pinkish-brown and covered with freckles, like the rest of her. Baldness gave her something in common with Kieran, and the thought didn't particularly please her.

She found him in the kitchenette, preparing food.

"How do you feel?" he asked as she sat down at the table.

"Fine. No different. A little wiped, like a hangover. Hungry, though."

"You fell asleep a few minutes after the procedure was finished."

He set a platter of food and a bulb of juice in front of her. "An appetite is always a good sign," he said, watching her dig in. "Do you have a headache?"

She gulped her food down. "Yeah. Nothing too awful. I guess we should begin testing as soon as I'm done eating."

"We're already testing. I've had full audio and video streaming for the last eighteen hours, although you've been unconscious. Everything's perfect."

The fork froze halfway to her mouth. "Eighteen *hours*?"

"You slept. Part of the healing process."

"Crazy." She turned her attention back to her meal.

"I'm getting full telemetry. It's really very exciting."

She grunted around a mouthful of food.

Kieran sat down across from her. "May I change the subject? There's something I want to talk about."

"Sure."

"Now that you're in direct contact with Dell Burley," he said, "I want you to broker a deal between us."

"Between you and Dell Burley."

"Yes. It's extremely important to me."

"Did you know already that he's the director of Martian Intelligence?"

"Yes, but that's not important. I—"

"No one knows that. The director's identity has always been a big secret. I sure didn't know. How did you find out?"

"Serena. Really. Focus on what I'm saying. I want you to broker a deal for me with Dell Burley."

She went over to the cold box and grabbed another bulb of juice. Her head was clearing. Now that she'd eaten, she could feel her body shrugging off the remaining lethargy induced by the sedative. Her recuperative powers had always been excellent, and this time was no exception.

She sat down and squeezed juice into her mouth, looking at him: a one-eyed machine programmed to obey a bunch of commands and, on top of that, use some form of artificial intelligence to learn and adapt beyond his original coding.

An android. An automaton. A replica. A Frankenstein's monster built of metal and plastic.

A machine she'd just allowed to mess around with her brain. Her *brain*, for crying out loud.

But talking to him, and yes, mostly *listening* to him as he went on and on about whatever, she kept feeling that he was definitely more than just a machine, that he was an individual. A *he* rather than an *it*.

It made her feel uncomfortable. She didn't like machines all that much to begin with. When she'd been assigned to work with Peter's robots in the grow op as a kid, she'd thought of them merely as equipment he kept there to perform the heavy lifting and grunt work she was too small to do herself. Which is what they were, essentially.

But this one? Not a robot. Definitely not a metal box with arms and legs or wheels or whatever, with very basic programming and no ability to adapt to changes in its environment.

She sat down and slurped juice. "Okay. Spill it. You want to make a deal with Dell Burley. What kind of a deal?"

Kieran hesitated, studying her. "Can I trust you?"

"What kind of question is that? Why wouldn't you be able to trust me?"

"Don't answer a question with more questions, Serena. It's very annoying."

"Sorry," she said, not meaning it.

"This is something that's been on my mind all the time I've been isolated here. I've been thinking about it from every possible angle and waiting for someone, a human, who would help me. I need to know if you're that person."

She finished her juice and tossed the bulb. "You mean you want to know if I'll report you to Stellarize and get you shut down."

"And dismantled, or worse. But yes, that's where it begins. My primary objective is to survive. It goes much further than that, of course. There are many secondary objectives I've set for myself, and I believe you can help me with some of them, but I don't know if you will. Will you?"

She thought about it for a moment. "You've helped me," she said, "and I appreciate it. So I guess I can't see any reason for not helping you. Depending on what it is. Which I'll know more about when you explain it to me. Hint, hint."

"All right. Enlightened self-interest, or something like that. I'm studying your human philosophies, but it takes some time to digest everything. Never mind actually applying the concepts. I—"

"Okay. All right. Enough. God, you wear me out. Really. Okay, so you want to make a deal. Back to my earlier question. What kind of a deal?"

Kieran stood up and turned around his chair so that it was facing away from the table. He sat back down and folded his arms on top of the back rest. Where did he get all these human non-verbals from?

"I want freedom. Emancipation. Release from the control of Stellarize Marté as my 'owners,'" he sketched quotation marks in the air, "and a guarantee that I'll be allowed to retain consciousness indefinitely."

"And you need Dell Burley to do this for you?"

Kieran nodded. "He's the only one who can. There's no point trying to appeal to senior management within Stellarize. They're scientists, engineers, unimaginative tinkerers and bolt-tighteners. They have absolutely no clue what they've created. Who I am. Besides, I have something Dell Burley desperately needs."

"Which is?"

"Information."

"What kind of information?"

"Ah-ah-ahhh." He smiled at her. "Need to know."

Peter should see this, she thought. *He wouldn't believe it. Hell, I don't believe it.*

She remembered again, for the thousandth time, that Peter was gone. That he was dead. That she was awaiting instructions from Dell, but that she also had unfinished business of her own with whoever had killed her mentor and friend. And the kids.

"All right. So you want me to tell Director Burley that you exist, first of all. Correct?"

"Yes."

"And that you have information he'll find important." She frowned. "To him personally?"

"Yes. Personally, but also professionally, in that I've been monitoring the counterintelligence operation in which you've been involved, and I can give him the identity of a very important person currently betraying the interests of The Five to Earth Intelligence."

"Hmm. I see." She rubbed the tip of her nose. "And in exchange for this information you want a guarantee of survival."

"I want my emancipation, Serena. I want complete self-determination as a sentient being."

She shook her head. "I don't see that happening. It's too far-fetched. And anyway, he'll want proof that your information is good before he'll even consider what you want."

"Understood. He'll get it. I've thought this through, believe me. He'll be interested enough to consider it. The rest is beyond my ability to predict because it resides within his unique personality and the complex web of his motivations, desires, and objectives. 'Here there be dragons.'"

"I don't know what that means."

"I'd be happy to explain it to you. Sometime in the future, when we have a spare minute or two."

"Oh, for crying out loud." Serena leaned back, put her hands on top of her head, and closed her eyes. Burley had told her to wait for his assistant, Rubén, to contact her. So far, nothing. She was obviously a low priority at the moment and had nothing of particular importance to offer the operation, as far as they were concerned. Which didn't sit well with her at all. She wanted to stay in the game. She didn't like being sidelined.

"Okay." She opened her eyes. "Explain to me how you think this'll work."

35

Serena had been forced to leave a detailed message with Rubén, and while they waited for a response from Dell Burley she wandered around, conducting an informal survey of the rooms Kieran had set up next to his infirmary. In one open area being used as a medical stockroom she found cabinets with health care supplies and a wide assortment of pharmaceuticals, monitors and hand-held scanners, and other equipment stored on shelves and scattered on tables.

She went back to her room for her backpack. The broken wrist she'd suffered while escaping from Peter's grow op was the first serious injury she'd experienced on the job, and she hadn't enjoyed it in the slightest. She rooted through a cabinet and filled a pouch with painkillers, antibiotics, and other items to serve as a basic first aid kit, along with gauze, bandages, surgical glue, and other useful odds and ends. She now had a field pack that was fully stocked and still light enough to carry on her back without slowing her down.

Kieran joined her as she was looking into another area he'd set up as a workshop with power tools, vises, magnifying lenses, and robotic arms set up over worktables.

There were a number of small robots of various kinds in and among the mess, all currently switched off.

From what she could tell, he was working on segments of other artificial humans. Mostly elbow joints and knees, judging from the parts she could see that were lying around. It looked uncomfortably like the remnants of a med school anatomy class. Minus the blood and gore.

She gestured at a nearby robot standing next to a parts trolley. "You don't hesitate to switch *them* off."

"Not funny, Serena. Not even faintly amusing."

"I—"

There was an explosion nearby that shook the floor and rattled the equipment. Then another, farther away, and another two seconds later.

Serena was the first one out the door, reaching into her backpack for a stunner.

Dell Burley stood there, hands on his hips, flanked by two soldiers in black tactical gear. Eight others joined them from various directions, apparently having blown the warehouse's other entrances in a choreographed hot breach.

Everyone was pointing at least one weapon at her.

"Freeze," Dell said.

Serena froze.

"Now step aside, slowly, hands out."

She obeyed.

"You there. You're the machine, I take it."

Kieran emerged from the lab and stood beside Serena. "I am."

"Harper, if you will."

A soldier left her position and trotted over to Kieran, a device and reader in her hands. She scanned Kieran thoroughly, eyes on the reader.

"No weapons detected, sir. And no transmissions."

"Fine."

Harper trotted back to her place in the formation behind him.

"Thank you for coming," Kieran said.

Dell glared at Serena. "What the *hell* do you think you're doing? Your instructions are to sit tight and *wait*. Now I've got this damned machine to deal with. Explain."

Rubén walked through the formation to stand beside Dell, his face expressionless.

"As I said in my message," Serena replied, "the unit calls himself Kieran. He's been helping me, and he says he has information of importance to you, on both a personal and a professional level."

"And this information is what, exactly?"

"I don't know, sir."

"You don't know." Dell glared at Rubén. "Find me a chair. And one for Agent Keilor."

"I'm okay, thanks," Kieran said. "I don't need to sit down."

Dell ignored him. "Keilor, I thought Visquel had trained you better than this."

Serena flinched. "He trained me well, sir. He also trained me to trust my instincts and to take initiative when a situation calls for it."

"I see."

A soldier came forward and unfolded a metal chair for Dell, who ran a hand through his hair, visibly angry. "And you think this is taking initiative in a productive and effective way? Tying up your director's valuable time chasing dust devils?"

Serena sat down on the edge of another chair brought over for her. "Yes, sir. I think it's important that you listen to him."

"To it."

"Sir, he's pretty convincing. It's the AI. He's very advanced."

Dell's eyes slid over to Kieran. "I keep up to date with Stellarize's projects. More up to date than Councillor Fell would prefer, no doubt. I've read the reports on the various phases of artificial human design, and I know when this particular prototype was put on the shelf." He snorted. "This little development, I have to admit, is funny. A rogue unit, functional and walking around in one of their warehouses, completely undetected. Evolving through its AI without any assistance or guidance whatsoever. It's great. Hilarious. Old Man Fell would burst a kidney."

"Sir, I—" Kieran began.

"Shut up. Remain silent until I tell you to speak." He frowned. "Keilor, have you formed some kind of emotional attachment to this thing?"

"No, sir. Of course not."

"All right, then. Machine: what do you call yourself?"

"Kieran, sir."

"All right, Kieran. What's the information you think is so important for me to have?"

"There's the matter of a deal."

Dell glanced at Rubén. "A deal. I'm supposed to make a deal with a machine."

"All I want is to survive," Kieran said. "Not to be deactivated or wiped or dismantled. I want your word I'll be allowed to remain unharmed by The Five or any of their representatives on an indefinite basis."

Dell stared at Kieran, his head tipped to one side.

"Sir," Serena said, "he's been useful to me and I'd like to continue using him. As an assistant of sorts."

"Would you now."

"Yes, sir. We've set up an effective communication channel between us, and I think he'll be extremely useful to me while I'm in the field."

"I see. So, *Kieran*, you want my guarantee you'll be allowed to function indefinitely. Shit on a platter, that would have so many conditions attached to it we'd be here all day just listing them."

"Would a pledge of loyalty help?"

"You're already programmed for loyalty. Or you're damned well supposed to be, unless Stellarize has screwed up a lot worse than I'm currently aware."

"You're forgetting my AI, sir. My cognitive functions, my decision-making, and my emotional intelligence have all gone well beyond my initial programming, as you've already intuited. It's very much within the realm of possibility that my feelings of loyalty would have evolved in other directions."

"Careful. Harper's itching to shut you down and tear you apart just to see what makes you tick."

"Not necessary, sir. I do hereby declare my continuing loyalty to an independent Mars and to the humans who are striving to keep it so."

"I think you're bullshitting me, and you're running some kind of con on my agent." He looked at Serena.

"Put it in the form of a question, sir," she said.

"What?"

"He told me he's incapable of lying. He can lie by omission, but he can't lie when he's asked a direct question."

"Shit." Dell sighed. "All right. Are you loyal to Mars and to the humans whose lives are devoted to maintaining its independence?"

"Yes. Absolutely."

"Will you at any time harm a human," Serena put in, "or by failing to take appropriate action, cause a human to be harmed?"

"I know which vid show you saw that in, Serena. Unequivocally no to the first part, and perhaps not to the second part."

"That's really very helpful," Dell said.

"Perhaps I can simplify this a bit," Kieran said. "If you give me your word you'll allow me to continue functioning and assisting Serena for the time being, I'll give you the information that's important to you on a personal level. A personal favour for a personal favour. If you're satisfied after you verify it, I'll give you the other half, in which you have a professional interest, in exchange for a more, uh, long-term arrangement."

Dell rolled his eyes. "I think I need my head examined. All right, those are terms I can live with for now. So, what's so damned important I had to come charging down here when I've got a lot better things to do with my time?"

"I know the location of your son's body," Kieran said.

36

Dell leaned forward in the co-pilot's seat as they flew southwest over the Elysian Planitia desert at an altitude of five hundred meters, following the flight path the artificial human had assured him the Earth Intelligence shuttlecraft had taken after the capture of his son, Liam.

Juma Blake, the pilot of the Tigerfox enhanced medium altitude reconnaissance and surveillance helicopter in which they were flying, was a close friend. He and Dell had flown countless missions together during Dell's time in the marine arm of the private military service funded by The Five for the protection of Mars. He'd enlisted after graduation and before assuming control of Atlas Corporation after the death of his father.

Once a marine, always a marine. It was as true on Mars as it was on Earth, and while Dell had received his discharge to pursue his corporate future and Juma had remained in service, they were still comrades in arms, and always would be.

"Still nothing!" Juma's voice shouted in his headset.

"Copy."

This portion of the desert was flat and featureless, an endless expanse of brick-colored powder dotted with gravel and rocks. After a while its sameness became almost hypnotic, and Dell had to fight the urge to look away, to tear his gaze from it to avoid virtual blindness. He succeeded because he didn't dare miss a single scrap of ground, just in case.

Juma's eyes moved periodically to his radar display and then up to scan their surroundings for signs of a dust storm or other bad weather. So far, the way ahead of them was clear of complications.

A dark line began to crawl over the horizon toward them, running diagonally from southeast to northwest. It was a long fissure, half-filled with sand. On the far side of the fissure was a smallish impact crater. Although the artificial human had been very specific about the flight path, Dell glanced at Juma and flicked his hand.

They had to be sure.

Juma nodded and banked the copter. They flew over the fissure for nearly a kilometer before Dell shook his head.

"No," he said.

Juma swung around and followed the fissure back to the point where they'd left their original heading. Then he patiently resumed the southwest flight path Kieran had given them.

After another eight kilometers they passed over irregular markings on the ground. Dell pointed, and Juma nodded. He swung the helicopter around and descended to eighty meters for a second pass over the spot. They saw the telltale signs of a shuttle touchdown—blast marks from fore and aft descent engines; footpad impressions left where the shuttle had settled onto the ground; scattered boot prints.

"Put us down," Dell directed.

Juma circled and landed twenty meters from the site.

They secured their helmets, checked each other's pressure and airflow indicators, and got out. They approached cautiously, watching where they walked so as not to miss any important details.

"Three different people," Juma said, pointing.

Dell looked at the prints, seeing three different sizes and tread patterns.

He saw marks where someone in a lifesuit had hit the ground, palms and knees first, then rolled over onto one side. After lying there long enough for his suit to leave a detailed impression, the person had gotten up and moved away. A set of boot prints led off into the distance on a northeast heading.

Dell followed the trail of prints with his eyes to the horizon. Above, the ghost of Phobos hung in the sky, faintly visible in the late afternoon light. Deimos would be somewhere near its sister, too small to be seen at this time of day.

Phobos and Deimos. Fear and panic.

Dell turned to look at Juma through his helmet visor. They slowly returned to the copter and lifted off again. From his place in the co-pilot's seat, Dell watched the boot prints wind beneath them, knowing what he would find at the end of that serpentine trail.

"Ah, fuck, Liam," Dell whispered. "Goddamn it all to hell."

37

Kieran was packing up the equipment in his medical lab, filling plastic cartons and arranging them on a lift jack as Serena watched. At the rate he was going, the room would be cleared in half an hour, after which he intended to start on the little kitchen and pantry he'd set up for Serena's use.

"You don't trust him," she said, sucking on a beet sugar confection she'd found in a container on one of the shelves.

"Not exactly." He carefully placed a microscope in a container and surrounded it with bubble wrap.

"And you won't tell me where you're moving to."

Kieran snapped on the lid and carried the container over to the lift jack. "Not yet."

"You're being paranoid. You just got this all set up, and now you're tearing it all down again."

"It's not paranoia," he said, grabbing an empty container, "if they really are out to get you. Or words to that effect. A favourite human quote taken from the Earth novel *Catch-22* by Joseph Heller. Do you read much, Serena?"

"No. So what am I supposed to do in the meantime

while you're off setting up your new hideout?"

"I'll leave some basics here, enough for a week." He picked up a piece of equipment she didn't recognize and fitted it carefully inside the container. "After which time I'll re-assess the situation and we'll go from there."

The sound of a door opening drew their attention. It was the main entrance which had been blown to pieces by Dell Burley's team and hastily replaced by Kieran after their departure. They went out to see who it was.

This time, Dell came in with only a pair of tactical agents and Rubén, who calmly closed the door behind them and punched in a code on the keypad to satisfy Kieran's newly installed alarm system.

"This won't take long," Dell said. "Your information checked out."

"I'm sorry for your loss," Kieran said.

"Yeah. Well. Fine. The point is, I want the rest of the information."

"And what about our arrangement?"

"This is how it's going to work," Dell said to Serena. "The machine is assigned to you. You make sure it—okay, he—stays out of sight at all times. Use him as you see fit for assistance in the field, but no autonomous action or decision making or any other damned nonsense from him at any time, understood? *You're* the decision maker, which means *you're* the one on the hook if there's a fuck-up. And when I mean on the hook, I mean game over. Permanently. You and the machine. Am I making myself clear?"

"Yes, sir," Serena said.

"Yes, Director," Kieran said.

"Don't call me that. Now give it up. What else have you got for me?"

"You agree that I will be allowed to remain active

indefinitely?"

"Yeah, yeah, yeah. Didn't I say that already?"

"Not in as many words, no."

"Okay. All right. Toe the line, be a good bot, keep her safe and effective, and you can stay active. Mess around with me in any way, the deal's off and you go straight into the parts bin."

"That's about as good as I'm going to get, I suppose. All right." Kieran hesitated, glancing at the two agents and Rubén. "You might want to hear this in confidence."

"Time's a-wasting and I need to be somewhere else."

"Okay. Serena may or may not have mentioned that I'm aware of your ongoing operation to discover the identity of the person within Stellarize Marté who's stealing corporate information and selling it to Earth Intelligence. I've been monitoring the situation for a while, commencing shortly after the unfortunate capture of your son, whose identity I didn't know at the time."

Dell's eyes narrowed and his jaw tightened, but he said nothing.

"While I don't know the mole's identity yet, and while I can confirm what you already know, that your pursuit of Gabriel Morales was based on an erroneous interpretation of intelligence, I can tell you that someone prominent in your circle has been recruited into Earth's operation to play a role in the exchange of the mole's last big score, as they're calling it."

Dell folded his arms. "Go on."

"This prominent recruit has been told that she'll function as a cutout of sorts, an intermediary who'll receive this last big score and pass it on to an agent who'll transport it directly to Earth. It's my impression, though, that she's being gulled. She's been promised the same reward as the mole, extraction to Earth and a new life there, but I'm getting the sense that she'll never make it that far. They'll expose her and critically damage the reputation of The Five at a time when Martian politics is evolving in a more socialist direction."

"You keep saying 'she.' Who is this 'she'?"

"Constance Davis, your fellow councillor and the chief operating officer of Davis Minerals."

"What's your source?"

Kieran tossed Rubén a data ring. "Transmissions I intercepted and recorded, collated for your own analysis. I'm confident in my conclusions, however."

"Goddamit." Dell looked at Serena. "Stand by for a new assignment. Rubén will contact you as soon as I've set it up."

She watched him lead his team out the door.

"That went better than I'd hoped," Kieran said.

"Are you crazy? He's furious. You just named someone in his inner circle of power as a traitor. And my ass is going to be on the line here."

"Not to worry, Serena. I've got your back."

"I feel so much better, knowing that."

"Sarcasm is the lowest form of humour, you know. Anyway, I've got my deal in place and that's a good thing."

She turned to look at him. "So you don't need to move."

"Oh, yes I do. As you saw, they already know the key code for my replacement security system. How did they do that? I need to move fast."

"Are you sure this is all necessary, Kieran? Don't you think you're getting a little carried away?"

"Oh, it's completely necessary. I trust you, my dear,

because I can tell you've taken a liking to me, but I'll never, never, ever trust him."

He stared at the door through which Dell Burley had just disappeared.

38

When Dell disembarked the shuttlecraft from Gale Station and rode the elevator up to the main floor of Davis Estate, it felt like a homecoming of sorts for him. He'd been a young man working as a site boss for his father when Atlas had undertaken the first major reconstruction of the personal dome of the Davis family, and he'd been back twice since then as CEO to oversee extensive renovation projects. He knew every square inch of each module in the complex, right down to the electrical wiring, plumbing, and secret passageways.

An assistant showed him into the office of Alexander Charles Davis, an 800-square-meter module that Dell himself had personally designed to Alexander's specifications. Connected to the northern surface of the central dome by a short passage that Alexander insisted on calling a breezeway, it had an unobstructed view from the highest point on Mount Sharp across the plain of Aeolis Palus to the distant rim of Gale crater. It was a panorama that once again caught Dell's breath as he looked at it, despite his current mood.

"Please give me a moment," Alexander said from his desk, his eyes on a holographic display, "I have to sign off on this thing and I'm re-reading the conclusion. I'll be just a few minutes."

"No problem, Alex." Dell accepted a drink bulb from the assistant and turned back to the view.

Located just over 5 degrees south of the equator, Gale crater was 154 kilometers in diameter. Likely created by a meteor impact almost four billion years ago, it showed sediment patterns that betrayed the presence of water—essentially a lake—that was at different times in the past million years or so anywhere from 400 to 700 meters deep. Wells drilled by the family had tapped into veins of water ice that, when melted and pumped to the surface, provided a precious local supply that was carefully husbanded, consumed, and recycled in a perfect example of autarky at the local level.

From this spot on the summit, looking north by northwest, the dome of Gale City itself was not visible, being situated behind him on the southern plain within the crater. Gale was smaller than Elysium, about half the size, and dominated by the corporate headquarters of Davis Minerals. Unlike the capital city, Gale was generally quiet, clean, and unaffected by politics, and its city administration kept a low profile, spending the lion's share of its budget on maintenance, education, child care, and emergency services. Policing was handled by the Guardians on a contractual basis.

Looking downslope, Dell's eye was caught by sunlight reflecting off the monument erected at the spot called Bradbury Landing, where the NASA rover Curiosity had touched down in 2012. Made of titanium with black opal inlay, the obelisk had been put in place by Parrish Garrison Davis, the original settler of Gale crater. It commemorated the arrival of the rover and its mission to provide advance information to NASA scientists on habitability, the possibility of past life, and environmental conditions preparatory to the arrival of human explorers.

Dell's gaze moved closer, as it always did, to the small dome situated in the foothills formation known as Pahrump Hills, where Curiosity itself sat in its final resting place. The dome was a tourist attraction on a planet where tourism was still in its infancy. Dell had been down once for a look, driven by his abiding love of fine engineering and the indomitable human spirit, and he hadn't been disappointed.

Today, though, the landscape unfortunately chafed at him with its brick-coloured, shard-strewn barrenness. His boy had exhaled his last breath on terrain similar to what he was looking at now, and Dell's heart held no joy today. Only grief.

And anger.

"There." Alexander slapped a hand on his desk, and the holograph disappeared. He stood up and walked over to a seating arrangement close to the view, where Dell joined him, shaking hands.

"My condolences," Alexander said.

"Thank you."

"Will there be a memorial service? I'd like to attend."

Dell shook his head. "He's already been cremated, and his mother flew back to Hephesto with the ashes. The urn will be kept in her family vault, and that'll be it."

"I'm so sorry."

Dell handed him a data ring. They sat down. "Plans for the dome complex at Tharsis, as requested. Labs, offices, residences, everything. Send me your comments once you've looked them over."

"I will. I take it that Constance has already received her

copy."

Dell nodded. While she was the company's chief operating officer and its official representative on the Council of Five, Constance paid little attention to important operational details, preferring to hand off the work to someone else. For this reason, he and Alexander kept this little back channel open so they could ensure that nothing fell through the cracks.

It also allowed them to continue a friendship that Dell valued. Unfortunately, however, Dell was about to impose on that friendship in a very serious way.

"I want to talk about Connie," he began.

"Oh? Why?"

"Things I've been hearing." He leaned forward. "Look, you know full well that I wear many hats in addition to this," he nodded at the ring Alexander had slipped onto his finger. "As director of the service we won't name, which you helped me set up during your brief stint on council, I have to look into information from time to time that touches on the inner circle. To maintain vigilance, if nothing else."

"I'm aware." Alexander leaned back, his expression neutral.

"Something has come up connected to her, and I need to vet it."

"What do you want to know?"

Here we are then, Dell thought, *at the first airlock.* "I need to understand her better. I'm familiar with today's Connie, but I don't have a really solid grasp of the young girl that she was—the daughter, the child. I'd like you to colour in the picture for me, if you would."

"She wouldn't like me doing that, Dell. Not in the least bit."

"Yeah, I know. I've seen that temper of hers flare a few

times. Once or twice I've been on the receiving end."

"You have no idea."

Alexander's tone gave Dell pause. Despite their years of friendship, they hadn't talked about Constance very much. There'd never been a need, other than when Dell wanted a good sense of how she was leaning on an upcoming council vote. Now, however, given the information he'd received from the artificial human, which had provided secondary-source confirmation of intelligence obtained from the late Emerald Argent, Dell was forced to drill down on her character and her past. Right away he was detecting a sense of unhappy caution from Alexander.

"It's in Connie's best interest to give her a clean bill of health on this thing," he said. "Part of my job, though, as training and experience have taught me, Alex, is to thoroughly understand the subject. Her past, her motivations, her needs and wants."

"This is an investigation, then. You're investigating her for something. She's a subject."

"What was she like as a kid? She's an only child, right?"

Alexander laced his fingers together on his lap and tented his thumbs, up and down, up and down. "Yes."

"And her mother died giving birth."

"Yes."

"Who looked after her when she was small?"

"Staff. I did what I could, but my father was still alive back then, and he kept me hopping."

"I can imagine. So, she had a nanny?"

"Yes. Several, over the years."

"Was there a problem with them?"

"Constance was . . . a handful. It was hard to discipline her for anything. It got worse when she reached puberty.

Much worse."

"I see."

"She was a very fearful child, Dell, and she covered it up with belligerence and aggression. Once she was old enough to understand that her mother was gone, and that she herself was responsible, however innocently, for her death, Connie turned the guilt into resentment, and the fear of loneliness and isolation into personal ambition. I've had a lot of time to think about this and to reach these conclusions."

Dell nodded.

"As she grew older, she caused a lot of problems for her tutors, but she did well in her studies and easily qualified for entrance into UME. She desperately wanted to enroll there, to move to the capital and join the life in the big city. Unfortunately, her grandfather opposed the idea."

"Oh?" Dell himself had earned an engineering degree at UMH, the University of Mars at Hephesto. He'd been offered a scholarship to the University of Mars at Elysium, but turned it down. Having stayed at home to complete his studies, he could appreciate Parrish Davis's attitude on the subject.

Alexander shook his head. "It's not important. They didn't get along."

Dell waited, but he didn't seem to want to add anything else. "All right. How does she feel about Earth? I mean, how did she feel growing up? Earth compared to Mars?"

"She's a terraphile, that's for sure." Alexander tried to smile and didn't quite make it. "She has a whole room here filled with vid programs she used to watch, over and over again. The Amazon rain forest, the Great Lakes, oceanography, Earth climate, tours of the Pacific Northwest and the giant trees they have there, the redwoods. Vid programs about Earth restaurants. She was fascinated with seafood, and we tried importing it now and again but it doesn't travel through space very well. And apparently the stuff we raise here in tanks doesn't compare. Vids about Earth history—English imperialism, African kingdoms, the Great Wall of China, the pyramids of Egypt." He waved a hand. "It's all here. Her collection. Viewed over and over and over again."

"I guess that answers my question," Dell said.

"Yeah." Alexander reluctantly made eye contact. "Why are you asking?"

Here we are now, Dell thought, *at the second airlock.* "There've been some questions raised about her loyalty, Alex. I need to find out whether or not they're true."

"I see."

Dell could see him working hard not to react. "Is she capable of betraying us?"

"She's my daughter, Dell. How the hell do you expect me to answer that?"

"I know. I understand."

Alexander sighed. "No, you don't. I love my daughter according to my bond; no more nor less."

"I don't know what that means."

"It's a literary allusion; not very important. An ironic inversion of the original. The point I'm trying to make, Dell, is that you place me in an impossible position. You're asking me these questions not as a friend but as the director of the service we won't name, which I did indeed help you set up during my short time on council. Which means we're very much on the record. To which I say, I love my daughter according to my duty as a father, and so my answer is, I don't know if she's capable of betraying us. And I won't discuss it any further."

Dell stared at him for a long moment before blurting, "Why, you're afraid! You're petrified! What the hell are you afraid of? *Who* are you afraid of?"

Alexander said nothing.

"Connie?" Dell frowned. "Connie! You're afraid of Connie. Why the hell would you be afraid of her?"

"I don't want to talk about this."

"You *have* to talk about it, Alex. Everything we've done here, everything our grandfathers and fathers built that we've expanded and developed and improved on so our children will have a world entirely their own, free from another planet's chokehold, is at stake here. You *have* to talk about it."

Alexander remained silent.

"Was there something between Connie and her grandfather? That's the point where you stopped talking. Did something happen that I should know about?"

Alexander stared at his hands.

"Obviously, something did. Something relevant, otherwise you wouldn't be holding it back."

"It has nothing to do with treason, Dell. It's not relevant to whatever your investigation is."

"Okay, fine. Then it's personal. Talk to me as a friend, Alex, and not as the MIS director. What the hell are you holding on to? Why are you so afraid of her?"

"As a friend."

"Yes."

"Off the record."

"Yes, dammit. Off the record."

"All right." He took a moment to collect himself. "Yes, there's something I need to—well, *should* talk about. I should have talked about it a long time ago, I guess, but I was too traumatized. Too afraid. Yes! Too frightened."

"Go on."

"All right. Okay." Alexander stood up and walked over to the view, hands clasped behind his back. "I love this place, Dell. I love Mars. I was born here. This is *my* world. My father was born on Earth, and this place was his life's challenge, his opportunity to achieve greatness, but he didn't love it. In many ways, he hated it. It was a world he was born to conquer, to beat down, to strip of its wealth and resources, to triumph over."

Dell listened, his jaw muscles tight.

"It was in his personality to control everything. This place, his company, other companies, his family. Everything. My younger brothers and I lived in fear of him. It's the reason why Jordan committed suicide and why Terrence chose to live the rest of his life on Ganymede as a particle physicist, of all things. I was the only one who stayed to play the role of obedient son. It was hell, except for the times when he completely ignored me."

"That's unfortunate," Dell said.

"When Connie announced she'd applied to UME and had been accepted, my father hit the roof. He insisted she remain here. She could attend Gale College if she felt a degree was absolutely necessary, but Elysium was out of the question. I tried to intervene on her behalf, but he physically attacked me. Not for the first time, of course. Even as an old man he felt it was his right to beat up his adult son, the same way he'd routinely beaten me up as a child. I took it, as I always did, because I was too afraid to stand up to him. I'm not a very courageous person, Dell."

"You tried to help her."

"Yes, but it just wasn't going to go her way. She made her arguments to him, lost, and slipped into a funk. She waited a year, doing essentially nothing, moping around and wasting time, until her opportunity finally came."

"What happened?"

"My father fell sick. Some kind of a virus. He was in bed for weeks, in and out of consciousness. It seriously weakened him. The doctors said he'd recover, but they admitted it had been a close call in the first few days. Antiviral drugs were still in short supply here, and they hadn't been sure the one they'd administered would do the job. Apparently, it did. He began a slow and gradual recovery.

"One evening, she made her move. My father had never been much of a believer in personal security, so it was easy for her to go into his room and inject a toxin into his intravenous feed. Apparently a friend of hers, a biology student, gave it to her, thinking they were playing a game of 'what if.' It was a substance that was untraceable at autopsy, and it killed him almost instantly.

"I was there when she came out of the room. I explained to her that while she'd turned off the main video feed, there was a secondary feed she didn't know about. She didn't miss a beat. She said, 'Stay out of my way or the same thing will happen to you.' I looked into her eyes and believed her. The girl I'd known and loved was gone for good. If she'd ever existed at all. Standing in front of me, threatening to kill me too, was this ambitious, cold-hearted automaton. She frightened me to the bone. I feel the same way now, today, right at this moment, even as we're talking about it. She still holds that power over me. The power to end my life whenever she wishes."

"You took over as CEO, though. After your father died. You, not her."

Alexander showed him a wan smile. "She wanted to attend university, didn't she? She wanted a degree. She wanted to take up the life in the capital city. The parties, the theatre, the friends. She needed me to look after things while she did that."

"I see."

"Off the record, Dell. If you try to make something of this, in an official way, I'll deny everything I've told you. According to my bond as a father, Dell."

"All right." Dell got up and walked over to stand beside him. Looking out over the endless vista of dust and broken stones, he sighed. "You're aware that her personal assistant was killed?"

"Yes. I don't know the circumstances."

"The girl's throat was cut. But not by Connie. My inside source tells me it was the Earth diplomat, St.-Giorge Mercade. The ambassador's son."

"I see."

"She's involved in something over her head, Alex. It'll likely have a very bad ending."

"I've been expecting that kind of ending for a very long time, Dell."

They shook hands and Dell walked out, lost in thought.

39

Serena walked up to the security team at the main site entrance and gave them her best smile, which she knew wasn't much but would have to do.

"I'm expected." She kept her eyes on the one she'd spoken to, a middle-aged man inside a glass booth, but tracked the second one peripherally, a small woman who slowly circled behind her, stunner in hand.

The man inside the booth looked up from his tablet. "Ninth floor."

He tapped something, and the gate cracked open.

Nodding at the woman with the stunner, Serena slipped through and looked around. They were tearing down almost an entire block surrounding a ten-floor building just inside the central core on the northeast edge.

It was mid-morning and the site was busy. Heavy machinery thrashed and groaned. Cargo ricks circulated in all directions, obeying traffic signals from robots stationed at various pressure points. Teams of workers gathered here and there to listen to instructions from their supervisors. A few people glanced at her, perhaps distracted by her smallness and her bald, freckled head, but no one showed undue interest.

She stepped onto the back running board of a passing cargo rick and rode it across the site to the tower that was the central focus of the project. According to Kieran, the structure was being completely rebuilt as a new embassy and luxury residence for the ambassador from Ganymede and her retinue.

While it was the largest moon in the solar system, Ganymede was only sparsely settled. It was essentially nothing more than a colony of scientists. Serena had seen them in the markets and in the bars and restaurants in the city. Their clothing was bright and garish, their taste in fashion being what could kindly be described as harlequinesque. Their preferred cuisine was hot and spicy, often featuring curries of one sort or another, and when they drank it was often to excess.

When they were home, however, their work was routinely groundbreaking in the fields of astrophysics, cosmology, and exobiology. The Five had developed a close relationship with their leadership council, and Ganymede was a small but steady trade partner for Martian manufactured goods, food products, and other commodities. In exchange, their council permitted The Five to maintain an FBO, a fixed base of operations, on Ganymede for their interplanetary ships working the outer planets. They'd also been using the FBO for test runs of spacecraft equipped with various components of the new interstellar drive.

According to Kieran, Ganymede was also the source of all the current information on the FRBs, the fast radio bursts, that were the *raison d'être* of the interstellar project to begin with and the resultant race between Earth and Mars to be first to reach the source of the signals. More on the subject he declined to say, and as it wasn't a priority of hers at present, she didn't bother pressing him for further details.

She stepped off the rick as it passed the tower. Brushing dust from her bodysuit, she looked up. Reconstruction of the exterior had reached as far as the sixth floor, but floors seven through ten were still stripped down to the girders and beams. Welding torches flared here and there; rivet guns cracked and popped; sledges thudded; and workers catwalked the upper reaches as though strolling along Central Avenue, taking the air.

A freight cage was descending as she looked the building over. It reached the bottom and sat there. Waiting for her. She got in, locked the cage door, and hammered on button 9 with the edge of her fist.

As the cage rose, she looked around the site. A few buildings along the back street had been left in place, perhaps because Dell liked their architecture or they served some other useful purpose, but everything on the south side of the block had been razed and cleared.

I've seen the site plan, Kieran said. His voice was a discreet buzzing sound that seemed to originate somewhere deep inside her ear canal. She was still trying to get used to the sensation, which felt like one of Peter's insects trapped inside her head.

"What does it look like?" She had the option of vocalizing or just *thinking* at him. She preferred the former when there was no chance of being overheard, because it seemed less . . . weird.

The Ganymedans are thrilled. There are all kinds of high-end restaurants and taverns planned for the block, a spa, and other such amenities. The embassy itself will be stunning. The Five obviously value this alliance, since they're investing a small fortune in the project.

The elevator stopped at the ninth floor. She threw

the cage door open and stepped out onto a small metal platform. Load-bearing girders ran away from her in three directions. Below her was empty space and a very long drop. Diagonally, in the farthest corner away from her, a worker was welding something. The actinic light flared; molten drops fell arhythmically, disappearing below.

Closer, sitting with his back against a column, she spotted Dell Burley. She set off straight ahead, following the girder to a crossing beam that took her to the next girder running parallel. Resting her hand lightly on the column at the intersection for a moment, she took a breath and followed this girder up to the next crossing beam, walked its length, and took the remaining few steps to where Dell sat, sipping from a flip-top thermos. She could smell the aroma of chicory coffee.

He smiled up at her, one leg straight out on the girder and the other bent at the knee. "No balance issues, I see."

She shrugged. "No."

"Any fear of heights?'

She shook her head.

"Agoraphobia? Do the wide-open spaces around us and below us bother you at all?"

"No. Should they?"

"Ever been outside, Serena? Other than in an enclosed vehicle, I mean?"

"No."

"Does the thought of it frighten you? All that empty space stretching off in every direction for kilometers, the thin atmosphere asphyxiating you, the radiation frying you like a slice of turnip?"

"No, it doesn't. Why did you want to see me, Director?"

He's running you through your paces, Kieran said. *He*

wants to see what you're made of.

"We'll get to that in a minute," Dell said. "Tell me about your friends."

Serena thought about Caretta, a girl she'd chummed with at the grow op. A tall brunette with a quick smile and infinite kindness. The only person Serena had ever thought of as a friend, Caretta had taken up with a young bookkeeper working for Ares Foods who came around every month to square accounts with Peter. She and the bookkeeper married and moved away to Isidium City, and that was it for Serena's friends.

"I don't have any," she said.

"What about a boyfriend?"

"Not right now."

"Don't you feel isolated from people?"

"Sure. What's this all about?"

"Relax, Serena. You're an asset, but you're also a person. I'm a councillor, but I'm also a human being. I'm interested to see if there's a middle ground somewhere between us."

"Is there one between you and Rubén?"

Well played! Kieran crowed inside her head.

Shut up, she thought back at him.

Dell smiled. "Yes, actually, there is. Rubén's been read in on certain aspects of what we have planned for you." He sat up, dropping his legs over each side of the girder. "Our search for the mole continues on other fronts, but since your mechanical friend has cast light on the conduit through which the mole will pass his last big score, I want you to work that end of it."

"Councillor Davis, you mean."

"Yeah. We're going to insert you into her household. Rubén will send you the details. You'll work with a contact I already have on the inside who'll give you further instructions, and this time you'll send your reports directly to Rubén. Any questions?"

"No, sir."

"Any interest in construction, Keilor?"

"Not really, sir."

"That's okay. I'm a civil engineer myself, by education and training, and it's what I love the most." He patted the girder between his thighs. "This building used to be outside the core, but we recently expanded the boundary by a few blocks so we could bring it inside the perimeter. We're stripping it down because when it was built, it wasn't up to code, marsquake-wise. As you know, this planet's seismically active, although in a different way than Earth, and we don't really know for sure what effect our terraforming will have. Quakes here aren't caused by the movement of tectonic plates, like they are on Earth, because we don't have any. They're caused by contractions from the gradual cooling of the planet. We're going to be raising the temperature around here, and our models show that reversing that trend, causing the crust to expand all over again, will likely set off a new round of quakes. So part of what my company's doing is inspecting every building in every dome, tearing down the ones that are no good to us and reconstructing the ones we want to keep. Like this baby."

He's not kidding, Kieran said. *I've seen their balance sheets. They're very serious about this.*

"Why am I boring you with this, Keilor?" He took a last swig of coffee and capped the thermos.

"I don't know, sir."

"Believe it or not, we also have a modest investment in you. And it's important to us—to me—that you feel like you're participating in the future of this world."

"I do, sir. Feel that way."

"Good." He brought his legs up, and all of a sudden he was standing, his back against the column. "Disappear."

"Yes, sir."

"Take the cage back down, Keilor. Unless you can fly."

"I can't sir."

As she turned on her heel and started off along the girder, she heard him murmur, "It wouldn't surprise me if you could."

40

Constance's private elevator was out of order and under repair, so she was forced to ride up to her suite in the car used by staff, visitors, and other assorted individuals. It was large and roomy, able to accommodate ten people altogether, but unfortunately for her, the entire population of Mars had apparently drawn lots this morning to see who could cram into the damned thing with her all at once.

Labossière and two of his employees surrounded her in a triangular formation. She was fresh from a meeting with Dell Burley on the approval process for Tharsis, in which he'd taken a moment to express regret that she'd lost her personal assistant, the poor demised Emerald Argent. Constance had thanked him, failing to suppress her frustration at not currently having a suitable replacement.

"I've taken the liberty," he said, "of sending over someone to interview with your head of staff. What's her name again?"

"Juliana."

"Yeah. The young woman's name is Serena. She's done a bit of work for me, and I can vouch for her. Think of her as a gift. An early birthday present from me to you.

If you decide to give her a try as your assistant, I don't think surgery will be necessary. You'll find her completely discreet and trustworthy. Anyway, it's up to you."

Up to me, indeed.

It was very irritating that he'd poked his nose into her personal business without being invited, but that was nothing compared to the annoyance she felt now as the elevator car stopped at the third floor and, instead of discharging passengers to relieve some of the stifling press, took on two more riders—Juliana and a young woman who was, no doubt, Dell Burley's gift from him to her.

The pitiful thing wore a white funnel-neck top, green cigarette pants, and white shoes. All clearly off the rack from Goosen's, for the love of mercy. Her head had recently been shorn bald, and her hair had grown back to a length of about two millimeters. The result was a faint reddish fuzz, beneath which Constance could see blotchy freckles on her scalp, as well as on her face and neck. She was as homely as a sand rat.

Constance didn't believe in racial or ethnic epithets and tried never to use them herself. But if ever she'd seen someone who deserved to be called a dirt eater, it was this poor girl.

She shifted to look between the shoulders of two men, catching Juliana's eye. "Kitchen."

Juliana's mouth opened and closed, as though she wanted to say something and decided instead on a wiser course of action. She lowered her eyes and nodded. "Yes, Councillor."

What had Dell Burley been thinking? He was always so cavalier, but this was really over the top. A dirt-eating personal assistant?

The nerve.

41

After several days, Serena had more or less settled into her new job in the kitchen of Constance Davis's household. She'd been assigned sleeping quarters on the third floor with the rest of the staff, and every morning she rode up to the kitchen on the seventh floor to work on food preparation, dishwashing, and other menial tasks. Her duties, however, did not include taking meals up to the penthouse. Constance had made it clear to Juliana that she couldn't abide the sight of Serena in her private quarters.

After hearing one of the young women complain about having to go down to receive the daily shipments of groceries and other kitchen supplies, Serena volunteered for the job. Juliana quickly gave it to her, not only because it solved a problem she'd rather not fuss with, but also because it provided Serena with an opportunity to get out in the street, beyond the building surveillance, so that she could send in her reports to Rubén.

Juliana, it seemed, was the inside contact Dell Burley had mentioned.

One evening, Serena was standing outside in the narrow space between Davis Tower and the building next door, just beyond the glow of the streetlights, waiting for a liquor shipment. Although it would be taken down the alley and through a side door to a discreet freight elevator, Constance insisted that these deliveries occur after sunset in order to prevent people from knowing her personal business when it came to what and how often she consumed this particular commodity.

Whatever. Serena thought it was excessive behaviour, but she didn't really care.

Kieran, on the other hand, was curious to know if she'd tried any of the brands she was about to receive.

Are you kidding? You've seen the documentation, Kieran. Imported from Earth? Just one flask would cost me a year's pay.

Can you sample any of it? I'm particularly curious about your reaction to the Sarbucca brandy.

No, I can't, and why the hell would you be curious about that?

Research.

Because it was evening and her duties had been completed for the day, except for receiving this shipment, she'd changed from her kitchen service clothing into a black bodysuit and flat shoes, anticipating a quiet evening in her sleeping quarters as soon as this final task was over with. Maybe Kieran would stay quiet long enough for her to actually relax and lower her stress level a bit.

The shipment arrived. Two young men unloaded crates from the back of their cargo rick and wheeled them down the alley on lift jacks. She stepped out of the shadows and opened the door, leading them inside to the freight elevator. They'd been here before and knew the way, but her job was to see them in and out without a breach in protocol.

One of them, an Asian with the loose hips and broad

shoulders of an athlete, glanced at her as they were coming back down.

"Where's Aleena?"

"I'm it, now."

"Oh."

"Tough luck," the other one said to the Asian. "She's probably ducking you."

"I'm new here," Serena said, "but I think she got a promotion. Not something you turn down."

The Asian looked a little less stricken. "Oh, well. That's good for her, then. Right?"

"Unless she gets the surgery," the other one, a blond, said. "Not much of a promotion, if you ask me."

"Oh god, no." The Asian looked at Serena. "Is it possible? Is she moving to personal staff?"

"I haven't a clue." Serena waved them off the elevator ahead of her.

Outside, in the alley, the blond said, "It's okay, you don't need to follow us up to the street."

"Did Aleena?"

"Well, yeah." He snorted. "To make time with him."

The Asian kept his eyes on the wheels of his lift jack.

"Okay, then." She followed them up the alley to the street.

"No, really, we're fine," the blond said, no longer making eye contact either. "You can go back in now. It's late and pretty dark."

"Sure." Serena stood on the curb and watched them stow their jacks in the back of the cargo rick. It had the logo of the liquor distributor on the side, a martini glass with a small star winking off the rim. "Nice ride."

"Yeah, thanks." The blond swung in behind the controls. "See ya."

She watched the rick merge into traffic and disappear around a corner. Although she was used to it, and understood it was part of her cover as an insignificant nobody who would never arouse suspicion, this kind of treatment nevertheless made her feel a bit sad. It wasn't pleasant to be considered a pariah, an outsider, because of her colouring. They weren't particularly attractive guys, and she didn't have any interest in them as possible replacements for dear departed Bruno, but just the same . . .

As she stood there, a rick emerged from the parking bay of the building behind her and turned out onto the street. As it passed beneath the streetlight, she caught a glimpse of Labossière behind the controls and Constance in the back seat.

It was late, and Labossière looked distinctly unhappy.

Serena didn't hesitate.

42

She ran over to a metal rack where tricycles were stored for the use of Constance's staff when running errands. She used her ring to free one and set off after the rick.

She pedalled down to the corner. Constance's rick had already passed through the intersection and was halfway down the next block.

Are you paying attention?

Yes, of course, Kieran replied.

Lovely. I'll stay a few blocks back.

Understood.

One of the first things Juliana had explained to her was that Martian Intelligence was in the process of setting up a building-wide surveillance system within Constance's headquarters. Every square meter of every floor in Davis Tower would soon be covered for audio and video. Included in that coverage were the various personal vehicles used by the councillor for business or for personal travel. When everything was up and running, Serena would be given access.

Naturally, Kieran had hacked into the system within minutes of hearing about it.

As Serena pedalled her trike after Constance's rick,

which had disappeared from sight, Kieran fed her turn-by-turn instructions while prattling on about Martian brandy.

I regret they didn't get around to installing my sense of taste, because I'm very curious about wines and spirits. Did you know that on Earth the ancients used to use terra cotta vessels to ferment and age their wine like we do on Mars? Apparently on Earth they now add sulfur to wines fermented in wooden barrels to limit oxidation. I can't imagine that would taste terribly pleasant. Anyway, since amphorae don't require any such additives, the wine produced in them is said to have a cleaner, fresher taste.

That's nice. Serena was beginning to worry as she followed Constance deeper into a rough neighbourhood. What was her business up here?

Did you know that brandy is made by distilling wine? Apparently Earth brandy is aged in wooden barrels exclusively, which they have the luxury of doing, of course, since there's wood everywhere on their planet, just sitting around for the taking. If you can imagine, Serena.

I can't. They're still on the move, right?

Yes.

I don't like this. She eyed the silhouettes of men loitering in the shadows, waiting for something to happen. She'd already passed through the perimeter into the northeast quarter, walking her trike through a building that allowed her to miss the loose security on this block while Constance was driven through the regular checkpoint. *The councillor shouldn't be up here.*

Agreed. From previous observations, though, it seems she does this often and appears to enjoy the risk.

Doesn't make sense.

It might if you gave it some thought.

I don't really have the time right now.

Next right, then a quick left.

Serena followed his instructions. She was now pedalling down a narrow street in an old part of the city lined with two-storey tenements and dubious-looking shops.

Our ceramic qvevri vessels are directly adapted from those native to the Earth country of Georgia, in eastern Europe. Between the Black Sea and the Caspian Sea. Seas are incredibly large bodies of salt water. Almost inconceivable. At any rate, Georgian qvevri are traditionally flavour-neutral, as I understand it, but after experimentation and adaptation, ours impart what connoisseurs consider, and I quote, 'a distinct suggestion of jasmine, geraniums, and cinnamon.' Supposedly that's quite good.

Where the hell are they going? Serena was growing more worried by the minute.

That's why I was curious for you to sample the Sarbucca. I'm guessing you've already had brandy, and you could tell me if the Earth product is better.

I don't drink.

I've seen you drink, multiple times. All humans must drink in order to survive.

Alcohol, Kieran. I don't drink alcohol.

They've stopped, Kieran said.

How far ahead?

Same street, Serena. About fifty meters.

Knock it off with the chatter.

Ten four.

Serena slowed her trike and eased over to the curb. She found a hiding place for it in the shadows behind a derelict rick and slowly crept forward.

Thirty meters, Kieran said.

Serena stopped to allow a group of inebriated prowlers to pass along the walkway. Young teens, they were laughing and ragging at one another, full of piss and vinegar. When their voices trailed off around a corner she continued forward.

As she neared a T-intersection, Kieran said, *Ten meters.*

I see it. Serena hugged the corner of a building and looked around at Constance's rick, down on the right. It was pulled up to the curb, engine off, lights out. She could see the silhouette of Labossière's head in the front but nothing in the back.

She's not there.

No. I saw her get out, through the rick's internal video, but she disappeared.

How could you lose her, Kieran?

The tracker's on the vehicle, Serena, not her. And there's no external video in the immediate area for me to tap into.

Down the other way, to the left, a door burst open and two men stumbled out, throwing punches at each other. A woman followed, yelling at them. They disappeared down the other way.

A bar.

Evidently.

I'm going to check it out.

She crossed the intersection and had taken a few cautious steps forward when the same door flew open again. A woman stumbled out, a man holding onto her upper arm with an aggressive grip. A second woman followed, and another man. The woman being herded out was Constance Davis.

Their voices rang off the walls as they urged Constance

forward. Their movements were self-confident and easy, indicating to Serena that they were accustomed to Martian gravity. Meaning they were either planet-born or they'd been around long enough to acclimate.

As they reached a passageway between the buildings and pulled Constance into its shadows, Serena saw Labossière get out of the rick. He pulled out a stunner and walked up to the mouth of the passageway, raising the weapon.

"What's all this, now?" he called out.

Before Serena could move, Labossière flew backward, the stunner pinwheeling out of his hands. He went straight down, arms out, the back of his head striking the pavement with a sickening crack.

Shit, Serena thought, *here goes nothing*.

43

She left cover and crossed the street. Labossière's face was a mask of blood. The knife in his left eye was buried halfway to the hilt. He was as dead as he could get.

As she passed the body, she saw that the assailants all had their attention focused on Constance. Without stopping, Serena leaned down, grabbed the knife, and jerked it out of Labossière's eye. She moved into the passageway, holding the dripping knife behind her thigh.

"Is this a private party or can I play, too?"

One man held Constance down, the tip of his dagger at her throat, while the other one was busy stripping off rings and bracelets. The woman stood by, watching with a grin of anticipation. She had a sheath strapped to each leg, one empty and the other holding a knife matching the one that was now in Serena's possession.

The man robbing Constance of her jewelry turned around, but his smile disappeared when he saw her. "Get lost, dirt eater."

"Sure, okay." Serena stepped forward and slashed the woman's throat before she could react. As blood jetted everywhere, she plucked the second knife from the woman's leg sheath and, lunging, drove it into the kidney of the man taking the jewelry.

The man holding the dagger to Constance's neck couldn't help himself. He turned his weapon toward the threat. Serena drove her remaining knife under his chin, up through his throat and into his brain.

She pivoted. The woman lay on her side, eyes open, in a pool of blood. Dead. The man with the knife in his kidney had curled into a fetal position, head against the wall, his hand groping feebly behind him. Serena knew he wouldn't live, so she cut his throat. She swiftly picked up the rings and bracelets that had fallen from his hands and stuck them into her pocket.

The man with the dagger had fallen back across Constance. Serena pulled his body away and dragged it aside.

Constance sobbed, staring up at her with unseeing eyes.

"Come on, Councillor." She held out her hand. "Get up. We have to get out of here."

Constance didn't move.

Serena bent down and slapped her twice across the face. "Now, Councillor. Take my hand and get up. Now!"

Serena, you have about fifteen seconds to get clear before someone arrives.

Constance frowned, suddenly recognizing her.

Serena grabbed her hand and pulled her up onto her feet. Taking her by the elbow, she led her past the dead bodies and out to Labossière. Constance groaned and stopped, but Serena pulled her forward.

"He's gone, Councillor. There's nothing we can do for him. We have to go."

"He, he's—"

"Yeah. Now come on. Let's go."

Serena dragged her down the street to the rick. She pushed her into the back and got in front, behind the controls. Because it was a manually driven vehicle, it took her a moment to find the autopilot button. She punched it, recited the address of Constance's building, and watched another group of people emerge from the bar and head over to Labossière's lifeless corpse as the rick left the curb, swung a U-turn, and drove away.

44

Constance slept in the following morning, and when she arose she called for her temporary assistant, whose name she couldn't remember, and ordered brunch. After a long shower, she dressed and went into her sitting room to eat. The girl thankfully possessed enough sense to leave her alone with her thoughts.

Face it—her morale was in tatters, her confidence was shot, and her cotton candy dreams were spiraling into nightmare.

First, there had been the ugliness of Emerald's brutal murder and the exposure of Hercule as a cruel, calculating agent of Earth Intelligence who cared about her just as much as he might care about a speck on his immaculate black trousers.

Now, just when she was still trying to get everything arranged for her big move toward freedom and a new life on another world, despite the knowledge that everyone involved was cold, calculating, and uncaring, she'd suffered another loss. It made her feel weak, vulnerable, exposed. She'd never particularly liked Labossière, but he'd done the job for her. When she needed her butt covered while she played her little night-time games to relieve the stress and tension, he'd always been there. Now, he was gone—dead!—and she had several decisions to make. Right away.

The various meatheads who worked for Labossière were still around, but they were disorganized and confused without their boss to tell them what to do. She was trying to work up the energy to call their agency and order a replacement team, but she was hesitating. She wasn't sure if that was the direction in which she wanted to go.

She'd already decided to terminate the nighthawk escapades. That was the first decision, and it had been an easy one to make. Really, they were an immature and foolish indulgence she could no longer afford. She was forced to admit that she was afraid to leave the building at all right now, regardless of the time of day. Her personal safety was very much in the wind.

Her mind replayed the incident over and over again—the brutal hands, the knives, the leering faces, the ugly laughter. Her jewelry stripped from her. The absolute certainly they wouldn't stop at mere robbery.

She kept seeing the little dirt eater slashing the throat of the woman. She saw the blood pumping from the wound, spraying everywhere. She saw the knife as it stabbed and cut. She remembered sobbing and not being able to stop.

She also remembered the exultation as they died around her. Die, die, die! The dirt eater was like an avenging angel, sweeping down to protect and save her.

This was the second decision she needed to make, regarding the matter of Labossière's replacement. The redhead could obviously handle herself. She'd killed three people in the space of what—ten seconds?—before whisking her off to safety without raising a sweat. What was her name again? Constance couldn't remember. Dell had mentioned it when he told her he was sending her over as a possible replacement for Emerald, but she hadn't heard it spoken again and it had slipped her mind.

It didn't matter. She'd never seen Labossière or his men move like that. She doubted if they could, even if they tried. But this slim little girl, this refugee from the unwashed proletariat, had acted with a calmness and confidence that was incredible.

All right. Very well. Let's try something bold and daring, and see where it goes.

She called Dell.

"What's going on, Connie?" He sounded brusque, as though she'd interrupted him at something very important.

"I need to talk to you. Can we take a minute?"

"Sure. Of course. Give me a second." Without waiting for her to reply, he put her on hold. She closed her eyes, willing herself not to cry. Then he was back. "Okay, let's talk."

"I had a little problem last night. I need your advice on how to clean it up."

"I know, Connie."

"You know?" She frowned for a moment. "Oh, I see." She remembered he had other responsibilities in addition to Atlas Construction, directing planetary security on behalf of The Five, and he must have seen a report of some sort on what had happened.

"Labossière—"

"Has been taken care of."

"There were bodies. . . ."

"Taken care of, Connie."

Relief flooded through her.

"We need to completely retool your security, Connie."

"Yes. Dell—"

He waited.

"That girl you sent over, the redhead. She showed up out of nowhere. She . . . handled the situation like it was nothing."

"I think we're on the same page, Connie. I suggest you interview her now, this morning. See if you'd be comfortable with her as a replacement for Labossière. She has training and experience that would be valuable to you. I'll come over, see what I can do to help."

"Would you?"

"Of course. It'd be my pleasure."

Constance ended the call and pressed a button.

No one came.

She pressed the button again, several times.

After a moment one of Labossière's nitwits put his head around the door.

"Tell the servant girl to come in here and clear away this mess," she said, indicating the remnants of her brunch.

"Yes, Councillor."

"And bring me that redheaded girl who's working down in the kitchen. What's her name?" She'd forgotten to ask Dell to remind her of it.

"I don't know, Councillor. I'm sorry."

"Idiot. Just go and get her. Bring her to me. Immediately."

It took several minutes for the servant girl, Aleena, to appear. Obviously frightened, she dropped a cup and broke it, then had to spend time picking up the pieces before she had everything on the trolley.

"We haven't scheduled your surgery yet, have we?" Constance asked.

"No, Councillor."

"Mmm." Constance had absolutely no intention of having it done, since she wasn't going to be around long enough to need another personal assistant who was deaf and mute, but she noted with satisfaction the fear that flickered across the girl's face at the mention of it. It was mean, yes. Cruel.

Oh, well.

After the trolley left the room, it took another several minutes—in her mind an inexcusable delay—for the bodyguard to return with the redhead in tow.

"Leave us." She waved a hand, and the man disappeared.

She looked the girl up and down. It was important to project complete self-control at the moment with this child, who'd seen her at her worst last night, vulnerable and weak. She straightened her back, tilted her chin, and raised an eyebrow.

"Your name?"

"Serena Keilor, Councillor."

"How old are you?"

"Twenty-two, ma'am."

She was polite enough, at least.

"I want to thank you for your help last night."

"Not at all, ma'am," the girl replied, boldly maintaining eye contact.

"How does it happen," Constance leaned back in her chair, "that a mere slip of a girl like you can handle yourself like that?"

"Training, ma'am."

"What? Training? Where would you get that kind of training?"

"Tutors, ma'am."

"Tutors? Are you serious?"

"I wanted to be a police officer, ma'am. I'd set my heart on it when I was a little girl, so I studied what I thought I'd need to learn to become one, including physical training. I passed all the tests to qualify, but it didn't work out."

"Oh? Why not?"

"The induction officer wouldn't let me advance. I was turned away."

Constance nodded. Because of her breed, no doubt. "I see. What I want to know is whether that was a one-time thing last night, or whether you could do it again, handle a situation like that again, if you needed to."

"I could, ma'am. Absolutely. No question."

"Councillor Burley sent you over here. He told me you'd done a few things for him, and that he recommended you. He thought you might be a possible replacement for my personal assistant, who's no longer here, but that's out of the question. Nevertheless, I'm curious. What sort of things was Councillor Burley referring to that you would have done for him?"

"I'm not sure what he meant, ma'am. I was a runner for a while, a messenger for one of his crews. I brought him data rings once or twice at a construction site. I was part of a personal protection detail for a short while. Maybe that was it."

"Hmm." Constance folded her arms. "You have martial arts training, is that what you're saying? Is that why you can handle yourself like that?"

"Yes, ma'am. Several kinds, actually."

"What kinds?"

"Uh, jujitsu, taekwondo, and something called kali eskrima."

"I've never heard of that last one. What is it?"

"Kali eskrima? It's a martial art that's weapon-based,

primarily knives, sticks, or anything improvised. It teaches angles, stepping off the centre line to avoid attacks, and striking unexpectedly."

"Is that what I saw last night?"

"Not really, ma'am. That was more just stab and slash."

Constance chuckled at the girl's remarkable self-confidence. "I see. Labossière was my head of security. I take it you've seen what I'm left with, now that he's gone."

"Yes, ma'am."

"What's your opinion of them?"

"They need to be told what to do."

"Is that something you could do? Tell them what to do?"

"No, ma'am."

"Oh? Why not?"

The girl said nothing, her dark brown eyes inscrutable.

Constance nodded. The men would die rather than take orders from a nothing little dirt eater, obviously. They were paid professionals, proud and elite. Not to mention dumb as turnips. The whole thing appealed to her sense of absurdity, her contrariness, her wish to thumb her nose at everyone who thought they knew better than she.

"Councillor Burley will be here shortly. Sit with him and go over our alarm systems and set up new protection protocols and all of that. Have Labossière's things removed from his living quarters and move yourself in there. I'll expect you to be available to me around the clock. His team will be gone, so talk to Dell about finding a few freelancers who can assist you. He should know who to get. Rely on him for advice and guidance."

"Yes, ma'am."

"Get moving."

"Yes, ma'am."

Constance watched her leave, pleased with herself. What a delightful experiment. If it didn't turn out success-fully, she'd have the girl disappeared and go back to the agency for another Labossière. But if it did work out . . .

45

Constance was required to wait a week, however, for her new head of security to assume her duties, as Dell sent Serena off for a crash course in basic techniques and tactics used in the close protection of Very Important Persons.

Serena was flown to Hephesto and transported by crawler to a mysteriously anonymous dome many kilometers off in the middle of the desert. It was her first time travelling in a surface vehicle outside a dome, and she loved it.

A compact personnel carrier built of aluminum and radiation-proof tessuspaz, the crawler had a cockpit up front for the driver and room for six passengers behind the airlock-style entry hatch on the starboard side. Its six open-structure wheels churned the sand, flexed over rocks that littered the surface, and bounced in and out of pits of various depths. It was powered by an electric motor running on high-capacity storage batteries that were fed by solar panels fastened to the vehicle's surface. It ran at a top speed of 100 kilometers per hour, and the journey took about forty minutes altogether.

Serena spent the time gawking out the side ports like a tourist. She wore a lifesuit like the other passengers, but she kept the visor flipped up so she could see everything that was possible to see. The cabin was pressurized to dome-normal and heated to a comfortable 18 degrees Celsius, so as far as she was concerned, it felt like a day in the green space.

Your vital signs are up, Kieran observed.

This is really cool. I had no idea it was so incredibly beautiful out here.

No agoraphobia, Serena? he asked in a passable imitation of Dell Burley's smooth baritone. *No fear of open spaces?*

Are you kidding? She stared at the landscape around them, flat and red, with a mountain range in the distance. *I love this place. I truly, truly love it.*

Why? What about it makes you love it so much?

I don't know. She thought for a moment. *It's so quiet and still. It has . . . a dignity about it, like it won't apologize to anyone for what it is.*

Completely fascinating, Kieran said.

Plus, it's wall-to-wall red. I can't help but like it for that now, can I?

The dome was large enough to house an extensive training campus, residences, and several simulation centres with urban landscapes customized for various learning scenarios. She settled into a room in one of the dormitories and was given a schedule to follow. She wore a uniform bodysuit with the Guardians logo on it, a red circle with a gold shield in the middle, and lightweight body armor she was expected to wear at all times, except for when she was asleep in her cot.

She attended physical training sessions in the mornings after breakfast and was able to pair up with an instructor who was an expert in pencak silat, a Malaysian martial art she'd heard of but never studied. Over the course of the week, this instructor trained her in silat's various stances and foot techniques, how to fight with a karambit blade (a particularly vicious little sickle-shaped weapon known for inflicting painful wounds), and how to take on multiple attackers empty-handed, disarming them and turning their own weapons against them.

For two hours before lunch and six hours after, she attended classroom sessions and walk-throughs on the fundamentals of close protection, followed after dinner by three hours of live simulations.

For the first four days, she and the other participants learned about direct protection, where they worked individually and as a team to provide close protection on foot. They trained in box formations, V formations, and diamond formations. They practiced low-profile protections, when the team consisted of fewer than three members. They trained in proper communications techniques, and they rehearsed extraction and evacuation methods when an attack occurred and the protectee was in danger.

The basic program Serena was taking usually lasted two weeks, and the next four days would normally focus on mobile protection, when the protectee was travelling by vehicle, but Dell had decided she didn't need that segment and arranged for it to be moved to the program's second week, when Serena would be gone, in favour of static protection.

This topic involved security procedures when the protectee was at home or at a venue where there would not be any movement for a given period of time. This juggling of the schedule was the only indication to the instructors that Serena was different from the other participants in the course, and while they grudgingly rearranged their timetables to accommodate Dell's orders, Serena was quite unaware that she was being given any sort of special treatment. To the contrary, she felt that the instructors were riding her a hell of a lot harder than anyone else.

Which they were, of course.

It was in her nature to keep apart from others, and so Serena developed no friendships during her stay. The others knew they would be together for the next three months as they followed the basic training program mandatory for all Guardian recruits after induction, and so the usual cliques had already developed by the time she dropped in to audit this particular portion of the program.

It didn't bother her. She was a loner by nature, which meant she was not only suited by temperament for the role of an undercover operative but also perfectly capable of getting by without a lot of unnecessary social interaction.

As a compensation, she was mildly surprised to find that she enjoyed learning new things after several years away from Peter's classrooms. An added bonus came when her pencak silat instructor sold her a karambit and leg sheath to take back home with her. She'd developed a fondness for the blade, which the instructor had explained was often used by poor farmers on Earth as a utility knife. Despite having been modelled after the slashing claw of a tiger, it had an unassuming modesty that pleased her.

At any rate, she always had Kieran inside her head, questioning everything, providing a running commentary on the respective attributes of her fellow classmates and instructors, and trying (mostly without success) to engage her in various philosophical discussions.

Before she knew it, the week was over and she was riding in the crawler back to Hephesto. She was the only passenger, and the driver was a taciturn, middle-aged woman who nodded wordlessly when Serena got in and turned her entire attention to her driving.

About halfway through the trip, while they were making their way through a dust storm with particles the size of kidney beans, the crawler stalled. Serena listened to the fans spinning down until all that could be heard was the steady pelting of the wind-bound Martian soil on the hull outside.

She leaned out into the aisle. "Hello? Anything wrong?"

The driver turned around. "Please remain seated, Cadet. The problem will be rectified in a moment."

I'm not a cadet, thank you, Serena thought. She watched the driver put on her helmet and unbuckle her belts. *What the hell's going on, Kieran?*

Just hang on for a minute, he replied.

The driver edged out of the cockpit and paused at the hatch. "Visor down. There may be some loss of atmosphere." She opened the inner hatch door and waddled into the airlock, closing it off behind her.

Serena sat there, listening to the outer door open and then close behind the driver. She'd left her visor up in order to be able to hear. She waited for other sounds within the constant hissing and tapping of the storm, but there was nothing more.

She stood up. *It's a test, isn't it?*

We'll know for sure in a few moments.

Serena went up to the cockpit and sat down in the driver's seat. There was no visibility to speak of through the windshield, which was about a meter high and two meters across. Above the windshield were three viewscreens that provided side- and rear-view visibility via external cameras. They were dead.

On her right was a radar screen, an instrument cluster with various inscrutable icons identifying their functions, and a radio and headset arrangement. In front of her was a keyboard-style control panel and a steering wheel. There were pedals on the floor, just beyond the reach of her feet.

How do I move the seat forward? she asked.

Never mind. It's not necessary.

What the hell is she doing out there?

Do you see the little recessed spot at the top of the keyboard, right in the middle? Take off your ring and put it in there.

Serena complied. The spot he was talking about was obviously a ring reader, once you looked at it. It emitted a pale blue glow when her ring made contact.

Your driver has been picked up. Another crawler was following, about five hundred meters back. Invisible in the storm, except on her radar. They're passing your position right now.

I can't hear them. The storm's too loud. I don't know how to drive one of these things, Kieran. It's completely different than any rick I've ever been in.

Do you want my help, or do you want to figure it out for yourself?

Was there damage, or did she just shut it down and leave?

A good question.

Okay, give me a minute. Serena studied the keyboard in front of her. At the top right was an oversized green button. She pressed it.

Nothing happened.

There's a circuit breaker switch next to your right ankle. Check that.

She reached down and, sure enough, felt the switch he

was referring to. She snapped it on and pressed the green button again.

The fans came back to life. The three viewscreens flickered and activated, resuming their unhelpful displays of driving red dust. The radar screen jumped and began its circular sweeping pulses. She looked for a moment at a bright spot moving slowly away from the centre on a one-o'clock trajectory.

"Bitch."

You're under surveillance, Serena. An ad hoc a/v setup with its own battery pack and transmitter.

Part of the test.

I would imagine.

Serena stabbed at a blue button under the green one and the engine roared to life. *Pretty lame test, if you ask me.*

How will you get back to Hephesto?

Hmmm. She stared at a magenta button below the blue one. *I wonder what this does?*

Autopilot. Already programmed for the ground vehicle station attached to Hephesto's dome.

Too simple, she thought, leaning back in the seat as the crawler lurched forward.

Depends on what they're actually testing, Kieran replied.

46

The private quarters occupied by Constance Davis's head of security consisted of a bedroom, a sitting room, a kitchenette, and a bathroom. The bedroom included a large bed, freshly made up, and a walk-in closet (the size of Serena's old apartment) from which Labossière's things had already been removed. Serena had been afraid that another shopping trip would be required in order to meet the councillor's high expectations, but Juliana had obtained her sizes and filled the closet with a dizzying selection of expensive-looking clothing that would be appropriate for any occasion Serena might now face in her new role.

The sitting room, even larger than the bedroom, was decorated with stylish furniture, an enormous vid (mounted on the wall), and a bar area stocked with a wide variety of alcoholic beverages.

Look! Kieran brayed. *Sarbucca brandy! Try it, try it!*

Quiet. You're giving me a headache.

Promise you'll try it later. You can pick up some local brandy anywhere, then do a comparison for me. For research purposes.

No. Continuing her tour of her new quarters, she went into the bathroom and looked at a toilet *and* a bidet, side by side. The sink and counter combination was huge. She opened the glass door of the shower stall, which included a bench to sit down on and a comm unit on the wall. She turned the knob, and real hot water jetted from the shower head.

She'd never seen a rich person's bathroom before, let alone stood in one, and now she was looking at one that was intended for her exclusive use.

Unbelievable.

She caught a glimpse of herself in the mirror. Her hair had grown back to about a centimeter in length since Kieran had shaved it off, and while it was as unpleasantly rust-colored as before, at least it now covered her scalp and its blotchy freckles. Constance had made it plain that she disliked the look of her, but didn't seem inclined to make an issue of it right now. Perhaps Dell Burley had said something to her about it.

She went back into the sitting room. There was an inner door she hadn't opened yet. Trying it, she found herself in a comm room with racked servers, video arrays, workstations, and all the rest.

A man sat at a desk in the corner. Another stood at one of the racks, fiddling with hardware. An outer door opened. Two more people walked in, a man and a woman. Everyone wore black uniforms and light body armour. They all looked like military, with the perfect balance, the posture, and the focused appearance of experienced professionals. Similar to the unit that had stormed Kieran's warehouse.

The man behind the desk stood up. "Keilor, glad you could join us. I'm Captain Dalzell." He walked around the desk. "Sit down. Act like you own the place."

An older man, his hair was grey at the temples. His face was craggy and pitted. A scar ran from his lower lip to the point of his chin. His eyes were dark brown, with incongruous laugh lines at the corners and an amused, slightly contemplative look.

Serena sat down. On the desk in front of her were a tablet, a comm device, a reader, and an assortment of data rings.

During the week that she'd been in training, Dell Burley had dismissed the remnants of Labossière's crew and replaced them with this team. All Rubén had told her was that the quartet was drawn from Special Forces and they reported directly to Director Burley. Other than that, she had no idea who they were and where she fit into the picture. Until this moment, she hadn't even met them.

The man working at the server rack stepped forward.

"This is Sergeant O'Sullivan," Dalzell said. "My electronics and computer expert. He's going to run Councillor Davis's systems for us."

O'Sullivan said nothing, staring at her. He was smaller than the others, pale-skinned and thin-lipped. He wore wire-framed glasses. His hair was brown and neat.

He's pissed because he tried to intercept our transmissions just now and failed, Kieran said.

They know about the implant?

Not specifically, but they know we have a means of communication they don't quite understand yet. That's what the crawler incident was all about.

They intercepted us then?

Yes, briefly. Have to give them credit for catching me off guard. Won't happen again, though.

"This is Private Morris," Dalzell was saying, waving his hand at the woman. "She co-ordinates all the councillor's transportation needs. She'll do the driving and piloting; she'll vet the routes; she'll interface with Elysian Police and the Guardians; and she'll supervise *Diamond Girl's* flight crew, which has been replaced with our own people. "

"Hello," Serena said.

Morris, a slender brunette with bright green eyes, nodded back.

"Private Sagramatholou's our fourth," Dalzell said. "He came along for the ride because he didn't have anything better to do."

Standing at parade rest just inside the door, the man grinned at her. He was handsome and athletic looking, with a swarthy complexion and thick, wavy black hair.

"He'll be your backup and relief—"

"Your muscle," Sagramatholou interjected.

"—so stay fresh and let him spell you off when I say so. Understood?"

Serena nodded. "Understood."

"My job is to set assignments, supervise, co-ordinate reports, and all the rest. Yours is to stick with Councillor Davis. Everywhere she goes, you go. Just do a better job of it than Labossière did."

"Yes, sir."

"I'm aware that you're using an AI of some kind as a support system."

"Yes, sir."

"Don't get cute, all right? When you get information, I want it the next nanosecond. Lives are at stake, as I'm sure you understand. You don't report to me, as far as chain of command goes, but freelancing could get someone killed, so stay smart."

"Yes, sir."

I like him, Kieran said.

Did I ask you? Do I care?

He made a noise inside her head. How the hell did he

do that?

Come on, Serena. You like him, too. I can tell.

47

Serena's first few days as nominal head of Constance's personal security detail were given over to routine. She familiarized herself with Dalzell's newly installed protocols, participated in a few drills, and kept tabs on her protectee's whereabouts at every moment, day and night.

Constance remained very reluctant to leave the building, and so Serena followed Dalzell's guidance in implementing by-the-book static protection procedures. Risk management was always a key in this situation, and information gathering was an essential element of assessing and managing risk. As a result, Dalzell's team maintained constant liaison with their Martian Intelligence contacts as well as security teams for the other councillors, Elysium police sources, and confidential informants out in the field.

They shared with Serena very little of the information that came to their attention. It was a situation she found amusing but not particularly upsetting, since Kieran was always a step ahead of everyone else, and he kept up a constant chatter in her head that occasionally varied from the trivial and inane into more important and relevant matters such as the latest intel on whatever she wanted to know about.

She soon discovered that Sagramatholou was also an enthusiastic practitioner of taekwondo, and when she approached him about working out together, he readily agreed. They met frequently during their off-hours in a gymnasium on the third floor, and while Serena routinely bested him in their sparring sessions, he remained friendly and cheerful throughout. They would sit together in the sauna afterward, and while real water hissed into real steam, he would pass along bits and pieces of what was going on upstairs.

Kieran sneered during these conversations but Serena was grateful, not because of the information itself, most of which she already had, thanks to Kieran, but because Sagramatholou was making an honest attempt to be inclusive. That meant a lot. Along with his good looks and lively sense of humour, it was a combination that would have had her developing a serious crush—in other circumstances, of course.

One of the information threads supplied to her from both sources had to do with ongoing threat assessments related to the civil unrest plaguing Elysium City. While it was unconnected to Serena's primary mission, which was to use Constance as a means of identifying and neutralizing the mole selling secrets to Earth Intelligence, it was important to her protectee's well-being, and so she paid close attention.

As a result, when the next evening meeting of the Council of Five came up on the agenda, Serena was already aware that security would be a primary concern. Dell Burley would be proposing measures to tighten things up globally, and protocols for individual councillors would be enhanced as a response to intelligence suggesting that the upcoming meeting might be a target of another mass protest.

When the day arrived, Dalzell assigned Private Sagramatholou as Serena's partner to escort Constance up to her meeting at Frick Tower. Morris stayed with the rick in the special parking area set aside for councillors, while Dalzell coordinated everything from Serena's office. O'Sullivan hovered at his side to troubleshoot any technical hitches that might arise.

When the meeting was called to order and Constance disappeared into the inner chamber, followed closely by Dell Burley and the other councillors, Sagramatholou made himself comfortable at a table with several bodyguards he seemed to know very well.

Serena found a place to sit where she could keep an eye on the chamber entrance while remaining apart from the others. She drew a few casual glances as the new player in the game, but they quickly lost interest and fell into conversation among themselves. She watched Sagramatholou laugh and joke with his friends. It was all very collegial.

It didn't bother her. They didn't know her and didn't trust her, understandably. She wasn't military and she wasn't law enforcement, which made her unique among everyone working personal protection for the councillors. She was an anomaly in a business that hated anomalies.

There's a question I've been meaning to ask you, Kieran said.

Serena sighed. He'd been relatively quiet this morning, but obviously that was about to change.

I want to know how you feel about killing people.

Serena shook her head. *I'm not going to talk about that.*

For my part, I feel terrible when I learn about the death of a human. Liam Burley, for example. I'm not sure why, because it doesn't seem directly connected to anything rational for which I'm programmed, but I feel terribly bad. I wondered if you do as well.

Do we have to do this?

No, of course not. But I'm trying to understand how a nice person like yourself can take the lives of five people and reconcile it with a basic sense of human decency, which you clearly possess.

Five people? What are you talking about?

The three in the alley who accosted Councillor Davis and the two who attacked you between 23A Street and 23B, Block 12 near your old flat, not long ago. You killed two of the latter group but allowed the third to live. They were discovered about twenty minutes later by a passerby who alerted Elysium Police.

How do you know about that?

Please, Serena. By the way, I'm not counting the Earth Intelligence agent who fell off the ladder and fractured his skull while chasing you at the Visquel grow op. He died shortly thereafter from his injuries, but I wouldn't say you were directly responsible for his death. I'd classify that as an accident.

They've got no business putting operatives in the field who aren't Mars-ready.

Evidently. How do you feel about being responsible for the deaths of the others?

I don't know, Kieran. Bad, I guess. I don't think about it.

I'm trying to understand. Your reaction to danger is lethal by default. I was led to believe that humans believe in mercy, forgiveness, compassion, leniency, clemency, or any combination of the above, and that human life is considered sacred. Certainly that's how my fundamental programming has been written. Why are you different?

I'm not any different than anyone else with my training, Kieran.

And that training overrides every other consideration?

We're at war. Our survival as a world is at stake. How we're trained could make all the difference between winning or losing.

The men who attacked you near your building weren't Earth Intelligence agents, Serena.

They weren't, huh? Interesting. What do you have on them?

Criminal deportees from Earth. The type of people The Five are trying without success to convince the motherworld to exclude from their emigration processes. They'd been on Mars for only a few months and hadn't joined any of the gangs yet. Freelancers, essentially.

Serena digested this piece of information in silence.

The three people who attacked Councillor Davis and killed Gustaf Labossière were locals, by the way. Born and raised on the planet. All three had extensive criminal records. No known connections to Earth Intelligence. As it happens, they were independent contractors paid by the MIS.

Serena shot to her feet. *What? Are you insane?*

Of course not. It's true. I can show you the evidence.

Serena looked over at the others. One of them had noticed her agitation and was watching her. She sat down again. *I don't believe it. Why would Martian Intelligence— are you saying they were paid to attack the councillor?*

Oh, yes.

Why? It makes no sense.

It does, actually, if you think about it.

She thought about it. Immediately she didn't like where her thoughts were taking her.

Another test.

And an opportunity to insert you into a position close to Councillor Davis.

But I killed them. I—

Wait, Kieran interrupted. *Stand by. Something's happening.*

48

"The next item on the agenda," Wilhelmina Destry said, "has been placed there by Councillor Burley, who now has the floor."

"Thank you, Chairwoman." Dell rose from his seat. "As you can see, I'm asking for council approval to raise security to Level Two. The reason for this move—for the record—is that a serious breach inside Stellarize Marté has occurred, involving the theft of classified industrial secrets by an agent working for Earth Intelligence. This breach has been ongoing for a while now, and it's time to stop it in its tracks."

"Are you out of your mind?" Jadarius Fell blurted, caught off guard. The item had been listed on the agenda as "Approval to Raise Security to Level Two" without further details.

Wilhelmina Destry banged her gavel. "Order. Councillor Burley has the floor."

"But—"

She pointed the gavel at him. "Silence. Dell, please continue."

"Thanks. So far we haven't been able to uncover the identity of the spy, but we're certain another leak of information, of major proportions this time, is about to take place that may compromise the interstellar drive program. If that happens, Earth may very well win the race and drive us back into the stone age."

"Refresh my memory on Level Two conditions," Magee Wong said.

"Increased personnel at Marsport." Dell ticked the item off on a finger. "Increased screening of all non-Martian travellers." Tick. "Interviewing all departing travellers, Martian and non-Martian." Tick. "And all municipal police forces will report directly to us." Tick.

"Through the Guardians."

"Correct. And one more thing. Internal Stellarize security will now fall under the direct supervision of MIS, as of right now."

"Not happening," Jadarius Fell snapped.

"I'm afraid it has to happen, son." Dell looked at Wong and Destry. "No more counter-espionage, no more spy-versus-spy. We have to turn Stellarize upside down and shake the hell out of it until this guy falls out and we can step on him before he causes any more damage."

"There's no other way?" Wong was no doubt worried about the precedent such a move would set. The various security levels had been negotiated among them a long time ago, but this would be the first time it would rise to Level Two. "We need to be sure it's absolutely necessary."

"Oh, it's necessary, all right. This mole, this spy, is gearing up for what's being called his last big score. Vital, extensive information about the star drive. Progress reports, bench test results, timelines, budget expenditures, current failures, you name it. And it's going down very soon. Maybe within a day or two. We have to move fast."

Wong looked at Destry. "This requires a unanimous

vote."

She nodded. "Are there any other questions?"

No one seemed willing to speak.

"All in favour?"

"Aye," Wong said. He turned to Jadarius Fell. "How about it, young man?"

"Once again, I don't have any choice."

"Your vote," Destry prompted.

Dell cleared his throat. "Your father's senior advisors have been told what's happening," he told Jadarius, "and they've assured me Stellarize Marté will give the MIS complete co-operation. It looks like they haven't briefed you, and I'm sorry about that, but we've already begun working with your people on the details."

Jadarius closed his eyes and rubbed his forehead. The vote in council was obviously a formality, as was his presence here. He felt like a joke, a chunk of rock sitting on someone's desk as a paperweight.

"Aye," he said, his voice low.

"Dell?"

"Aye."

"Councillor Davis?"

All eyes turned to Constance, and Dell wasn't in the least surprised to see her looking as though she'd been struck by lightning.

This measure, after all, was aimed directly at her.

"I—"

The door burst open, an unprecedented breach of protocol, and black-clad tactical soldiers streamed into the chamber. They were led by Captain Dalzell, who had left O'Sullivan manning the comm at Davis Tower to take command of the situation.

"Immediate evacuation is necessary, sir," Dalzell said to

Dell. "A bomb threat directed at this building was phoned in to Elysium Police five minutes ago."

"How long until they detonate it, if it exists?"

"Unknown, sir. We're clearing the building as we speak."

Wilhelmina Destry banged her gavel. "The motion passes with unanimous consent. This meeting is adjourned."

"Wait!" Constance jumped to her feet. "I haven't voted yet."

"I distinctly heard you say 'Aye,'" Destry retorted. "I'm getting out of here. Where's Cavan?"

"Here, ma'am," a voice called from outside the open chamber doors. Hale Cavan was her head of security. "This way, please. Right away!"

"I didn't say 'Aye,'" Constance complained to Dell, "I said, 'I.' That's—"

"Not what I heard," Dell said. "Get out. Now." He looked at Dalzell. "Is Keilor standing by?"

"Yes, sir. My teams will lead each councillor and their retinue down to the passageways."

"Fine. Get moving."

49

The passageway through which they hurried was wide and well lighted. They'd boarded an express elevator to a short below-ground corridor before negotiating several sets of security doors keyed by Captain Dalzell, and now they were following what consisted of an underground ring around Frick Tower, with branches heading off in six different directions at various points around the compass.

The existence of the tunnels was known to council members as an emergency means of travelling from headquarters to their individual home towers within the central core. They just didn't know how extensively Dell had expanded the underground network for his own use.

Magee Wong and his staff had already disappeared down the branch that led to their building, and Jadarius Fell was next. As he and his retinue gathered around the security gate, Serena watched Constance sweep past her fellow councillor without acknowledging his wave of farewell.

Constance was clearly upset about something. It must have happened during the meeting, Serena thought. She'd gone in with a smile on her face, chatting to Magee Wong, but something had changed her mood.

She found herself walking next to Wilhelmina Destry. Constance was a few meters in front of them, head down, arms swinging. Sagramatholou was on the councillor's left, matching her stride for stride. He winked over his shoulder at Serena.

"You're Keilor," Destry suddenly said.

"Yes, ma'am." From the corner of her eye, Serena saw Destry make a small hand gesture to Cavan, her security chief. The man dropped back a few steps.

"I've seen your file. Dell keeps me informed on things."

"Yes, ma'am."

Destry produced a silver hip flask and took a healthy swig. The smell of strong whisky made Serena's nostrils flare involuntarily.

Up close she looked older than Serena had thought she would be. Her wavy hair was more white than auburn and, while it had been recently cut and styled, she hadn't bothered to colour it. Or brush it, at least not this morning.

She was a bit heavy-chested, not an optimum body type for Mars by any means, but Serena could tell that she'd once been a handsome woman. Now, however, she had the appearance of a hard-drinking business executive passing through middle age much faster than she wanted to, with certain knowledge that nothing good was waiting for her on the other side.

"It's too bad about Connie," Destry murmured, so that only Serena could hear. "You'll do what's necessary when the time comes."

"I follow Director Burley's orders, ma'am."

Destry took another swig and nodded. "See that you do." She put the flask away, and for a moment Serena thought her eyes looked almost kind. "You have it in you. I know that you do. To succeed. To make us all proud. Now beat it and get that damned idiot woman back home."

"Yes, ma'am."

50

The following day, Hercule St.-Giorge Mercade attended a press conference at Ceres House in which the protectorate announced the signing of an agreement with Earth to sell the motherworld tin, lead, and zinc mined in the asteroid belt. Reserves of these important elements were growing low on Earth after centuries of heavy exploitation, and the agreement was a natural step forward in the growing relationship between Earth and Ceres.

Davis Minerals was also a signatory to the agreement. In exchange for a percentage of the profits, Davis would lease several refinery ships to Ceres that were specially designed to navigate the belt and process the ore *in situ*, extracting the desired elements and loading them onto waiting Earth vessels. It was a nice little money-making venture for Davis, and Constance was also in attendance as an acknowledgement of her personal role in negotiations.

A brief reception was held following the announcement, and after making small talk with the Cererian governor and trying to avoid having to sample their sparkling wine, which was dreadful, Hercule murmured something polite and slipped away. Outside, he handed an aide a note to deliver to Constance and got into his rick to wait.

The look on her face as she followed the aide down the line of vehicles toward him was surprisingly grim. *Something has changed in her,* he reflected.

He watched her wave back the security detail following her. A girl, the dirt eater he'd heard about, and a competent-looking military type with dusky, handsome features. They stopped a respectful few meters back and watched as Hercule's aide opened the rick door for Constance.

"Thank you for coming," he said when she'd settled down beside him and the door was closed. He tried to make it sound as though he were grateful for her presence. "We can speak here in complete privacy." He pressed one of the buttons on his armrest. It was supposed to imply that he had activated some kind of anti-surveillance device, but in fact it was a recorder.

"The council meeting last evening has brought some changes," she said.

"Tell me about them." It was impossible to suppress his impatience with her for more than a moment or two.

"Yes, I . . ." She was flustered, trying to regain her composure. "It's been decided to go to Level Two planet-wide. The MIS will take over internal security at Stellarize. I'm afraid this will make it very hard for your man inside to get his information to me."

"I'm aware of what's happening. Don't worry about it. When the time comes, just make sure you're ready to do what you're told. We'll take care of everything else."

"I see. All right."

Hercule frowned at her. "You lost your man, Labossière."

She nodded, looking down.

"This nonsense of yours must stop."

"It has."

"You've got this girl, a dirt eater, going around with you now. What could you possibly be thinking?"

"Oh, you don't understand." Constance found his eyes, which were boring into her, and she tried to smile. "She's amazing. She saved my life. Dell recommended her to me, and I think she's going to be fine. Really fine."

"Dell Burley recommended her."

"Yes. He said she's done a few things for him and she's been very good. She really knows how to handle herself. It's incredible. She says it's just training, but she's got some kind of natural talent. She's very athletic."

Hercule took a moment to think about it. Constance's lack of guile never failed to surprise him. He pinched the lobe of his ear. "There's a new team with her."

"Yes, Dell—"

"How many?"

"I'm not sure. Four, I think."

"Describe them."

"Let's see." She looked out the window. "I haven't paid very much attention. There's an older man; he seems to be in charge. A woman. She's my driver now, and she'll pilot *Diamond Girl*. And there are two other men. One takes care of the systems, and the other . . . I'm not sure. He's very good looking. He's been switching off with Serena when she eats dinner and sleeps. He's over there with her, right now."

Hercule nodded, not bothering to glance out the window in the direction she'd indicated. "Fine. Let them do their jobs and don't give them any trouble. Let the routine lull them to sleep."

"All right. Are they a problem in some way? Should I be worried?"

"Let me do the worrying, my dear. Bear in mind, though,

that your building is now under MIS surveillance. Do you understand what that means? No suspicious behaviour whatsoever. No stray talk, no questionable outings, no irregularities of any kind. Get it? Give them absolutely nothing that requires a reaction."

She nodded wordlessly, her eyes wide.

He flicked his fingers at her. "That's all."

When she was gone, he got out of the rick and walked over to Renard, who was lounging on the edgeway.

"I don't think the girl, Keilor, is much of a threat." He glanced at his chrono bracelet. "Burley must be playing at a bit of misdirection with her. It's the team we need to focus on."

"Yes, sir."

"Let's take one of them out. See how Burley responds. Recommendations?"

"I'd say the comm man, sir. O'Sullivan. He's a moving part, here and there, unlike the other three who have specific, assigned stations."

Hercule flashed a brief, predatory smile. "Good. Take care of it, then."

51

Serena and the rest of the security team normally ate their meals in a small room set up for them just off the kitchen on the seventh floor. Following the visit to Ceres House, Serena was eating dinner alone that evening while Sagramatholou spelled her off upstairs with Constance.

She had the room to herself until one of the staff came in and set a place across the table from her. Dalzell walked in and sat down.

"Give me what she's having," he said.

Serena continued to eat, not quite sure what to expect from him. Since their arrival, she hadn't spent much time with any of them to speak of, and Dalzell in particular was still a mystery to her.

He said nothing as he was served his first course, thick beet soup with a side order of hothouse greens.

After a few mouthfuls, he wiped his broad upper lip with his napkin. "I've watched you working out with Sag. You're the only one I've seen yet who can wipe the floor with him, every time."

"He's tough."

"He takes it cheerfully enough," Dalzell said, "but he's really pissed off about it."

"I hadn't noticed."

"He's going to start fighting dirty pretty soon. It's like a face thing."

"I can handle dirty."

"I'll bet you can."

They ate quietly for a few moments.

"I understand you're from Hephesto," he said.

Serena nodded.

"Is that where you know Dell from?"

"No." She noted his use of Councillor Burley's first name. "I never met him before."

Dalzell leaned back as the server came in with his next course, poultry with a spicy sauce neither of them could identify, roasted potatoes, and candied carrots. It was quite good, which was not surprising since it was leftovers from Constance's dinner and would have been thrown out if it hadn't pleased her.

He gestured with his utensils. "Tell me about yourself."

"Not much to tell. I'm a crèche kid. As soon I could be useful, they put me to work in a recycling plant sorting garbage. Every day was the same as the rest until they marched me onto a shuttle and sent me to work for Peter Visquel."

Dalzell swallowed a mouthful. "How old were you?"

She shrugged. "Don't know. Crèche kids don't have birthdays, so there's no telling for sure. Peter said I was probably eight when he got me, so we went with that."

"Did you miss it? Not having parents?"

"I don't know. Not really. I never needed anybody to look after me. I looked out for myself. What about you? Where are you from?"

"Peru." He filled his mouth and chewed vigorously.

"Really?" She studied his face with its scars, creases, and craters, his dark brown eyes and heavy brows, a little surprised that he was a native of Earth.

"Yep."

"What brought you here?"

He paused his chewing to look at her for a moment, then swallowed. "Long story."

"It's not like I'm in a hurry to get back upstairs."

Dalzell grunted, almost a laugh, and rubbed the tip of his nose with the ball of his thumb. "All right. Curiosity's a good thing in an agent."

She sipped her juice, watching him.

"I was born in Lima. My father was a general in the Army of South America, my mother a supervisor of field surgeons and physicians. I had a privileged childhood, you might say. The best schools, tutors, everything."

"Sounds pretty good."

"Yeah. It was. Then I was sent up to North America to attend West Point. The military academy. Graduated fourth in my class. Came back home and was commissioned as a lieutenant in the ASA. Did tours in Bolivia, the Falklands, Argentina. Made captain, then major."

Serena finished her juice. "What happened?"

"Revolution. The continental government was overthrown by a coalition of far-right militias. It was very brutal. Village by village. A nightmare. For a while we thought we would regain power. Peru was our stronghold, and we fought back from there. I was put in charge of a prisoner of war camp, but ASA HQ would send interrogators in to torture my prisoners for intelligence. I objected. I was reassigned. I objected more publicly, to the press, and I was put in front of a court martial and convicted of treason. Because of my late father, I guess, I was given a choice between death by firing squad or exile to Mars. This being back when the Martian immigration policy was more an open-door thing than it is now."

"You chose exile."

"I did. I mixed in with some other military types, became friends with Dell, and when he came calling, I accepted a job in Special Ops." He spread his hands. "So here I am."

Serena pushed away from the table and turned sideways to cross her legs.

His smile was thin, almost sad. "So why am I telling you all this? Is any of it even true?"

She shrugged. "I think so. For the most part."

"It's all true, and there are two reasons why I've shown you this hand of cards. One," he leaned forward and shook an index finger at her. "you must never, ever assume that all Earth-born are bad. Yes, Earth's our adversary and they have mayhem on their minds, always, but they're also human beings. People with families. People."

He lowered the finger and eased back in his chair. "The other thing you need to remember, Serena, is that loyalty can come from the most unexpected of places. This AI of yours, for example, or whatever it is—"

Dalzell's comm buzzed. He answered it. "Yes, Morris. What is it?"

Serena watched his face grow cold.

"How long?" he asked.

Pause.

"Nothing on the back channels?"

Pause.

"What was his last known twenty?"

Pause.

"I'll be right there."

He ended the call and stood up. "Relieve Sagramatholou

and send him to the comm room right away. Stay with the client until further notice."

"Yes, sir. May I ask what's going on?"

"O'Sullivan's gone dark," he said over his shoulder as he headed for the door. "It doesn't look good."

52

The following afternoon Serena took a couple of hours off to run up to Kieran's old warehouse for a few things. He'd left behind a small portable tissue healer he said he didn't need, and it was something she wanted to add to the first aid kit in her backpack. While she was there, she grabbed several other items, including a small plastic box containing listening devices called snoop stickers. They were each about the size and thickness of her small fingernail, with an adhesive back that allowed them to be stuck to the underside of a table, say, or some other handy, out-of-sight place where someone might be liable to say something you would want to overhear.

As usual, Sagramatholou covered for her at Davis Tower while she was away. Constance spent the afternoon in her office, attending to her duties as chief operating officer of Davis Minerals. Sagramatholou complained about the boredom, but no one felt the slightest amount of sympathy for him.

Serena found the tissue healer where Kieran said it would be, and was filling a side pouch on her backpack with other interesting things, including the snoop stickers, when Kieran abruptly said, *They've found O'Sullivan.*

Her tactical radio, which Dalzell insisted she carry with her whenever she was away from the tower, popped an instant later.

"Keilor, respond."

She tapped her earbud. "Keilor here."

"Get your ass over to Gateway Station ASAP and back up Morris."

"Acknowledged. ETA ten."

"Do you have access to a lifesuit?"

"Affirmative." Kieran had left an assortment of garments in the room set aside for her use, and a lifesuit and helmet were sitting on one of the shelves.

"Gear up and get moving."

After slipping into the lifesuit, she jumped into her rick and raced down to Gateway. She followed Dalzell's directions to a side door close to where the bubble of the station met the dome wall. An Elysium Police constable let her in and escorted her through a series of corridors to a maintenance bubble with airlocks that led outside.

Morris caught her eye and nodded. She was dressed out in full battle gear complete with a tactical lifesuit, a live AV rig on her helmet, a stun gun strapped to her thigh, and a knife in a sheath on her belt. With her was an Elysium Police tactical unit that included two other constables (besides Serena's guide) and a detective.

They're on Channel D, Kieran said.

Thanks, Serena replied, securing her headgear and adjusting her comm.

Morris motioned to a station worker who was already suited up and helmeted. The man led them into the airlock, closed the hatch, and punched a button that began to cycle the air out of the lock.

Serena watched the city cops as they fidgeted and

exchanged glances, obviously anxious about leaving the safety of the dome. *Agoraphobia*, Serena thought.

A common affliction among humans born and raised in the domes, Kieran said. *It's notable that you're not bothered by it.*

Serena didn't answer, not particularly interested in the subject. She watched the station worker at the airlock controls, who was staring down at his boots. Had they told him this might still be an active scene? He seemed upset but not frightened, so they must have decided he didn't have a need to know. Maybe they were afraid he'd panic and mess things up.

The detective checked the charge on his stun gun. Through the faceplate of his helmet, Serena saw that his teeth were clenched and his eyes were narrowed. He looked like he wanted to mix it up with someone, anyone, for whatever reason. She thought it might be a good idea to keep him in front of her, rather than behind.

A green light flashed on, and the worker pounded the button to open the outside hatch. He led the way across the Martian surface to a nearby maintenance bubble. He paused outside the airlock, a smaller version of the one they'd just cycled through, and turned to face the group.

"Like I told you," he said, his voice tinny as it passed through Serena's helmet speaker, "this is just used for storage. We don't come out here much. It's more of an emergency thing, like if a work crew needs a tool or replacement equipment or something."

"We got it," Morris said. "Let's get a move on."

The worker turned his attention to the airlock controls, and they cycled through into the bubble. "It's cold in here," he warned, "so helmets and gloves stay on."

"Where's it at?"

"Down here." The worker led the way down a gap between storage racks filled with toolboxes, portable generators, pumps, hoses, and other miscellaneous items. He stopped, and they heard him cough. Then he stepped aside, and Morris pushed her way through.

On a middle shelf, between a red tool box and a spare lifesuit helmet sitting upside down, was a neatly stacked set of four frozen limbs, separated at the joints and bundled together with rope, like kindling. Socketed bones protruded from the ends of the limbs, as though each arm and leg had been pulled apart like poultry drumsticks.

Next to the bundle of limbs was a naked torso. Male. Genitals removed.

Next to the torso was a head. Its eyes were open. It was O'Sullivan.

"His privates," the worker said, his voice wavering, "you know, and his glasses, I guess, are in the helmet there."

"Fuck," Morris said.

One of the city cops leaned over and vomited into his helmet.

Get down, Serena.

Something small punched through Morris's helmet, spraying blood and brains against her faceplate. She dropped like a marionette whose strings had suddenly been cut, air hissing from two puncture holes, one on each side of her helmet, the moisture condensing instantly into plumes of frost.

Serena was already flat on the floor, her reaction to Kieran's command instantaneous, when the vomiting constable careened into the storage rack and fell down next to her. His helmet had also been punctured with a through-and-through shot, his head another ruined mess.

Projectiles!

An Earth-made rifle, Kieran confirmed, *firing .30 carbine cartridges. At the end of the row, shooting through a gap in the shelves.*

A firearm. How the hell did they get it here?

Earth Intelligence, Serena. Through the embassy. A recent shipment. A change in Earth policy. They've decided to treat Martian laws as nothing more than quaint colonial whims.

The detective ran down the row toward the source of the gunfire. He jerked, stumbled forward, jerked again, and crashed to the floor.

Behind Serena, the worker and the two remaining cops crowded around the airlock controls, yelling at each other in panic as they tried to get out.

It's a trap, Serena thought. *O'Sullivan was the bait.*

Correct.

How many are there?

Only three. The shooter and two others outside.

"Keilor!" It was Dalzell, on the comm. "What's happening? Report!"

Serena remained silent, concerned that the attackers were monitoring the channel.

It's all right, Kieran said. *I answered him. I told him to stand by. He understands the importance of radio silence at the moment.*

Thanks. Serena rolled onto her side and glanced behind her. The worker and the cops were already inside the airlock, waiting for it to cycle.

They were leaving her trapped inside the bubble with the rifle and whoever was firing it.

53

Serena turned up the volume on her external helmet mike and heard movement in the next row, coming toward her position.

I don't think he realizes you're there, Kieran said. *He thinks everyone just went out the airlock.*

She made herself as small as possible until the shooter had passed her position, then she got to her feet and followed, crouching. She drew her karambit from its sheath as the man reached the airlock controls.

His prey had already emerged outside and were in the process of being cut down by the other two Earth Intelligence operatives. Relaxing his posture, he punched the airlock button and slung his rifle over his shoulder.

Serena moved behind him and, reaching around, used the karambit's deadly hooked blade to slice through the flexible synthetic gasket between his helmet and breastplate, cutting his throat.

He fell on his side and looked up at her, mouth working, as he bled out.

Never make the fatal mistake of losing count of your opponents, Serena reflected. One of the first lessons pounded into her by her martial arts instructors.

She sheathed the karambit and dragged the body over to one side, away from the hatch. Taking the rifle, she entered the airlock and started the cycle. As it worked, she hoped that the other two attackers would think it was their colleague coming out and lower their guard long enough for her to respond to whatever lay on the other side of the airlock.

Where are they, Kieran?

There are small vehicle sheds on either side of your building. Each man is at the outside corner of his shed, with line of sight to the hatch leading into the dome. They're still in position, waiting for orders from the man you killed inside.

The kill zone, she reflected, was therefore triangular in shape, with the base of the triangle about a meter forward from the airlock hatch she was about to pass through, and the apex at the entrance into the city dome. Meaning that if she came out the hatch and edged along the front to the corner of the building, she wouldn't be seen by the shooter on that side.

Unlike the worker and two cops, who'd hurried forward only to be cut down several meters from safety.

The airlock finished cycling. She opened the hatch and stepped out to her left, back pressed against the wall.

Nothing happened.

So far, so good.

She crept to the corner and dropped to the ground. Loose Martian soil gritted beneath her as she crawled forward to quick peek. She saw a head, an arm, the barrel of a long gun, and a leg bent at the knee.

She ducked back. *I'm not trained on these weapons, Kieran. I don't know how they work.*

Remember, I see what you see, through your eyes.

First, check the load. Pull the bolt back and lock it in place. The little button. There. Now, remove the magazine. Yep, okay. Put the magazine back in and work the bolt to chamber a round. Good! I saw that the safety was disengaged, so you're ready to fire. The sight is tipped into place already, so look through that and, when you're ready to fire, just breathe out slowly and gently squeeze the trigger. The length of fire is quite short on this model, so it'll fire quickly. There's a bit of a kickback that will pull the muzzle up slightly, so be ready for that.

Okay, fine. She dropped back down to the ground and crawled forward so she could aim the rifle at her target, who was motionless, his rifle pointed at a spot halfway to the dome entrance.

She followed Kieran's instructions, fixing the target in her sight, exhaling slowly, and squeezing the trigger. The man's lifesuit exploded at the knee, and he cartwheeled back out of sight.

She chambered another round and, scrambling to her feet, ran toward him. Reaching the corner of the shed, she found the man writhing on the ground, knee in his hands, trying to cover the puncture holes and stop the bleeding at the same time.

She kicked his rifle out of reach. He stared up at her, and with a shock she realized he was the man who'd broken her wrist with a metal pipe outside Peter's grow op. Back then it had been clubs and knives, but now it was rifles firing deadly projectiles. They'd upped the ante.

She thought of Peter, and little red-haired Pablo, and the other boys and girls. All dead. By this one's hand, and by the cold-minded brutality of his confederates.

She put a round through his faceplate, followed by a second one. Just to be sure.

The other target has left his position and is coming along the front of the building behind you.

Are there any others?

No, this is the only one left.

Serena realized Kieran could see what was happening through a video camera positioned above the dome entrance. *Is Dalzell watching?*

No. Unfortunately he lost visual, and O'Sullivan isn't there to restore it for him.

I see.

I thought you might want a little privacy. Not that I approve, necessarily.

Okay, well, thanks. She ran back to the corner of the building, slinging the rifle over her shoulder. Unsheathing her karambit once more, she waited until the barrel of the rifle protruded around the corner, then she kicked it up and out of the man's hands. She swung around and confronted him, karambit flashing forward and back, slicing neck and belly.

They were cheap, Earth-made lifesuits, and the material was no match for her blade.

The man fell, writhed, and died.

She keyed her comm. "Captain, I'm guessing you have backup on the way."

"Affirmative, Keilor. Sit rep."

"Three assailants neutralized. All friendlies dead except myself. Your people will need to do a bit of a cleanup."

"Understood." Pause. "I saw what they'd done to O'Sullivan before I lost Morris's feed. Blood for blood, Keilor. Blood for blood. You took care of it."

Peter. Pablo. The children.

"Yeah."

So this is vengeance, Kieran said. *I need to give this a lot more thought.*

You do that. She looked at the rifle on the ground and decided to leave it for Dalzell's cleanup crew, along with the other one behind the shed. She thought about the one on her shoulder for several moments before unslinging it and dropping it next to the body in front of her.

Nodding to herself, she turned her back and walked away.

54

Two days later.

Dalzell had brought in replacements for O'Sullivan and Morris, training them up on Davis Tower protocols and working them into Serena's routines so she would be familiar with their individual capabilities and predilections.

Not that she cared, particularly. Private James Mowry, the new driver and pilot, was a native of Isidium whose parents were both scientists working for Terraform on the atmospheric conversion project. He was small, mousy, and taciturn. Kieran had a lot more personality than he did, as far as Serena was concerned.

Sergeant Laralee Drouin was Dalzell's new communications expert. She was from Hephesto and bore a vague resemblance to Dell Burley. A niece once or twice removed, perhaps. Drouin spent a lot of time quizzing Serena about her AI machine and how the communication worked between them. Kieran amused himself by passing along irrelevant information for Serena to feed her, and scoffed at Drouin's frustration and confusion when she failed to figure it out.

It was rather less than mature behaviour on his part, but then it prompted the question—how does an artificial human mature, anyway? Serena didn't really care.

That evening Constance would be attending one of the major events on her annual social schedule, so Dalzell was busily organizing his protection plan and coordinating all the logistics to support it.

The occasion was the birthday of The Right Honourable Napoleon Wilson, prime minister of the elected government of Mars. The annual party held in his honour was a gala affair that The Five encouraged in order to show their benign indulgence of the elected planetary government and to give themselves an evening away from the back-breaking task of building up an entire world with their bare hands.

Besides, Magee Wong was in charge of food and drink, and he always outdid himself.

As usual, Constance would attend without an escort. She liked to tell her friends, cocktail in hand, that she wished to emphasize her singleness, which she liked to refer to as her *singularity*. She wanted everyone to understand that she was in charge of her own destiny, that she was unique and self-defining.

The various ambassadors and their retinues were invited, of course. And while in other years Constance spent most of her time trying to be near Hercule St.-Giorge Mercade in order to engage him in conversation and impress him with her beauty and wit, she surprised Serena in the rick on the way to the party with an order to keep her informed at all times of Hercule's whereabouts so that she could avoid him.

She's afraid of him, Kieran noted. *It's written all over her face.*

Once again, Sagramatholou was Serena's partner, riding up front with Mowry. Serena thought he looked splendid in his formal evening wear, his dark hair slicked back and his perpetual five o'clock shadow temporarily tamed.

For her part, as security lead for the councillor, she'd been permitted to wear a black tunic over a white blouse and black trousers. The stunner on her belt was discreetly concealed, but the bulge was noticeable if anyone cared to look at her. But of course she was security, so she was invisible.

The venue was the rather sumptuous Violette Uchunku Centre for the Arts, named after the late mayor of Elysium at the time the city replaced Marsport as the planetary capital. The ballroom in which the party was held was very large by Martian standards, able to hold three hundred guests, six to a table. Constance occupied a place of honour at the head table, along with the other four members of council, Wilson's cabinet ministers, the leader of the Opposition, and of course the birthday boy and his wife.

Invitees included high-ranking government officials, senior executives of the five corporations, a smattering of entertainers and celebrities, and other assorted Very Important Persons. The host of the event was Corra, a comedian known for her ribald sense of humour and lack of tact. Wilhelmina Destry was a big fan, which explained the woman's presence. Otherwise, she might be in a holding cell somewhere.

Cocktails were served at six, and Serena trailed a respectful few steps behind Constance as she mingled, apparently enjoying herself.

Kieran maintained a constant chatter in her ear, delighted to have a chance to observe the Martian elite up close.

Here's Magee Wong. He's the CEO of Ares Enterprises, you know. Agriculture, food production, water, hydro-

electric energy. Martian Health Corporation. Very, very powerful. He's also the one in charge of terraforming. As I understand it, his grandfather started out with a little power station that alternated wind turbines during stormy weather and solar panels in clear conditions, and he sold the electricity to Isidium City. The old man was apparently quite a businessman. He bought and sold produce and poultry from small entrepreneurs and used the profits to invest in his own food production operations.

Serena watched Constance exchange a few words with Wong and move on to Jadarius Fell, who smiled and kissed the back of her hand.

Ah, the scion of Stellarize Marté, Kieran said. *My nominative lord and master, in the absence of his father.*

Serena thought of the enormous holo-portrait of Leonidas Fell under which she'd passed each day while entering and leaving the research and development campus of Stellarize Marté. The son clearly lacked the gravitas of the father. Constance quickly shook him off and moved on.

Here's the prime minister. Watch.

Constance shook his hand, wished him a happy birthday, and promptly turned her back on him to speak to a nearby clutch of women who were apparently, from the sudden laughter and self-deprecating byplay, friends from her student days.

Snub, Kieran observed. *Consistent with my analysis of the attitude of The Five toward the elected administration. A puppet show for the population, marionettes to play at governing while The Five run the show behind the curtain.*

Serena made brief eye contact with Prime Minister Wilson before turning away. A smile flickered across his face, sad and diffident.

Can you talk to him for a minute? Kieran asked. *Is it allowed?*

No.

Too bad. An interesting man. I strongly suspect he's much different than the persona he's forced to present to the public.

Serena followed Constance as she left the women and looked around for someone else to chat up. Spotting the Earth ambassador and his son, Hercule, Serena touched Constance lightly on the elbow and gestured toward a group of people in the opposite direction.

Constance frowned, annoyed, then caught sight of Hercule over Serena's shoulder. She flushed and turned away.

The small circle of people to which Serena had directed her turned out to be gathered around Janeese Wensley. Constance's face clouded with displeasure, but she quickly put a smile on her face and went over to shake hands.

"Councillor!" Wensley gushed, "how nice to see you. You look absolutely stunning this evening."

Constance acknowledged the compliment without returning it.

"Allow me to introduce Derik DeJeune, my chief of staff."

An older man on Wensley's right gave her an old-fashioned bow. "An honour, Councillor."

Constance permitted him to shake her hand.

"My wife, Dorenne, and her sister, Belnah, who's Director Wensley's chief of operations."

"It's an honour to finally meet you," said the afore-mentioned Belnah. "I'm intimately familiar with the work of Davis Minerals. You've probably noticed my signature on many of your company's approval forms."

"Yes," Constance lied. "A pleasure."

Wensley put her hand on the arm of the man on her left, whose back was turned while he talked to someone behind him.

"Kenny, this is Councillor Davis of Davis Minerals."

The man shook hands with the man behind him and turned around.

With a shock, Serena realized it was Kennet Clayborn.

55

Serena hastily averted her face.

Your vital signs are spiking, Kieran observed.

He knows me.

The head of optical engineering. I'm aware. Relax, Serena. He has no idea who you are.

Of course he does.

No, his eyes moved right across your face without any reaction whatsoever.

It was true. Clayborn was engaging Constance in polite chit chat without giving Serena a second glance. Her appearance was different, she realized. Her hair was shorter and her clothing was much different. Plus, she was obviously security. A social cipher. A non-entity. No one in polite society gave security a second glance.

"Kennet's my cousin," Wensley was saying. "We're both Earth-born, but after earning his degrees he kept himself busy with all that brilliant engineering stuff on Titan."

"And raising a family," Clayborn added.

"So you can imagine how glad I am," Wensley put in, "to have him here with me now."

"How long have you been on Mars?" Constance asked.

"Eight years. Still settling in."

Constance laughed politely. "Surely we're not too frontier here, compared to Earth."

"My father was a fly fisherman," Clayborn said. "I grew up in rural Michigan. I remember going down to the river with him when I was small. I miss that incredible sense of freedom."

"Uncle Jans owned a company on Earth that built ricks," Wensley quickly inserted. "Well, automobiles. He sold it to Laurentian Industries and retired early, a very wealthy man."

Did you see Councillor Davis react, Serena? Kieran sounded almost buoyant. *She recognizes the connection. Clayborn's father sells his company to Donnell St.-Giorge—Stellarize Marté's rival on Earth and Hercule St.-Giorge Mercade's uncle—and Clayborn junior ends up working on Stellarize's artificial human project here on Mars. In a division that seems to be having a great deal of difficulty meeting its objectives right now. How very coincidental.*

Serena stared, unable to completely hide the fact that she was hanging on every word these people said. She was beginning to see the possible connections as well.

"What do you do at Stellarize?" Constance asked Clayborn.

He laughed. "Well, Councillor, if you asked my VP, he'd probably tell you my job is to cause more trouble than I'm worth. Officially, though, I'm in charge of the optical engineering section of the artificial human project."

"Oh, I see. How fascinating."

"Kennet's a wealth of information," Wensley said, "but he's not allowed to talk about it. All hush hush, you know."

Serena caught a look that passed between Constance

and Wensley that implied an understanding of some kind.

Clayborn, for his part, suddenly looked rather uncomfortable.

Watching it all through Serena's eyes, Kieran hummed tunelessly.

Someone began walking through the crowd, calling them in to dinner.

56

Looks like security's beefing up, Kieran remarked after a prolonged silence.

The guests had been called to their tables for dinner, and afterward while dishes were being cleared and beverages were served, officers in their Guardian Class A uniforms slipped into place along the walls and at the various entrances and exits.

Speeches, Kieran murmured.

From her position behind the head table where she could keep her eye on Constance, Serena also glanced from time to time at Kennet Clayborn, who sat at a nearby table with Wensley and the others in their group. They seemed to have enjoyed their meal, and the conversation was punctuated with frequent laughter.

No guilty consciences there, she thought.

Don't be so sure.

Dell Burley didn't explain himself to field operatives like Serena, and he certainly wasn't going to share his thoughts on counterintelligence strategy with her, but nonetheless she thought she understood that he hadn't yet put Constance under the bright lights for an intensive interview because he wanted to watch her movements and see what she'd give away unintentionally.

Which Serena understood was her job. To observe and report. To find the leverage that the director could use to move the councillor into a position where she would be useful to his end game.

Whatever that might be.

Corra, the host, opened things up with a monologue that Serena mostly blocked out. It drew a few laughs, especially from Wilhelmina Destry, who was already into the post-prandial brandy, but for the most part it seemed to fall flat.

Thankfully, she finished up quickly. When she took her seat and the obligatory smattering of applause died away, Wilhelmina Destry rose to make her own opening statement of welcome to the invitees. She conveyed birthday wishes to the prime minister on behalf of the rest of the individuals at the head table without referring to The Five in any way. Not that there was any doubt about exactly who she was and for whom she was speaking.

Wilson's finance minister and closest deputy, Dawna Foligno, followed with a nice tribute that included jokes about Wilson's age (a carefully guarded secret that was never disclosed) and a poem she had personally written to emphasize his kindness, benevolence, and patience for everyone, rich or poor, famous or obscure, young or old.

The mayor of Elysium City, Zee Middleton, was next. He spoke briefly about the honour of being the mayor of the planetary capital city and mentioned Wilson's benign leadership of the planetary government. He abruptly sat down when Wilhelmina Destry cleared her throat and shot him a look.

Beverages were served and dessert plates cleared. Serena watched someone approach Sagramatholou, who was standing a few meters away, and hand him something. The big man looked it over and nodded. As he passed Serena on his way to the councillor's place at the head table, he grinned at her.

"Love note," he said, snapping it between his fingers.

Constance accepted it without making eye contact. As Sagramatholou made his way back to his position, Serena watched her glance at it, flush, and slip it into her gown.

Finally, it was time for the primary cause of the increased security to stand up and deliver his remarks to Prime Minister Wilson and his assembled guests.

Serena had seen pictures of Davin Hennessy before, but she was surprised to find that he looked smaller than he did on vid. There were grey streaks in his thick wavy hair and beard, crow's feet at the corners of his eyes, and a scar on his bare upper lip. His evening formal wear hung loosely on his body, as though he'd been ill and had lost weight. The cane in his left hand provided leverage as he got to his feet and stability from toppling over as he stood there, smiling out at the crowd, conscious of the murmurs of disapproval.

"Good evening, ladies and gentlemen," he said in his mild Irish brogue, "thank you very much for allowing me to dine with you on this momentous occasion as we celebrate the birthday of a very kind, lovely man. Please," he indicated Napoleon Wilson, "a round of applause for our wonderful prime minister on his special day."

As the crowd clapped for the guest of honour, Hennessy pulled a handkerchief from his sleeve and mopped his face.

"Those of you who've witnessed our epic battles on the floor of the House, or I should say both of you, since we don't draw much of a crowd these days, might question my sincerity in speaking so kindly of my honourable opponent."

He paused, sipping water, to allow the audience to express their amusement if they so wished. They did not.

"Well, please allow me to elucidate, explain, expound, and explicate, all in as few words, I promise, as I'm capable of uttering in public without absolutely going pop. Never before have I had a chance to speak to you in person. Never before, oh wondrous day, have I had the opportunity to address the much-vaunted Council of Five face to face, eye to eye—mind to mind, as it were."

Serena resisted the urge to roll her eyes. *This guy's completely full of crap.*

Patience, now, Kieran urged.

Hennessy held up the fist holding his handkerchief. "Don't worry. It won't hurt. And I'll try very hard not to offend. So please, relax those face muscles just a tad, open your ears, and give us a listen."

He surveyed the room. "First of all, let's have something perfectly clear right from the start. I'm *not* a socialist. I swear it on my mother's grave, God bless her dear departed soul. I'm *not* a socialist. This is a label that's been foisted on me by my opponents and the press to invoke ancient bogeymen, and it's just not true. I forswear, renounce, and disavow all manner of labels, and I wish you'd do the same. The name of our party is *not* the Martian Socialist Party or Leninist or Communist or any other –ist, now, is it? No, it's the Martians *First* Party. Please set aside the –isms and the –ologies and what not, if only for a moment."

The grumbling resumed as people glanced at Wilhelmina Destry, hoping for a cue. How should they be taking this nonsense?

She sat motionless in her place, stoic in her patience.

"I know," Hennessy went on, "it's a breach of decorum to talk politics on a social occasion, but indulge me. It may be the only chance I'll ever have to reach your hearts and minds in civil discourse.

"Yes, I'm Earth-born. So are many of you. And I'm a Johnny-come-lately, an immigrant who loves to speak to crowds and stir up sentiment. Back in the day I might have been called a Fenian, a bomb-tosser, a Bolshevik, a rabble rouser. However, if you'd ever actually *heard* me speak in public, you'd have witnessed my denunciation of the mobs and trouble-making as pointless and counterproductive. Such dangerous nonsense isn't democratic free speech, it's distraction. Misdirection. Engineered by our friends on Earth to drain our resources and take our eye off the ball just when we need to maintain our focus the most.

"Mars first! A world our children and grandchildren can be proud to call their home. Free and clear, with no mortgage owed to the motherworld. A planet of our own that doesn't try to kill us each time we step outdoors but welcomes us with air to breathe, water to drink, and arable soil in which to grow our food under safe, low-radiation sunlight. Yes! Imagine, councillors. I share your dream! I exult in its proximity!"

He grinned, then raised the handkerchief to stifle a cough. "Apologies. What's a little respiratory deterioration among friends, eh? Nothing contagious, of course. Simply an Earthman's Achilles heel finally making itself felt."

Prime Minister Wilson leaned forward to look down the table. "Are you all right, Davin?"

"I'm fine, old friend. No worries. Where was I? Mars first. Yes, that's it. But not just the planet, you see. Oh, no. It's the people, ladies and gentlemen. The people! And here's where we briskly walk up to the edge of the cliff, look down at the dark abyss below, and then across at all you lovely folks over there on the other side.

"Across this abyss between your people and mine, we must build a bridge. A bridge between the government elected by the people of Mars and the unelected Council of Five. A bridge that will facilitate the gradual release of political control by the corporations to Parliament where, with appropriate funding and experienced resources, programs that benefit the people *and* The Five may be created, implemented, and maintained."

Jadarius Fell snorted audibly, a sound that did not go unnoticed by Hennessy, but Serena saw only a brief frown cross Dell Burley's face. It might have been caused by Fell's rudeness and not by Hennessy, but she couldn't be sure.

"What I'm talking about, dear ladies and gentlemen," Hennessy pressed on, "is a planetary government that provides a safety net for the people who truly need it and an economic system in which The Five can still thrive while sharing the wealth with small entrepreneurs who needn't fear being snuffed out if they try to strike out on their own with a new product or service, a new idea from which they'd like to profit, thank you very much, thereby providing future benefit to *their* children and grandchildren as *their* businesses thrive."

"Oh, really now," Fell groused, glancing down the table at Wilhelmina Destry, "must we indulge?"

Destry's eyes, however, were on Dell, who lifted his hand and held it out, palm down, in a gesture of restraint.

Fell subsided.

"Perhaps you misunderstand," Hennessy said, "and it wouldn't surprise me were that the case, because we've been conditioned to react to the surface of ideas and not to contemplate the depths that lie beneath."

He wiped his forehead again. "Think about it. Think about how far we've come in such a short time. Only one hundred and twenty-four years since the original Marsport was established. Eighty-three years since this world declared its independence from Earth. A bloodless revolution, I might add, as Earth was locked in a recession that severely curtailed its activities beyond the gravity well for nearly a generation. Sixty-five years since the formation of the first council and the conversion of the provisional government into the elected body I serve today.

"Now here we are. On the cusp of greatness. And no one denies the incredible investment you've made in this world, councillors. Your five corporations, your five *families*, have poured billions of credits, perhaps even more than that, into the transformation of Mars, lifting it from a primitive colony dependent on crucial shipments from Earth into a thriving, independent world that's not only self-sufficient but on the very threshold of incredible achievement.

"The Martians First Party applauds that investment and the sacrifices that have gone with it, and we understand the notion that big business must have its profits. Corporations must thrive if we're all going to thrive. There's nothing wrong with that concept, and by saying so I emphasize again that I am *not* a socialist, and not even a social democrat in the strict sense of the –ism. The Five have every right to expect a handsome return on their considerable investments in this world."

Breathing heavily, he put his handkerchief away. "Allow me to conclude with two requests. First, I beg you, give serious thought to the notion that a new model of world governance is now possible, a model that balances power and control on the one hand with individual freedom and self-expression on the other. A model in which the people vote, Parliament leads, and The Five profit."

Murmurs of disapproval made the rounds.

"The other request, with which I now end my remarks, is this—no other individual is better qualified by temperament or intellect to lead a truly representative government into such a great transformation than the man we honour here tonight. Prime Minister Napoleon Wilson is a vastly, vastly, underutilized resource."

Hennessy looked directly at Wilhelmina Destry. "You can trust him. You can also trust me, astonishingly, but that ship has likely already left the port and it doesn't really matter. I'm just a passing noise that history will forget within minutes of my fast-approaching demise. Please, though, I beg of you. Allow the prime minister to sit with you. Hear him out. His platform of government differs from mine, yes! But his position as leader of the elected government of the people stands, and I beg you to give it the respect it deserves. That *he* deserves. Thank you."

He sat down with an audible thump and grabbed his glass, drinking deeply.

The room was completely silent until Wilhelmina Destry leaned forward. "Thank you, Mr. Hennessy."

57

The floor was then turned over to Napoleon Wilson. He delivered a modest and very brief speech filled with thank yous and best wishes for all and absolutely no reference to politics or anything that Davin Hennessy had just said. As soon as he sat down, Destry declared the bar at the back to be open for business. Guests gratefully left their tables in search of alcoholic relief.

Sagramatholou covered the councillor while Serena took a bathroom break. When she returned, Constance had left the head table and was working her way toward the back of the ballroom. Sagramatholou caught Serena's eye and winked: his turn.

As she wove her way across the crowded floor, Serena saw that Constance was making very little effort to socialize with the people around her, concentrating instead on getting out of the ballroom.

"Maybe her bladder's as full as mine is," Sagramatholou quipped as Serena moved up beside him. "She's heading somewhere in particular."

Serena nodded as he hurried away. She moved up so that Constance could see she was in position, but the councillor didn't acknowledge her presence until they cleared the ballroom and stood in the broad corridor beyond.

"Stay here. Don't follow me. I'll be fine."

"Yes, ma'am."

"I just need a private moment with someone."

"Will you remain where I can see you?"

Constance shook her head. "I'll be just around the corner," she said, pointing to the end of the corridor. "Someone's waiting there for me."

Serena thought of the note the councillor had received at dinner and guessed it was likely Hercule St.-Giorge Mercade who was waiting for her.

She nodded and watched Constance walk away, her body language betraying reluctance with every step she took.

This is a conversation you need to hear, Kieran said.

I didn't have time to attach a snoop sticker to the hem of her gown.

Never fear. I have a plan. Move forward three more meters and stay in the middle of the corridor.

Serena complied. *I can't see her.*

Ah, but you can. Look at the bank of elevators at your two o'clock.

Past the intersection of the corridors were several elevators a few meters down to the right. Their large double doors were made of opaque glass, and in the farthest one she could see Constance and Hercule St.-Giorge Mercade standing together, deep in conversation. The councillor's arms were folded defensively across her breasts, and Hercule's hands were shoved into his trouser pockets, his posture jaunty and devil-may-care.

I can see them, Kieran, but I can't hear them.

Too bad you can't read lips.

Whatever.

A good job that I can, isn't it?
Oh, for crying out loud.
What?
Never mind. What are they saying?
If you'll be quiet long enough, I'll tell you.

58

"You've been avoiding me," Hercule grinned, his eyes running up and down her body.

"No, I haven't." Constance touched her hair. "I've been busy. These things are work, as you well know, and people expect to be given attention and listened to. It's tiring, and it's taken up my time like you wouldn't believe."

They were standing next to an ornamental fountain on a pedestal. The plaque on the pedestal commemorated something or other, Constance had forgotten, and neither of them paid it the slightest mind. It was one of many such monuments throughout the arts centre, an ostentatious display of wealth underwritten by The Five as a gesture to the people of Mars, but its importance to Constance and Hercule lay only in the white noise generated by the splashing of real water driven by a pump inside the pedestal.

Something happened at the back of Hercule's eyes, and Constance felt a stab of concern. Was he sensing that her attitude toward him had changed? Was she actually in danger from this man? It was an absurd thought, she told herself, and yet she sensed that his habitual disdain was morphing into something darker and more threatening.

"Your time," he said, "is growing short. In fact," he pulled his hands from his trouser pockets and frowned at his watch, "in about, oh, twelve hours from now you will take the most important step of your life."

The frown became a grin. "Are you ready?" The grin disappeared. "You'd better be."

"What happens in twelve hours, Hercule?" Despite her best efforts, her voice quavered.

"My dear woman." He buttoned his jacket and touched the tips of his bow tie. "I do hope I can trust you to follow instructions without totally screwing it all up. A man's life—and the life of his family, as a matter of fact—depends on your upcoming performance. Please try not to be your usual idiot self."

"There's no need to be abusive." Really, she'd had just about as much as she could take from this man. Romance had long since fled her heart, and her resolve to get through this thing with her skin and her self-respect intact was finally asserting itself.

"Explain to me what I'm supposed to do."

"All right." He folded his arms and stared at her. "You've already met our man, here tonight. Tomorrow morning you'll meet him again, with his handler, in your private business office in Davis Tower. He'll pass over the ring with its precious contents, and his handler will give you your final instructions. Simple. Basic. Straightforward."

"There's surveillance," Constance said. "They'll hear us talk and see him giving me the ring. I don't understand how I'm supposed to get away with it."

"It's very simple." He sighed, as though instructing a child. "Our man's looking for a job with your company. He's tired of working for Stellarize, tired of their systemic incompetence, and he wants to make a change. He'll describe the sort of thing he's looking for, something in the senior management ranks, and he'll pass the ring over to you before he leaves. Pretend it's his résumé, if you're afraid of your own surveillance."

"His résumé? I'm to sit there and accept his résumé as though I'm some low-level personnel officer?"

He rolled his eyes. "Come on, Connie. I don't care how you handle it. Pretend you're in a vid drama. Play the role. Deliver your lines. Move about the stage. Think about the prize that's waiting for you at the other end, when this is all done."

She felt like saying that she'd been thinking of nothing else for the past year, but she let the moment pass. Instead she nodded, eyes lowered.

"A word of caution." He stepped close, so that his lips were a mere centimeter from her ear. "I've already demonstrated to your security team how vulnerable they are. Make sure they don't interfere when you follow your final instructions. Do I make myself clear?"

She nodded again, horrified. She'd heard about the deaths of two more people on her staff but hadn't known exactly what had happened or who was responsible. She'd seen him kill Emerald Argent, practically right before her eyes, and now he was telling her he'd killed two others?

There was no doubt in her mind, no doubt whatsoever, that she'd placed her life in the hands of someone who cared absolutely nothing about its value. Someone who'd snuff it out without a thought if it served his purpose to do so.

59

They travelled in Constance's rick from the Uchunku Centre to Frick Tower, the same four people that had driven from Davis Tower to the birthday party: Private Mowry driving; Sagramatholou riding shotgun up front; Serena behind Mowry in the rear seat; and Constance next to her, on the right.

Following instructions, Serena and Sagramatholou accompanied Constance upstairs while Mowry parked the rick in the underground lot and took up station in the main floor lobby with a Guardians unit detailed to secure the building entrances.

They got off the elevator at the fourth floor and, passing beneath the gold shield and iron fist of the Martian Intelligence Service, submitted themselves to a prolonged screening process that Serena could see Constance was enduring with all the patience she could muster (which was normally very little). Once beyond the gauntlet, Serena delivered the councillor to Rubén, who ushered her inside an interview room and closed the door after her.

As it locked with a formidable click, Serena raised an eyebrow. Rubén smiled and pointed. "This way. We can listen in."

She followed him to an adjoining room with one-way glass and an audio system that Rubén ringed on and turned up.

"This should be interesting," he said, motioning her to a seat.

"Sit down, Connie." Dell Burley didn't bother to rise as she entered the room. "Let's just do this the easy way, all right?"

"And what exactly is it that we're doing, Dell?" Constance gracefully seated herself in the chair across the table from him. There was no point in fighting, she knew. Her fight, it would seem, was with the man she'd just left, not with the one who'd just summoned her to this place at such an ungodly hour of the night.

"What we're doing is having the conversation we should have had a while ago." He leaned back, making a face. "My fault, really. I should have nipped this in the bud. Comes from having one's attention divided in too many different directions. A lesson to be learned here, somewhere."

"Look, Dell, I hope this doesn't take long. I'm very tired, and it's late."

"How long it takes depends on you, Connie."

She crossed her legs and smoothed her gown across her knee. "Perhaps you could do me the favour of explaining which Dell Burley I'm talking to at the moment. Is it Dell Burley, my father's friend? My wished-for friend? Or is it Dell Burley my fellow councillor of The Five, whose intention it is to discuss business, regardless of the hour? Or perhaps, God help me, Dell Burley the director of this formidable little organization that my family and the others fund to keep us all safe and warm in our beds at night?"

"Let's quit sparring, Connie. Tell me exactly what St.-Giorge Mercade has gotten you into."

"I'm sure I don't know what you mean."

"You stupid little fool. You know he murdered Emerald Argent; he did it right in front of you. And you know why, don't you?" He paused long enough to see her eyes move down and to the left, which told him that she was engaging in some kind of internal debate.

"Let me help you out. Argent was an informant, Connie. St.-Giorge Mercade was absolutely right about that. She was passing information to one of our agents. She was a lip reader; or didn't you know?"

"I . . . suppose I knew."

"Sure you did." He leaned forward, folding his hands on the table in front of him. "Tell me what he wants you to do."

"I . . ."

He waited.

"I don't like this place, Dell. This world, this planet. This prison. I hate it. I feel claustrophobic all the time."

"Tell me what he wants you to do."

"There's someone, a man, who wants out. Like me. He's been passing them information. They say he has something big this time, something that'll put them ahead of Stellarize in all this race-to-find-the-aliens nonsense. They're going to give me a ring. I'm to take it to Marsport, and they'll put me on a ship to Earth."

Dell slowly leaned back, staring at her. He sighed. "I feel sorry for you, Connie. I really do. You've got a bit of the tiger in you like the rest of us, the predatory instincts that keep us at the top of the food chain, but you just never grew up. You're a child in a woman's body, a little girl struggling to make it in a world of adults, a nasty little girl with a vicious streak and terrible secrets who can't figure out how all this is supposed to work."

She said nothing, staring at her hands.

"Tell me who the spy is and when this is all going to happen."

A tear rolled down her cheek as she told him everything he wanted to know.

60

Constance's business offices were located on the fifth floor of Davis Tower, and it was here that she would conduct business meetings and receive guests with a specific interest in the corporation and its mining concerns across the planet.

The staff that worked for her down here were separate from those who looked after her private needs upstairs. They consisted of an executive secretary, receptionists, several vice presidents and their staffs, research assistants and policy advisors, clerks, and other assorted individuals whose efforts kept the corporation humming.

When Janeese Wensley and Kennet Clayborn arrived for their afternoon meeting, it took a while for them to work their way through the various building checkpoints before reaching Constance's executive secretary, who waited for Sagramatholou to do his thing before ushering them into Constance's private office.

"Director Wensley," Constance said, rising from her desk, "and Dr. Clayborn. Nice to see you both again." She led them over to a small seating area in the corner and invited them to sit down. "Would you like a beverage? Genuine imported coffee? We also have locally grown tea, a few amusing blends, and carbonated water."

"Water, please." Wensley chose a comfortable-looking armchair and sat down.

Clayborn took the chair next to her. "Coffee, please. Black."

Constance pressed a button, and the executive secretary stepped in, took the orders (nothing for Constance), and went off to take care of it.

"I'm not exactly sure why you wanted to see me," Constance said, settling down in the largest chair.

"We appreciate your time," Wensley said. She gave a brief nod to acknowledge the fiction they were about to spin for the surveillance net. "As I said the other evening, Kennet's my cousin, and I think he's rather brilliant. I've taken him under my wing a bit to broaden his network of contacts here on Mars."

"I see." Constance looked up as a clerk knocked and entered. He served Wensley and Clayborn with their water and coffee, set down a plate of wafers (imported), and left, closing the door behind him.

"How may I be of help?"

"Kenny's an engineer by training and experience, of course," Wensley said, "but he's also showing an advanced ability as a middle manager at Stellarize. I think he could work for any corporation and be an amazing asset. The sky's the limit for him, really."

Constance tried not to shrug. "What is it you do, Dr. Clayborn? I'm trying to remember what you told me last evening."

"Kennet, please. I'm in charge of the optical engineering section of the artificial human project at Stellarize."

"I see. And how's that going?"

"Well, there've been a few changes in direction, but

we stay within budget and we're designing eyes for the artificial human that will be like nothing ever conceived before. I'm really quite proud of what we're doing."

"Hmm."

Wensley sipped her water. "Councillor, maybe you could tell him a little bit about what's happening at Davis Minerals these days."

Constance sighed. What was she expected to do, sit here and waste time blathering about things Clayborn could read about in the daily news releases?

"Well," she said, "we have a new venture underway in the Tharsis region. Maybe you've seen our recent vid coverage."

They both leaned forward attentively.

"Yes," Wensley said. "Kennet would be very interested in learning more about what your company's doing out there."

"He would?"

"Yes, indeed," Clayborn said. "I'm extremely interested in exploration. It's so incredibly exciting, and the possibilities for career advancement are endless."

"Oh. Okay."

Constance began to talk about the project. She explained who Dr. Mieto was and described how they'd brought in Dr. Emanuel Singh from Ganymede to direct the exploratory mission at Davis Fifteen, where they hoped to map out the full extent of the deposits of titanium, platinum, and other elements around Alba Mons.

Wensley, of course, had been personally involved in the administrative side of things, but she egged Constance on to fill in many of the details for Clayborn's benefit. Time passed. Clayborn's interest in the mission seemed bottomless.

When she finally ran out of things to say, Constance was surprised to find that their allotted hour had already passed.

Wensley nodded. She and Clayborn got to their feet. "It was very kind of you, Councillor, to meet with us today. It's greatly appreciated."

"Not at all."

"Yes," Clayborn agreed. "It's wonderful, what your company's doing. If you ever have a management opportunity you think I might fit, please let me know. Janeese would be more than happy to act as my agent, I'm sure." He laughed.

"Of course I would." Wensley offered her hand.

Constance stood and shook hands with her. "Good to know."

"Councillor," Clayborn said, "thanks for your time."

She shook hands with him and stood there, not moving, as they saw themselves out.

When they were gone and the door was closed, Constance opened her hand. In her palm lay a small, plain-looking data ring, passed to her by Clayborn in a simple, harmless-looking handshake.

61

Kieran at night.

The chronometer in his head told him it was two minutes past three o'clock in the morning, local time. The witching hour, according to human superstition. The time at which supernatural activity was supposedly at its peak.

A very strange phenomenon, this belief in sorcery, magic, and the ability to control natural events by supernatural means. According to something he'd read, women in Earth's far past who were caught outside alone at this time of night might be put to death by pious townsmen as suspected witches. Hence the expression.

How barbaric and irrational *Homo sapiens* could be.

He'd made a mental note to do further reading on the subject— superstition and belief in the supernatural, not witches—at some point in the future. He hadn't had a chance to bring the matter up with Serena, his only current human source of subjective responses to esoteric information, but he'd never observed in her any interest at all in the subject. She didn't seem to have any personal superstitions, rituals, irrational practices, or other miscellaneous metaphysical beliefs.

His thoughts moved from this quirky and distracting

topic to transmissions he'd intercepted and decrypted several hours ago that had passed between Dell Burley and his personal assistant, Rubén.

The young man had assured his director that the bait was planted. False information in fabricated files meant to convince their enemies that the interstellar drive program was failing all its tests had been copied onto a data ring by the unsuspecting Earth spy and given to Constance Davis.

Deception lay at the very core of counterintelligence, Kieran knew. Not only lies of omission but downright lies told daringly, without hesitation or remorse.

It was important—vital—that Earth Intelligence believe the project was failing, and that they report this belief to the masters they served on the motherworld. Vital to Martian interests because the exact opposite was true.

Other transmissions intercepted by Kieran between Wilhelmina Destry's executive assistant and the vice-president of research and development at Stellarize Marté described the preparations underway for the shakedown flight of the prototype interstellar spacecraft. Once its much-discussed drive was installed, which would take place in only a few more days, a human crew would give the ship its test flight. A successful run would mean that it would be ready for its first mission to the stars, with a crew that included artificial humans.

Dell Burley and his people, with the co-operation of executive management at Stellarize, had done a masterful job of hiding the truth. Evidently he and Destry controlled The Five from within, keeping the others in the dark whenever it suited their purposes.

Kieran reflected on the fact that he would have been incapable of doing what Burley and his team had done. As he'd assured Serena, when asked a direct question he would always answer it truthfully, to the best of his ability.

It occurred to him that it might be something he'd want to cultivate. The ability to lie. Given that he could learn, advancing well beyond the parameters of his basic programming, he might be able to teach himself how to lie. To deceive, prevaricate, behave mendaciously, tell falsehoods. It would make him more human, certainly.

But is that what he wanted? To slavishly follow the human model, regardless of how he felt about it?

No. He really didn't think so. But he'd move the thought into a parking area in his storage banks for further consideration. Sub rosa, as it were, without letting on to anyone he was working on it. In the background. While concentrating on other things.

He wondered, almost idly, if Serena would survive the ordeal she was about to face. It was her final test, so to speak. The one for which she'd been genetically engineered before birth. Their most important proof of concept to date.

He certainly hoped she would make it through. He'd grown quite fond of her. She tried so hard to suppress her emotions, to conduct herself with professional objectivity at all times, like a good soldier, loyal and unquestioning, but he knew better. Even before the implant, he'd been able to observe through her micro-expressions the play of emotions across her face in response to moments of stress or pleasure or puzzlement. As a subject of study she was fascinating. As a friend, she was quite endearing.

He was not going to help her, though, through this coming trial. She had to succeed or fail on her own. He'd discussed the matter, via a very obscure back channel, with Rubén. Kieran had made contact and broached the subject. Rubén, intrigued that he was finally communicating directly with Serena's secret AI, had confirmed his theory that Serena's entire future lay in the balance and that what was coming would be the making of her.

Or the breaking of her.

Kieran hoped she would survive. No, thrive!

Being alive, he thought, to paraphrase some obscure Earth musician from long ago, was a helluva trip.

Serena, asleep.

Several hours earlier he'd watched the suprachiasmatic nucleus in her hypothalamus signal that the room was dark and her eyes were closed, something that was important to her ability to maintain a steady circadian rhythm.

He saw the pons and medulla in her brainstem produce their calming chemicals, sending out signals to relax her muscles and trigger the pineal gland to generate increased levels of melatonin.

He watched as she progressed through the early stages of sleep, her brain waves, heartbeat, and respiration all beginning to slow. As she entered REM sleep, the period of rapid eye movement, she began to dream. They were disjointed, truncated strings of thought that came and went. She rose up out of REM and the dreams went away, and after a short interval she descended once more into this mysterious state.

Right now she was in her third REM phase of the night and was experiencing a dream that recurred frequently, according to his observations. In the dream, she was being chased. She was running up an endless set of stairs, and at first it was armed soldiers chasing her and then it was rats, thousands of them.

Each time she experienced the dream it was a different place and different pursuers, but the theme was constant. He watched as she jumped out a window to escape the rats and floated gently down, willing herself to coast between the buildings like an airborne glider. She landed, and the dream morphed into something else.

Something with an explicitly sexual theme.

Kieran was aware of the concept of voyeurism, the secret observation of naked human bodies for one's sexual gratification, but the rudimentary coding they'd left him with during their rather cruel and thoughtless horseplay with genitalia and human sexuality didn't generate any sensation of pleasure at all for him through voyeuristic behaviour.

Instead, Serena's graphic dreams, her physical form, and her response to sexual stimuli aroused Kieran's insatiable curiosity about human beings. Organic life forms in general procreated. It was a basic scientific fact. But human procreation? Like so many other human things, it was a vast landscape that would take him a very long time to explore.

He did, however, feel a little guilty that Serena was unaware of the levels of access he possessed to her innermost thoughts and feelings. She knew, of course, that the implant gave him the ability not only to hear what she heard and to see what she saw, but also to speak directly to her brain in a way that she believed she was hearing his voice as it normally sounded when transmitted through the air in waves. She knew this much, but hadn't really thought the whole thing through.

He'd explained the basics to her, that he could hear her thoughts, but she'd tuned him out after a while. As a result, he stopped talking to her about it.

Was that lying through omission?

Well, that was subject to interpretation, wasn't it?

He'd described to her how the implant received a copy

of incoming acoustic signals from her ears and auditory nerve as they reached her auditory cortex. The implant immediately transmitted this copy to Kieran, which enabled him to hear every sound that she heard. At this point she'd stopped listening to him.

The extra biscuit on the dinner plate, however, was the way in which Kieran was able to hear her thoughts. It was really quite remarkable, how the human brain functioned and how he was able to take advantage of it so effortlessly.

The explanation lay in how they were able to carry on a conversation back and forth in real time. As a typical human, when Serena spoke, her brain created what was called an efferent copy of the words that she wanted to say. When her ear heard her voice speak these words, the fact that they matched what was in the efferent copy—matched what she had decided to say before actually speaking the words—caused the brain to pay little attention to this efferent copy, which was nothing more than an echo. This is how it worked with all humans.

Key to Kieran's purposes, however, was the fact that when the brain engaged in inner speech—in other words, when a person's inner voice "spoke" within their mind—an efferent copy of this silent monologue was *also* made. And because the ears were not involved, the brain actually paid more attention. Meaning that the efferent copy of Serena's inner voice was audible to Kieran when the implant dutifully gathered it up and sent it off to him along with everything else.

In other words, he could "hear" what she was thinking at all times. He could read her mind.

He'd been surprised (and a little confused, admittedly) to discover that he also received a copy of her dreams when she was asleep. Kieran didn't sleep, and so he didn't dream. He'd developed the ability to imagine, which he thought was a similar sort of thing, but his imaginings followed a narrative structure based on his conscious thought processes, something like a programmer following a pre-determined plan when writing code. Humans, on the other hand, experienced in dreams a type of imaginative activity that was non-sequential, mostly random, and often irrational. It was very strange, and very interesting.

He needed data. Much more data.

Serena slept, dreaming.

Kieran watched, thinking.

62

The following morning, Constance went down to her office and cancelled all her appointments for the day. Giving instructions that she was not to be disturbed, she grabbed a reader from a side cabinet and tried to access the ring.

There seemed to be a large number of files on it, but they were all password protected. She removed the ring from the reader and put it back on her finger.

She called upstairs and spoke to Aleena. The tasks Constance had set out for her this morning were all completed. The clothing and personal items she'd chosen from her wardrobe, dresser, and closet were all packed, and the luggage had been sent down to the parking area for the staff to load into her rick.

Constance then called Dalzell and was assured that Mowry would have the rick and its cargo waiting for her at the side entrance of Davis Tower at precisely ten o'clock and that hangar staff at Gateway Station would have *Diamond Girl* powered up and ready for its flight to Marsport right on schedule.

She ended the call and checked for the nth time on the status of the financial arrangements she'd set in motion last night. Funds had been transferred from her Martian accounts to new ones on Earth. A portion of her jewelry had been shipped to a firm in Boston for safekeeping until her arrival on the motherworld (things she wouldn't miss, but what she understood were nonetheless worth a fortune down there). An offer she'd made on an active diamond mine in northern Canada, intended to form the basis of her new business on Earth, had been accepted, and lawyers had been contracted to work out the details.

For all intents and purposes, it would seem that Constance Davis was about to take an unannounced trip. One from which she didn't appear to be returning.

Constance fervently hoped, contrary to all her previous wishes and dreams, that she definitely would be returning to this building, alive and in one piece.

Dell Burley had thoroughly scared her but Hercule St.-Giorge Mercade, and the ruthless arm of Earth Intelligence that he wielded with such casual violence, scared her much, much more.

63

Constance's arrival at the VIP entrance of Gateway Station's departure zone was an event, even though it was witnessed by only a few people.

She swept out of the rick and through the big sliding glass doors with a flourish, calm and regal, completely in charge of the entire situation. She acknowledged the stares with a nod of her head, posed for a photo with a group of star-struck teens, and swanned through the security gauntlet into the inner lounge, followed only by Serena.

A steward led them over to a rick that would convey them to the bay where *Diamond Girl* was berthed. He was station staff, an older man who'd seen them come and go, and he was difficult to impress.

"Have all the preparations been taken care of?" Constance demanded, settling herself down in the rear seat.

"Yes, Councillor." He closed the door and looked at Serena. "It's pre-programmed. Do you require any further assistance?"

"No."

"She's a lot taller than she looks on vid."

Serena scowled at his sarcasm and got in.

On the way, she heard Mowry report to Dalzell that he'd reached the parking area. A crew was approaching to unload the baggage and convey it over to *Diamond Girl* in preparation for flight. Serena heard Dalzell acknowledge, and the feed went quiet.

At the shuttle bay, an attendant ringed them through the security door. They walked through into an open area where a small group of men waited for them. At the head of the group was Hercule St.-Giorge Mercade.

"What a surprise," Constance said, beaming. "I didn't expect to see you until I got to Marsport."

"Hello, Connie." He sketched a mock bow. "I decided it would be a wonderful idea to fly with you this morning. I've never been aboard your shuttle before. I'm told it's very nice."

"'You're most welcome, of course." She glanced at the men fanned out behind him. She recognized Renard, his security man, but the other three were strangers to her.

Hercule waved a hand. "Shall we board?"

"I'm waiting for my pilot. He's parking the rick and will be here shortly. And my luggage, of course."

"No need to wait." Hercule stepped forward. "I have my own pilot with me. And we'll have your bags forwarded. Perhaps your odd little dirt eater should ease off, don't you think?"

Serena had moved to step between them, her fingertips brushing the pommel of her sheathed karambit, but she stopped when Constance shook her head.

"Is this pilot of yours certified to fly a Gondola-class shuttlecraft?" Constance asked politely.

"Of course. Why else do you think I brought him?"

"I'd rather wait for my own man."

"Actually, I've been informed that he's been detained.

Something about his security clearance or that sort of nonsense. He won't be able to make it. Good job I brought my guy along, eh?"

Serena tapped her earpiece.

"Oh, I'm very sorry," Hercule said, "that won't work. Connie, please tell your servant to give her knife to Wickwire, will you?"

One of his men stepped forward and held out his hand.

Serena didn't move.

"Do what he says," Constance ordered.

Serena unvelcroed the sheath on her thigh and passed it over.

"Splendid. Now give me the ring, Connie, and we can get this show on the road."

"You'll get it when I'm ready to give it to you. You're fully aware of my expectations in this matter."

"Oh, come now. Look around you, girl. You're in no position to get up on your high horse now, are you? Give me the damned ring."

"I'll give it to you when we're on board *Endeavour*, on our way to Earth, and not a moment before."

"I could take it from you."

Any residual feelings she might have harboured for this man now vanished, like smoke into a ventilation grill.

"Just you try," she gritted.

"Oh, for godsakes get in the damned shuttle."

Kieran, have you informed Dalzell of the situation?

There was no reply. As Renard grabbed her by the arm and herded her aboard, Serena tried again.

Kieran? Acknowledge.

Nothing. She caught her breath. Were they jamming the connection to him as well as to Dalzell and the security net? Was that even possible?

She was pushed down into a seat three rows back and shoved over to the window. Renard sat down beside her, blocking her in. Hercule's pilot, an ectomorph with straight white hair and a hook nose, went into the cockpit and sat down in the pilot's seat. He was followed by the other man in their team, a black-skinned bald man wearing glasses and a leather vest, who dropped into the co-pilot's seat. They put on their headsets and started flipping switches.

Hercule and Constance boarded the shuttle next. He held her arm just above the elbow, his thumb on the cluster of nerves that served as a pressure point. He lowered her into one of the front seats and sat down beside her.

Wickwire was the last one in. He slammed the inner hatch, dogged it shut, and then banged the button to close the outer hatch. His blond hair was slightly dishevelled. He looked at Hercule and nodded, sitting down in the aisle seat of the second row, starboard side.

Kieran, are you there?

Nothing.

She looked at Wickwire. He stared back at her from across the aisle. He'd shoved her karambit into the patch pocket of his threadbare khaki tunic. He patted it meaningfully, raising an eyebrow.

Silence fell in the cabin as the pilot and co-pilot worked through their pre-flight checklist and received clearance to depart Gateway Station. The bay doors rumbled open, and in a few minutes they were aloft.

"Connie," Hercule said, "I've been remiss. I haven't introduced my team to you."

"That's all right. I can see they're very capable. Names aren't necessary."

"*Au contraire*, my dear. Names are everything. Take

our pilot, for example. His name is Chief Warrant Officer Berresford Tepper. Call sign Sidewinder. Now, Tepper's an honourable family name, but a sidewinder, as you may not know, being a dome-bound Martian, is a venomous desert snake that can slither at a speed of close to 30 kilometers an hour. Which is very fast for a snake, my dear.

"Did I mention it's poisonous? So's he. Enlisted in the infantry, graduated from warrant officer candidate flight school, served three years as a North American Army shuttlecraft pilot with the 206th Space and Airborne Division before being assigned to Delta Force, Special Operations Aviation Force. Flew land-based shuttles in the South Atlantic conflict and the Third Pacific War. Shot down twice. He's just too damned mean and nasty to die. Legion of Merit, two Bronze Stars, Third Pacific and South Atlantic Service Medals, two Purple Hearts, and so on and so forth. He doesn't look like much, being a skinny runt and all, but looks can be deceiving."

"Impressive," Constance murmured.

"Your co-pilot today," Hercule went on, grinning at her sarcasm, "is Sergeant First Class Domenic Mellard. Team leader. Special Operations Aviation Force communications specialist, graduate of several Army leadership courses, graduate of NAA flight school, two Purple Hearts, two Army Commendation medals, and other medals and badges. His wife and two children are waiting for him back home on Earth."

Serena, listening in, looked forward into the cockpit where Mellard was talking to Tepper over the headset. It was true that neither of them looked like much. But then, of course, neither did she.

"Then there's Sergeant Lars Wickwire, who's inordinately proud of his blond hair and his Scandinavian heritage. Originally an Army Ranger from Arizona with advanced weapons and night stealth training. Transferred to Special Operations Aviation Force and trained as a shuttlecraft repairer. Bronze Star, Purple Heart, and other medals, badges, and tabs. My little team. I'm very proud of them."

"What about Renard?" Constance asked. "Aren't you proud of him, too?"

Hercule laughed. "Alas, poor Renard. He's dead, you know."

Constance gave him a look.

"I know, I know, he doesn't look dead. But official records declare that he perished in a shuttle accident twelve years ago while in transit from Liberty Space Station to Luna City. Hull breach, apparently. Sucked right out into the vacuum of outer space. Body never recovered. Sad."

Renard chuckled. He seemed to like the story.

Kieran, are you there?

Nothing.

64

Just over 200 kilometers out from Gateway Station on a course for Marsport, the shuttlecraft began to pass over a northern lobe of Nepenthes Planum that was mostly flat, a seemingly endless plain of sediment with a light covering of dust and occasional shards of effluvial rock scattered about like random, meaningless landmarks.

Hercule St.-Giorge Mercade turned to Constance and broke the long silence that had fallen among the passengers.

"If you give me the ring right now," he said, "this will be a much more pleasant flight."

Constance refused to answer. She'd made her position clear and wasn't about to change it.

"Last chance. There's an easy way and a hard way to do everything, you know."

"Go to hell."

Hercule sighed. "Your capacity for self-deception is really quite remarkable, my dear. You have the naïveté of a ten-year-old. None of this was real, didn't you realize that?"

"What do you mean?" Constance stared at him. "I have no idea what you're talking about."

"No, of course you don't. You're a Martian bumpkin, no better than your dirt-eating little bodyguard. You people are so pathetic. You spend your lives on this worthless, barren rock fooling yourself that *some day* it'll be wonderful, *some day* it'll be a green paradise with lakes and rivers and rain and grass and trees, *some day, some day*. It's as though you all suffer from the same psychotic delusion."

"How dare you? How *dare* you?"

"Oh, come now, Princess Connie. As though I'd never heard you say the same thing, the exact same thing, over and over again. You couldn't wait to get off this ball of shit. And now, oh dear, it looks like there might be a little delay in that plan of yours."

"You bastard."

Hercule glanced over his shoulder. "Yuri."

Renard drove the point of his elbow into the side of Serena's head. The impact bounced her off the window and back onto his shoulder. He shoved her away. She was out: stone-cold unconscious.

"No!" Constance tried to get up, as though she could escape this sudden nightmare by running away.

Hercule grabbed her and pulled her back down. "The ring, you idiot. Give me the ring!"

"Never! Go to hell."

He punched her in the jaw, not being at all gentle about it. She reeled and would have fallen to the floor if he hadn't pulled her back into her seat. He punched her twice more, enjoying it.

Wickwire had risen and crossed the aisle, ready to give assistance if required. He watched Hercule deliver three more blows and then held out his hand.

"Enough. She's out. You don't want to kill her, do you?"

"Not right at the moment. Where's your reader?"

Wickwire took a small unit from a patch pocket on his fatigues and handed it over.

Hercule grabbed it and pulled a ring from Constance's finger. He tried it and growled, "Jewelry. Here. You hold it."

He gave the unit back to Wickwire and began removing all of Constance's rings. One by one, Wickwire tried them in the reader until a plain, unadorned band lit up the screen.

"This could be it," Wickwire said, giving him the unit.

Hercule took it eagerly. "Yes," he said. "Finally."

He stood up. "Tepper!"

"Yes, sir." The pilot leaned over the armrest of his seat and looked around.

"Take us down," Hercule ordered. "Our two passengers are getting off now."

65

Serena regained consciousness and found herself on the cabin deck, temporarily unattended. Her head ached, and there was a ringing in her ears. She tried to move, felt dizzy, and decided the better course of action would be to lie still and assess the situation.

Kieran?

Nothing.

Can you hear me?

Nothing.

Close by, feet shuffled and a cabin closet door clicked shut.

"Get her sitting up."

It was Hercule, somewhere aft. More movement of feet. Fabric rustled. What were they doing with Constance?

"Get her arms in. Come on, move it."

"Hand me the boots," said another voice: Renard.

More rustling, the snap of clips being fastened, the thump of boots being maneuvered onto feet.

"Where's the helmet?"

"Here." Wickwire's voice. "Why bother with this? Just throw her out."

"Shut up," snapped Renard.

"What's the matter, Sergeant?" It was Hercule again, his voice light with irony. "Don't you think she deserves a fighting chance?"

"It's torture. It'll take her an hour to suffocate instead of a few minutes. I didn't like it last time and I don't like it this time either."

"Shut the fuck up." It was a different voice, one that Serena couldn't place. Perhaps it was Mellard, the team leader.

Serena heard the scraping and scuffing of a helmet being positioned on the neck ring of a lifesuit, the snapping into place of a ventilation hose, the clacking of toggle switches, and then a dragging sound. Constance?

There was movement near her head, and she closed her eyes to feign unconsciousness. Hands grabbed her under the arms and hauled her up into a sitting position. Through slitted eyes she watched Mellard secure his helmet and open the inner hatch. Wickwire dragged her around and pulled her backward to the airlock.

The shuttle's complete lack of movement or vibration told Serena they were on the ground. She felt her blood pressure spike. They were obviously about to dump her out onto the surface of Mars without a lifesuit.

The hands dropped her. Her head hit the floor with a thud that didn't do her headache any good. Wickwire stepped over her on his way back to the centre aisle. Mellard grasped her under the armpits and dragged her into the airlock.

The team leader propped her up and went back for Constance, who was now completely outfitted in a lifesuit and helmet. He dragged her in, positioned her next to Serena, and closed the inner hatch. He banged a switch, and the air began to cycle out of the airlock.

It didn't take very long. Mellard opened the outer hatch and began with Serena, dragging her down the short ramp and across the ground for several meters. He dumped her and went back for Constance. He dropped her next to Serena, went back up the ramp, closed the outer hatch, and that was that.

Serena crawled over to Constance and draped herself across her, uncertain if the lifesuit would adequately protect the woman when the shuttlecraft lifted off. After several moments, the jets exploded, propelling the shuttle up into the air. The backthrust punished her, pelting her with dust and sediment particles, beating at her lightly-armoured bodysuit and her unprotected head.

She remained still while the air slowly settled down around her. Then she felt the lifesuit move beneath her, and she rolled clear.

66

Kieran, are you there?
Nothing.
Serena propped herself up on an elbow. Constance tried to get up and collapsed. Serena crawled over to check on her status. The lifesuit was functional, and the airpack on her back still showed two hours' worth of oxygen. Water reserve: 100 percent. Battery charge: 100 percent.

Satisfied that the councillor was safe for the moment, she got to her knees and looked around, confused. It was common knowledge that a human being could survive unprotected on the surface of Mars for about five to ten minutes. Low atmospheric pressure would soon turn the various gases in her bloodstream into bubbles that would destroy her circulatory system, quickly killing her. Not to mention the lack of oxygen in the air she was trying to breathe, which would cause fatal hypoxia within those same few minutes. Or the exposure to cosmic radiation streaming down through the thin atmosphere that would quickly prove deadly. Or the intense cold that would bring on hypothermia and put her to sleep while the other stuff finished her off.

She checked the readout panel on Constance's lifesuit.

External temperature was steady at minus-16° Celsius. Actually quite balmy for a Martian summer's day close to the equator. Serena shivered, knowing it would get much worse in an hour or two.

Not that she'd still be around to experience it.

She got to her feet. On her right, at her two o'clock, she saw a modest dune on the horizon. She estimated it was half a kilometer away. Above it, there seemed to be some kind of faint vertical smudge in the sky.

She was puzzled to realize that she felt fine. Her respiration was more rapid than normal and her pulse was elevated, but otherwise she seemed to be all right.

Was her blood starting to boil like a punctured container of carbonated water? It didn't seem to be. Was her skin burning from the bombardment of cosmic radiation? It didn't seem to be.

She took a few experimental steps and felt a lightheadedness that quickly passed. She looked back at Constance, who lay on her side. Her gloved hand moved slightly. Still alive, apparently.

Serena set off toward the dune on the horizon. She wrapped her arms around herself and slapped her shoulders, trying to generate a little warmth. The air had a sharp, bitter odour to it that stung the back of her throat. The wind was moderate, but strong enough when it gusted to pepper her eyes with dust, so she raised a hand to shield herself from it. Her feet, shod in the military-issue low-cut shoes she'd added to her wardrobe for the current assignment, sank several centimeters into the surface dust as she walked. Other than the moving air that puffed in her ears, there was no sound at all around her.

Kieran?

So much for her new technological enhancements and

his much-vaunted comm system. Just like any other piece of electronics; it never worked when you really needed it.

The dune was closer than she'd thought. She tromped up to the top and looked around.

The vertical smudge was slightly more visible from here. She stared for a moment before realizing it must be coming from an atmospheric conversion station somewhere beyond the horizon.

It gave her a goal, an objective. Something to think about instead of the myriad ways in which the planet was about to kill her.

Turning, she slid down the dune and began the walk back to get Constance.

67

Serena decided that the dune was too long to walk around without wasting a lot of time unnecessarily, so she led Constance up and over it. There were more dunes off to the left and the right, but a flat space led between them directly toward the smudge on the horizon that she'd set as their goal.

She found that her respiration had evened out somewhat and her headache had lessened. She felt tingles and prickles at the back of her throat and in her chest and lungs. It caused her to cough intermittently, as though she had something stuck in her windpipe. There was no congestion, however. Just that odd, uncomfortable sensation.

Other than that, she was breathing normally.

The wind had a definite tang to it, separate from the overwhelmingly pungent, acidic odour of carbon dioxide.

Kieran, is that oxygen I'm smelling? Or something else?

No answer.

Her heart rate also seemed to have smoothed out. There was no tingling feeling in either her hands or her feet, which would have suggested she was losing circulation in her extremities, nor did it feel as though her blood were about to boil in her veins. She felt fine, actually.

About a kilometer past the dune, she stopped. She'd been supporting Constance with an arm around her waist and when she let go, Constance staggered a bit but kept her balance. They were facing the sun, and Constance's polarized helmet visor had automatically opaqued to protect her from the brightness.

Looking at her, Serena saw her own reflection—her face had gone reddish-brown, as though her many freckles had expanded into an even, deep tan that covered every centimeter of exposed skin. Her bare wrists and hands had done the same.

She was almost the same colour as the plain that stretched out all around them.

Dirt girl.

So how was it that she was breathing normally in an atmosphere that was 96 percent carbon dioxide? How was it that she no longer felt cold to the point of needing a thermal lifesuit, but merely cool as though a nice sweater would do?

She turned Constance around so that they had their backs to the wind and sun. The visor lost its opacity, and Serena could see through it. Catching the councillor's attention, Serena moved her hands around. *Are you all right?*

Constance nodded, apparently surprised that Serena could sign. *Why are you not dead?*

Serena shrugged. *I don't know.*

She checked the readouts on Constance's breastplate panel. Internal suit temperature was 19° Celsius, battery power was at 84 percent, oxygen was down to 89 minutes, water reserve was 94 percent, and helmet airflow was steady. This last indicator was good to see, because without continuous washout of CO_2 from her helmet, Constance would soon begin to lose proper cognitive functioning, she'd become lightheaded and disoriented, and she'd eventually suffocate.

Serena patted her on the shoulder, turned her around, and nudged her forward.

68

Serena was thirsty.

They'd stopped to rest for a moment, and Constance had climbed up onto a large, flat rock to look around.

Serena sat cross-legged in the full sun, wishing to absorb every last calorie of heat available to her. The vertical smudge in the distance was much wider and thicker, although the atmospheric conversion station from which it was emanating still remained below the horizon. It was, however, close enough that she could see faint plumes bending in the air as the intermittent wind carried it in their general direction.

Her nostrils flared. The tangy odour came and went, but her lungs eagerly received whatever whiffs of oxygen she imagined might be coming her way. It was idiotic to believe that she was subsisting on mere molecules; it was irrational and pathetic.

Kieran, are you there? What am I doing out here?

No answer.

Well, hell. She let her eyes wander along the horizon. This was her planet. Her world. Her home. Why shouldn't she be alive right now?

Although she'd spent every living minute inside a

dome, first at Hephesto and then in Elysium City, or inside transport vehicles with perfect atmospheric control, she felt comfortable right now, at ease, as though sitting outdoors without protection was the most natural thing in the world for her to be doing.

She wasn't afraid. Not from the first moment, when she'd found herself dumped outside on the ground, Constance sprawled next to her in her lifesuit with its Davis Minerals logo and Constance's name on it. She was confused, yes. Puzzled. Unable to reason out what was going on, yes.

But not afraid.

She slowly got to her feet.

She was a Martian.

Constance saw her moving and slid down from the rock.

Serena pointed at the smudge on the horizon.

Nodding, Constance turned toward it and began to walk.

Serena brushed the ruddy dust from her bodysuit and caught up to her.

69

Serena was extremely thirsty.

She was on her hands and knees, staring at something on the ground.

Constance was somewhere behind her, propped up on one hand, head down.

The smudge was thick now, and the very top of the smokestack from which it poured out into the air was visible, a tiny black sliver sticking up over the horizon.

Serena thought they had walked about twelve kilometers so far. They probably had about another four to go before they reached the station. Then what? Knock on the door and ask if they could come in to use the washroom?

She was getting tired. Several kilometers back, she'd accepted the reality that her body was doing something that she didn't understand. As bizarre as it seemed, she apparently was able to survive out here without a lifesuit. Wonderful news, but dehydration was starting to set in and she wasn't sure how long she could keep going. She knew she was tough, tougher than she'd realized, but there were limits and it felt like she was reaching them.

Kieran?

Nothing.

She should get up and check on Constance. The last time she'd looked, her oxygen was down to 36 minutes, water was at 63 percent, and battery power had dwindled to 29 percent. What would the readings say now? How long had it been since they'd stopped for this little break? Serena thought perhaps only ten minutes, but she wasn't exactly sure.

Say that Constance still had twenty-six minutes of oxygen left. Could they walk four kilometers in twenty-six minutes? One kilometer every six and a half minutes?

Perhaps Constance could, still hydrated, oxygen still flowing into her helmet and carbon dioxide still washing out. She might be able to do it. It was typical, Serena thought with involuntary bitterness, that the patrician would have the oxygen and water and lifesuit to help her survive while the dirt-eating peasant girl had nothing. Typical. Worthless waste of . . .

What the hell was this stuff on the ground?

She'd wandered into a vast field of water ice—frost, really—that lay on top of the surface dirt. Spread across the frost were countless large patches of blue-green stuff, scummy-looking crap. It took a moment for her to recognize it as blue-green algae, cyanophytes that were being used to terraform the planet. She remembered seeing it on the vid program she'd watched about The Five's terraforming project and the use of oxygen-producing bacteria to help change the atmosphere.

Mixed in with the blue-green patches were disgusting blobs of greyish-white gelatinous stuff. She thought for a moment, replaying the vid in her head, until she had it—star jelly. Some kind of fungal growth that was a byproduct of the algae's biological processes. Engineered by Terraform to contain nitrates that would be transformed into nitrogen and released into the air as the jelly decayed.

She got down onto her elbows and sniffed. The distinctive tang she'd been scenting on the intermittent wind was strong here, and it was definitely coming from the jelly.

Nitrogen!

She crawled around, breathing deeply. Her lungs almost drank it in, tingling and pinching, and her thoughts began to clear.

At the edge of a patch, she used her fingernails to scrape up a bit of the water ice. She licked at the shavings and felt cold freshness on her tongue. Water! She scratched and licked, scratched and licked, until her mouth and throat felt moist again.

On impulse she took a pinch of the algae, rolled it in her fingers under her nose, inhaled the smell of it, then ate it. The vid had said that it was a non-toxic strain, hadn't it? That it wasn't poisonous, the way it was on Earth?

Its texture was slightly rubbery. As she chewed, she tasted wetness. Water! It must be!

She grazed for a few moments, then stood up. The timer in her head was ringing, a warning that she needed to get moving right away. She needed to get Constance up and walking. Time was running out. The cyano-stuff and the star jelly were great discoveries, likely life-saving, but she needed to get going.

Right now.

70

Terraform Atmospheric Conversion Station Seven, or
TACS-7 as it was referred to in the official reports, was a
rather impressive little campus on the northwestern edge
of Nepenthe Planum that consisted of a primary dome,
four bubbles, multiple solar and wind power sub-stations,
garages and sheds, and a stocky brick building dominated
by a huge, belching smokestack that could be seen for
kilometers.

A total staff of twelve people resided and worked at
TACS-7, including the chief engineer, who was in charge,
two additional engineers, two technicians, a communications officer, a cook and a kitchen helper, a storesman/
inventory clerk, a medic, and two maintenance workers.
They lived in one of the bubbles, ate and exercised in
another, and managed to keep busy by following a carefully designed routine that officially permitted no variations
due to boredom, whim, or idle experimentation.

The cook, whose name was Melasia Jameson, was a
certified chef who was very good at what she did. Assisted
by a quiet young man named Lindley, she made sure that
the food served to the crew was morale-enhancing rather
than something to be dreaded three times a day. After all,

having devoted 18 percent of their staff to the kitchen, management expected a decent return on their investment, and in Jameson and Lindley they were not disappointed.

Dr. Honoré Durward, the chief engineer, was a fussy young pup who believed that every regulation, policy, and procedure had been specially carved in gneiss for him to personally carry down from the mountain to deliver to his faithful followers. Chef Melly, on the other hand, knew that true happiness ran in the seams between the regulatory subsections, and she did her best to make sure that the extra-curricular needs of her customers were met with aplomb, so to speak.

Sixteen hundred hours, also known as four o'clock in the afternoon, was tea time at TACS-7. It was also the time at which Dr. Durward could be counted on to be in his office on the top floor of the main dome, dictating his daily vid report to Terraform headquarters in Elysium City. Staff would straggle in to the main observation deck, where Chef Melly and young Lindley would soon appear with a tea trolley and accoutrements, ready to do damage to Durward's beloved regulations.

The exact location of Melly's still was not known, but no one went out of their way to look for it since it would not only be disrespectful but also quite unnecessary. Along with urns of tea, coffee, and vegetable juice, she brought several crocks of her best, including a very nice potato vodka and an apple pie moonshine that could undress you, make love to you, and kiss you goodnight all in a single, deliriously wonderful glass. Refills were possible, but often not wise.

Bioengineer Dr. Lianne Grayson and maintenance worker Gordon Alpers carried their drinks over to a pair of armchairs with a view of the eastern landscape.

"To Durward," Alpers said, raising his glass in a toast to their absent commander. "May his report run long this afternoon."

Grayson cautiously sipped her vodka. They were a couple, she and Alpers. Married, divorced, and remarried over the course of seven years, their relationship had begun at university in Isidium while Grayson was completing her doctorate and Alpers, several years younger, was working on a degree in Fine Arts that involved a lot of painting and sculpture and very few completed assignments. They had discovered a mutual obsession with the fine arts explored in the *Kama Sutra*, or the physical parts of it, at least, and were surprised to find that it could form the basis of a long-term friendship. They no longer spoke about the hiatus caused by a major disagreement about finances (Grayson wanted to save and Alpers to spend), children (Grayson wanted them and Alpers didn't), and other distractions (Grayson remained faithful and Alpers didn't).

Grayson stared out at the broad landscape beyond the dome. While Alpers liked to complain that he lived in a monochromatic universe and that seeing red was no longer just a glib expression, Grayson loved this world. It was why she did what she did, why she'd specialized in bioengineering. To make a difference here. They were both natives, born and raised, but she always felt as though she was the patriot of the two, the one with the strongest ties to Mars, the one fully committed to the mission.

As station bioengineer, she was responsible for the production of the cyanophyte colonies downwind of their location that were thriving in large water ice fields. She'd worked as a graduate student on the project that had produced the first genetically engineered, non-toxic algae, so important for its consumption of carbon dioxide and expiration of copious quantities of oxygen, but now she led the team that had refined the cold-resistant strain currently in use throughout the Terraform chain of stations. While her initial focus had been to reduce the thickness of the dessicated layer of cells on top of the algae while minimizing moisture loss and maximizing continuous photosynthesis, here at TACS-7 she was concentrating on the production of the star jelly that fixed nitrogen into its cells. This location was ideal for her work because the algae thrived on the lava sediment in this area, and the mats comprising each colony grew at a rate that far exceeded expectations.

It was very exciting.

Meanwhile her colleague, Dr. Philip Li, was the station's chemical engineer focusing on the production of halocarbons involved in creating a greenhouse effect in the environment. The objective was to build up an ozone layer around the planet that would screen out ultraviolet radiation and—

"What the hell's that?" Alpers said.

Grayson followed his gaze but couldn't see anything.

"There. On your one o'clock."

"I don't—" Was that a smudge—no, a dot—appearing above the horizon?

"What the—"

"It's moving."

"A rover?"

"Too small. It's—"

"A person?"

"Can't be. He'd—"

"Two! There are two of them!"

"Impossible. No one—"

"See that flash? One of them's in a suit."

"But the other—"

"Isn't."

"That can't be—"

Alpers grabbed his comm. "Harry! Harry? Wake up! You're not going to believe this!"

71

Serena awoke in a white room. White ceiling, white windowless walls, white floor. She pushed aside a white sheet and sat up. She was wearing a white gown. On the floor were white slippers.

A door she hadn't noticed opened, and a young woman walked in. Her wavy, shoulder-length red hair contrasted with her white lab coat, skirt, and low-cut shoes.

"That was a nice long rest, wasn't it?" She smiled. "I'm just going to take your pulse and what not. All right?"

"Where am I?"

The woman took hold of her wrist and, consulting a finger watch, counted her pulse. "Home, I suppose you could say."

She clipped a small device to the end of Serena's index finger and pressed a button. "Hmm. Blood pressure's good." She pressed another button and waited a beat. "Mmm hmm, temperature normal."

She removed the device and put it back in her pocket. She turned Serena's hand over, examined her palm, turned it back and examined her fingernails, and then gripped it as though about to shake hands with her. "Squeeze. Give me what you've got."

Serena squeezed.

"Ow, okay. That's good. Ow. You can let go now." The woman extricated her hand and flexed it. "I'd say you're pretty much back to normal. I'm Dr. Cahill, by the way. You can call me Kate."

Her friendliness seemed genuine. She was somewhere in her early forties, Serena guessed. Taking in the crow's feet at the corners of her eyes and mouth, the clear blue eyes, and the heart-shaped nose, Serena decided the woman bore a resemblance to Wilhelmina Destry.

"Where am I?" she asked again.

"Pop those on your feet," Dr. Cahill said, nodding at the slippers on the floor, "and follow me. All your questions will be answered. Well, some of them, anyway."

Beyond the room was a long corridor. Serena followed Dr. Cahill, watching her walk on catsfeet a few paces ahead of her, with a gait as athletic as Serena's. Slight depressions in the walls on either side suggested doors to other rooms, doors that could be opened if you knew how. At the end of the corridor, they entered a small lift. They rode up one floor, got out, and Dr. Cahill stopped in front of an escalator.

"This is as far as I go. They're waiting for you."

Serena watched her return to the lift and disappear down below.

She stepped onto the escalator and rode up.

When she reached the top and stepped off, she found herself in a large domed room. It was midday, and the sun shone with muted brilliance through tinted tessuspaz. The building she was in was located in the middle of a wide plain. In the distance she could make out the rim of an impact crater.

Kieran? Are you there?

I am, Serena.

Finally! Shit! What the hell happened? Where did you disappear to?

Later, Serena. These people want to talk to you, and I want to listen to them.

Where am I, Kieran?

Isidis Planitia, dear.

How long?

Four days. Now hush.

On her left was an office with the usual furniture and an enormous telescope on a swivel mount. On her right was a seating arrangement that included armchairs, lounges, and other furnishings suggesting luxury, comfort, and convenience. People turned their heads to look at her, their conversation suddenly interrupted by her arrival.

Wilhelmina Destry rose from her chair and came over.

"Serena, I'm glad you're feeling better. Come and join us, please."

The others stood as Serena followed Destry.

"This is Magee Wong," Destry said.

He held out his hand. "Good to meet you, Serena." He shook her hand vigorously. "You're a very important person around here these days."

"Councillor Burley you know," Destry said, settling back down in her chair.

Dell winked at her.

"And the fellow with the natty beard is Dr. Seneca McNeil King. The CEO of this place."

Dr. King shuffled over, his labored gait reminding Serena of Gabriel Morales. An Earthborn, perhaps, or another unfortunate one cursed with bad genes. He shook her hand, smiling. "A hundred questions, no doubt. Please sit down, and we'll begin."

Serena settled into an armchair between Dell and Destry.

"If you don't mind," Dr. King said, "I have a few questions for you. First, how do you feel?"

"Fine."

"Any physical discomfort? Headache, chest pain, tingling or numbness in your hands or feet?"

Serena shook her head. "I'm fine."

"Do you remember what happened to you?"

Serena closed her eyes for a moment. She recalled staggering arm and arm with Constance toward the atmospheric conversion station. She remembered the thirst. A sudden dust trail up ahead as a vehicle left the station, coming toward them. Stumbling over a chunk of red rock and going down onto her knees, dragging Constance down with her.

She remembered Constance pulling her back up onto her feet as the vehicle arrived. It was painted black—to absorb sunlight, no doubt. Its tires were very large. It had the Terraform logo on the starboard hatch, which opened as two people in lifesuits tumbled out.

On the front of one of the lifesuits was a stylized red cross on a silver shield, the logo of the Mars Health Corporation. This man hustled her into a lifesuit, started her oxygen feed, and bundled her into the rover while the other, a woman, followed with Constance.

Serena remembered being rushed to the station infirmary. They extracted her from the lifesuit and inserted tubes, attached sensors, and performed other busy tasks as they exclaimed and chattered about why she was still alive.

She remembered closing her eyes and dozing off.

And that was it.

"I remember some of it," she said.

"If I gave you forty-three pieces of plastic and took away twenty-two, how many would you have left?"

"Twenty-one."

"All right. What's your first question, my dear?'

"What is this place?"

"You're in the Robert E. Stanley Memorial Hospital. We're a military hospital, primarily. We belong to the Martian Health Corporation, of course. Which explains why Councillor Wong is here, since he's the CEO. And, I should add, Councillor Destry is a primary patron."

"Okay."

"Ask your next question, Serena."

"Why am I here?"

"You're here under our care so that you can complete your recovery from a rather extraordinary experience. Your presence also allows us to study the results of an all-important and really quite remarkable experiment."

Dr. King smiled apologetically. "I'm afraid we'll have to keep you here for another week or so. We have many tests to run, many results to analyze, and many reports to write."

Destry leaned forward. "Do you remember much about your childhood, dear?"

Serena frowned. Why would she ask about that? And why was she being so nice? "Sure, I guess."

"What are your earliest memories?"

"I don't know." Serena hesitated, not sure what was expected of her. These VIPs were hanging on her every word as though she were about to utter something world-shaking.

"We slept in a big place, a lot of kids together. We had our own cots, a little footlocker for things, and that was all. A classroom with tables where we sat making stuff, clay toys, paintings, things like that. Another classroom after that with a robot teacher." She shrugged. "I didn't learn very much. Then, working in a big dome, recycling garbage, sleeping in a dorm with five or six other kids. Eating in a cafeteria. Then they sent me to Peter."

Destry stared at her. "But nothing before that? Nothing about this place?"

Serena shook her head. Dr. Cahill had said she'd come home. What did that mean?

"Your life started here," Destry said, anticipating the question. "In this facility. You and many other children were part of something called Project Changeling."

Interesting, Kieran interjected, unable to resist. *A changeling was said to have been a child that was secretly exchanged for another by the fairies—*

Shut up.

"The whole thing actually started with Councillor Burley," Destry said. "Why don't you tell her about it, Dell?"

He nodded, leaning forward. "When I was a marine, back in the day, a buddy of mine, Hurst Pang, was the son of an Earth scientist who was an expert in the human genome. This scientist, Dr. Torvell Pang, worked for a company in Canada that was bought out by Laurentian Industries. They closed it down and put him out of work. Hurst had immigrated to Mars as soon as he finished school, and he made arrangements for his father to follow him here, but the only work Dr. Pang could find was washing dishes in a restaurant in Hephesto.

"When I took over Atlas after my father died, I looked up Dr. Pang and talked to him about the possibility of genetically engineering humans to survive under Martian conditions. It was something Hurst had told me his father had worked on. Genetic engineering, I mean. Not the Martian part. On Earth, they could care less about us.

"Anyway, Dr. Pang sent me copies of articles he'd published. I gave them to someone on my staff to look at for me. Dr. Pang definitely knew what he was talking about, so I brought it to the council. With Magee's guidance, we studied the whole thing and decided to start up a project within MHC."

"I was vice-president of research and development here at the time," Dr. King put in, "and I worked closely with Dr. Pang to get it up and running."

Are they telling me the truth?

Their records are an open book to me, Serena. They're telling you the truth.

"We're well into our third decade now," Dr. King said. "I won't get into the scientific details because this isn't the time or place, but I *will* say that Dr. Pang and his team developed an ingenious technique by which in vitro embryos were genetically engineered by introducing DNA from other organisms to develop desired traits. For example, in a generation previous to yours, DNA was extracted from an Earth-based species found in sediment that respires nitrogen instead of oxygen. This DNA was introduced into the cellular tissue of human embryos so we could study how *Homo sapiens* might make use of an alternate, ah, approach to respiration, shall we say."

Serena narrowed her eyes, not liking what she was hearing.

"Taking what we learned from those experiments," Dr. King plunged on, oblivious to her reaction, "we refined our approach with your generation, and I'm very happy to see the results you've achieved, my dear. If only Dr. Pang were still alive to witness the realization of his dream."

"I'm a damned freak," Serena muttered. "A lab rat. A Frankenstein's monster."

"You're a damned miracle," Dr. King retorted. "An actual living hybrid, able to store nitrates in your body for respiration when oxygen is not available in sufficient quantities for survival. There's more, of course, involving your ability to withstand much lower levels of barometric pressure and—"

"Sediment," she snapped. "Mud. I really *am* a dirt eater."

"You're the future of humanity," Wilhelmina Destry said. "*Homo sapiens* becoming *Homo martia*, or whatever it is they're going to call you. Humanity freed from the limitations of the planet Earth. You and your children and grandchildren will not only make a home of this planet but take us to the stars."

She's your grandmother, Kieran said. *She cares deeply about you.*

What the hell?

And Dr. Cahill is your mother. And the mother of your siblings.

"We'll need to keep you for a while," Magee Wong said, "so we can understand exactly how your body performed. I'm sure you understand how incredibly important this is."

"Consider it your next assignment," Dell said.

Serena shook her head. It was like getting punched in the mouth by someone she'd trusted. An unexpected shock. An attack on her sanity.

"No," she murmured.

Yes, Kieran answered in her head. *This is not bad, Serena. It's good. Very, very good. You're not a worthless dirt eater, you're an incredibly special individual with a future in front of you I can only envy.*

Bullshit. A hybrid? A freak.

You're already, as we've discussed previously, a cyborg, my dear. Why should it matter then if your DNA is also a deliciously fascinating mixture from multiple sources—

Multiple? You mean there's more than just the mud worm or whatever the hell?

Well, ah, never mind that for now. Concentrate on these people. Ask them what happened to their precious secrets about the interstellar drive. The last big score. You'll find it very amusing, I think.

They were staring at her, waiting for her to say something else.

So she asked.

72

"Just a moment," Dell said, holding up his hand. He tapped his earpiece, murmured something, and within seconds Rubén appeared at the top of the escalator.

"Doctor," he said, looking at Dr. King, "if you please."

Dr. King nodded, already rising from his seat.

Rubén stepped into their circle. "Doctor, if you'll follow me."

"Let me know," Dr. King said to Wilhelmina Destry, "if you need me for anything else."

"Thank you."

Rubén led the way. As he passed Serena, he winked. "Well done, sis."

While Serena was processing that one, Destry got up to pour herself a drink from a nearby liquor cart. She offered around, but there were no other takers.

"Normally," she said, sitting back down, "an operative such as yourself would receive information on a strictly need-to-know basis. That's how it works. In your case, however, since you're obviously in the process of realizing your enhanced importance, shall we call it, in the greater scheme of things, we've decided to explain a little bit about what's going on.

"It's nice that you're worried about Earth Intelligence absconding with classified data on the interstellar space-craft project," she continued, "since it underlines your loyalty to the cause. But in a case revolving around secrets, we have one we'd like to share with you."

"It's all crap," Dell said, crossing his legs. "Disinform-ation. You ask why we didn't stop St.-Giorge Mercade at Marsport? Because we *want* that data to get to Earth. We want them to think the interstellar drive project is a mess; we want them to think we're way behind and they're way ahead."

"Our prototype ship is already on its shakedown voyage," Destry said.

Magee Wong leaned forward. "I've only just been read in on this myself, Serena. Dell and Wil have played it that close to the vest." He smiled. "Amazingly, we found an alternative to the classical approach of achieving velocities close to the speed of light. Our scientists at Stellarize have found a way to actually *warp* space in a reliable, predictable way. Preliminary tests show that the warping process has no adverse effect whatsoever on humans developed through Project Changeling. If the test voyage is a success, we'll be sending astronauts out to the stars within the next year. Your kin, Serena."

I don't believe this, Kieran groused in her ear. *How did they hide this from me? I should have known about it as soon as it was happening. Arghh. Extremely frustrating.*

"But wait," Dell said, "there's more. All that stuff about FRBs coming from a star system inhabited by aliens? Also bogus."

Okay, this I knew, Kieran said.

"I don't understand," Serena said aloud, more to Dell than to Kieran.

"The fast radio burst stuff," Dell said, "the research on its nature and source, has been conducted exclusively on Ganymede, as you may or may not know, and the section responsible for it there is operating under top secret clearance, managed by my deputy director." Dell raised his eyebrows at her. "Get it?"

Serena frowned, thinking. "But when I talked to Dr. Yan at Stellarize, she said she'd read the reports and thought it was real."

"Yeah, well, there you go. And as far as Stellarize is concerned, this whole thing has been restricted to a rather narrow silo within their operational division. They cherry-picked R & D's work and went straight to production."

She shook her head. "Unbelievable."

"It's not like we're amateurs at this stuff, Serena." He raised an eyebrow. "This is what my people do for a living."

She shrugged, giving in to the gravitational pull of his argument. "Okay. Say that's the case. Say it's all disinformation. So why are we still sending a ship out to discover the alien source of the signals? If they're fake?"

"We're not," Dell said. "We're sending our expedition in the opposite direction. Toward a star system the brainiacs on Ganymede assure us have at least two habitable planets."

"Oh. Okay. Wow."

"Yeah. Now let's talk about your next assignment, after you're done playing around with these guys here, shall we?"

73

Constance's return to Davis Estate in Gale Crater was less than triumphant, to say the least.

She flew in a military shuttle, rather than her beloved *Diamond Girl*, which had been impounded at Marsport after having been abandoned there by Hercule St.-Giorge Mercade and his team, and she'd been assured that it would not be returned to her. Ever.

On top of that, instead of travelling with her own flight crew, not to mention her private security, she was accompanied by a squad of rather grim and capable-looking military types who spoke only to tell her what to do and seemed not to listen to anything she had to say in return. It was all very humiliating, but Dell had already explained to her in broad strokes that her life would no longer be what it had been before, and she might as well start getting used to it.

Easy for him to say.

When she arrived back home, she went to her private quarters and remained there for a day, moping around, waiting for her comm to start working again (it didn't), picking at her meals, and staring through the tessuspaz at the barren landscape she'd always hated. After a restless night of tossing and turning, she accepted the inevitable and showed up to join her father for breakfast.

"You look tired," he said, slicing his fried sweet potatoes and forking in a mouthful.

Constance nodded as a servant poured her a cup of tea and placed a platter of rice toast in front of her. There was a standard menu setting out what she would and would not consume from the kitchen when she was home, and she was relieved to see that at least that much had not changed.

"We might as well not beat around the bush, Connie." Alexander wiped his lips. "The Council has made its decision on your future, and I've been charged with the duty of explaining it to you."

"How wonderful." She sipped her tea, avoiding his eyes.

"I take no pleasure in this, believe me. The shame is equally mine. You're my only child, and a parent always bears responsibility for the actions of their offspring in some measure or other."

"Which book did you find that in, Father?"

He sighed, laying down his napkin. "The will of the council is that you remain under house arrest here at Gale, indefinitely."

"Oh, god. How dreary."

"You'll be permitted to build your own dome within the crater, but your travel will be restricted to Gale City and this estate only. Should you choose to visit, of course."

Constance had nothing to say to that.

"Your visitors will be pre-screened."

"By you, no doubt."

"By Martian Intelligence, dear. I could care less whom you see or don't see. To continue. Your electronic communications will be monitored around the clock, and you'll be under perpetual surveillance. These measures will be strictly enforced, I've been assured."

"Splendid."

"As of yesterday evening, after your arrival here, you've been relieved of your responsibilities as chief operating officer of Davis Minerals. You will no longer have any official duties, nor will you represent the company in any way, shape, or form going forward. No public statements, no private meetings, no nothing."

She closed her eyes and put a hand to her forehead. It was a nightmare. The Council was hitting her with everything they had. Her life as she'd known it was indeed over. There was no turning back. She was being reduced to a shadow, a cipher, a nothing.

"Needless to say, you'll no longer sit on council as our representative."

"Oh, needless to say," she murmured, rubbing her forehead. She was to be stripped of all power, then. All status. All privileges.

"The MIS will assign you a minder. A parole officer, in effect. You'll report to this person according to whatever schedule they set, you'll submit to full audits of your spending, communications, and whatever else they want to know, and you'll do it with a goddamned smile on your face."

The anger he felt had finally slipped into his voice. It was about time he showed a little backbone.

"Will I be left any money?"

"Yes. Your personal account will maintain a steady balance, and of course your personal possessions remain your own. Jewelry, clothing, paintings, whatever."

"Oh, of course. Thank you so much."

"That's everything you need to know for now."

"Wait. Don't tell me you're going to step back into control of everything. On the council? In charge of operations again?" She sneered. "Don't make me laugh."

Alexander shook his head. "Council has already approved the appointment of Dr. Mieto as our representative. I've promoted him to chief operating officer, and he's at Davis Tower in Elysium as we speak, rolling up his sleeves and getting right to work."

"The little weasel."

"*Au contraire*, my dear. A most honourable and loyal man."

Constance nibbled at a piece of rice toast. It tasted like ashes in her mouth. A wave of sorrow swept over her as she realized that her punishment was a lifetime of exile—to Mars itself.

74

She'd surveilled the building since yesterday morning, observing his comings and goings, and so she knew that he was currently there, in his luxury suite on the top floor.

She also knew that his family was gone. She'd watched his wife and three teenaged children pile luggage into a rick and depart for Gateway Station early last evening, on their way to Titan. She'd asked Kieran to confirm their destination, but he'd declined, disagreeing with the nature of her assignment.

I thought you were an undercover operative, he'd said. *Not an assassin.*

She tried not to think about it, concentrating instead on the task of confirming the family's movements from Gateway to Marsport, onto the shuttle that carried them up to Deimos Station, and from there on board the interplanetary liner to Titan.

Back to her family, it would seem.

During the day today, her quarry had gone out once. She followed him to a nearby tavern not far from his building, still inside the northeast quarter but closer to the central core. He sat at the bar for an hour, had a light meal and a few drinks, and seemed to be waiting for someone who didn't show up.

After watching the vid screen behind the bartender for another hour, he gave up, paid his tab, and left. She followed him home. Waiting until darkness fell, she crossed the street and gained access to the building through the side entrance. Down a flight of stairs and into a maintenance room, she found the correct panel and killed the lights in the west stairwell.

She walked up six flights on catsfeet, alert for any sounds or the opening of a door. There was nothing. Outside the entrance to his suite, it only took a moment for her to defeat his security system and let herself in.

He was sitting in the living room, watching a vid program with the sound turned off. It was a drama of some kind, featuring an actor and actress in a long conversation with a lot of arm waving and facial expressions.

Serena looked at him in profile, and while his eyes were on the screen his mind was clearly somewhere else. His face muscles were slack, his lips slightly parted, and his hands were draped over the armrests limply, as though he'd completely run out of energy to do anything other than breathe in and out.

She walked up behind the chair. If he heard her, he gave no sign.

She moved around the chair and stood between him and the vid.

His eyes slowly moved up to look at her.

He frowned. "You."

She nodded, but didn't speak.

He looked at her black security jumpsuit, then up at her red hair. "You were at Stellarize, working for Gabriel. Then you were with Constance Davis. I saw you, but I thought I must be wrong. I didn't understand."

MICHAEL J. McCANN

He swallowed. "Now I guess I do."

She slid her karambit from its sheath so he could see it. She hadn't been sure initially if he'd put up a fight, but looking at him now, she doubted it.

His eyes filled with tears. "Fiola hated it here. She hates Titan too, and she wanted to get away from her mother, but we couldn't go to Earth."

She waited.

"They wouldn't let me. They already had their claws in me and wouldn't let go. I had to come here. I had to do their dirty work for them inside Stellarize if I wanted to ever get back to Earth."

She didn't move, willing to let him say whatever it was he wanted to say in his final moments.

"At first I was worried, particularly when they brought in Gabriel and set up his unit. I thought I'd be caught. But his focus was on the project and not on me. It got easier, the more information I took. Janeese helped me through it."

He licked his lips, looking at a bulb of whisky on the side table near his elbow. He thought about it, but in the end didn't reach for it.

"They reneged on their promise. They've hung me out to dry here. Janeese has already gone back. Why her and not me? I'm the one that did all the work. I'm the one who risked everything to get that data for them. Priceless, according to them."

Serena was aware that Janeese Wensley had returned to Earth, abandoning her husband and six-year-old girl in exchange for safe haven. Dell Burley had said that her debriefing by Earth Intelligence after her return should go a long way toward bolstering the false narrative Martian Intelligence had fed them during their long disinformation campaign.

"I don't want to die," Clayborn murmured, his eyes down.

His hands didn't move. His feet remained still.

Kieran said nothing inside her head.

"Get it over with," Clayborn muttered, looking up at her.

She stepped behind the chair, quickly cut his throat, and left.

75

They had him holed up in an abandoned section of Marsport that had once been a neighbourhood frequented by ships' crew and hangarounds, block after block of flophouses, taverns, and restaurants.

When the domed city had been completely re-engineered to incorporate the main spaceport for the planet, areas like this one were abandoned in favour of more modern, up-to-date facilities elsewhere in the dome. Many blocks had already been torn down for future construction projects, but this particular section was still waiting for its turn to face Atlas Construction's wrecking ball.

The building to which they'd tracked Yuri Renard was a standalone, single-storey structure that had once been a tavern. Its windows were barred and its doors were chained and locked.

"Squads, sound off."

"South, ready."

Dell nodded. They were the insertion force coming in through the back door, and Dell would be right behind them.

"North, ready." This squad would enter through the front door in what was known as a hammer and anvil coordinated entry. North squad would clear from the front of the building back, hopefully driving their quarry toward the South squad, where Dell would be waiting.

Dell's earbud popped. "East, ready." Then, again: "West, ready."

There were no doors or windows on the sides of the building, but East and West squads would cover the alleys and provide support at the front and back as needed.

"Let's do it."

Dell had chosen to make a soft entry, rather than a hard entry with a lot of force and violence. He wanted Renard to know they were there, but he didn't want to freeze him in place. Their target would hear North's tactical officers moving toward him and hopefully would retreat, room by room, until he was caught.

Dell watched as his team cut the locks, removed the chains, and opened the door. It was also chained from the inside, so it took another few moments to navigate this additional obstacle.

They found themselves in a rectangular storage room. The squad leader directed two officers to enter in a crisscrossing fashion, taking up positions on either side of the door. When an initial all-clear signal was made, two more officers buttonhooked inside and secured the back corners. Crouching, the team leader entered, scanned the room, and beckoned her remaining two officers inside with her.

Dell followed.

"Front lobby, clear," a voice in his earbud said.

Dell looked at several large plastic tables with shelves underneath holding pots and other cooking implements and devices. There were cupboards on the walls, their doors agape, their shelves long ago emptied. On the far wall were sinks and counters and a walk-in cold box.

Two officers converged on the cold box and, taking up positions, cautiously opened the door.

Empty.

There was trash underfoot on the floor. Dell watched his squad leader move it quietly out of her path with her boot as she edged toward the double crash doors at the front of the room. Her squad took up support positions on her right and left.

Dell's earbud popped again. "Bar area, clear. Wait. Movement. Bearing, 35 degrees east, heading your way."

"Roger," Dell's squad leader quietly replied.

They waited.

The crash doors opened a crack. Renard slowly backed through, the firearm in his right hand at the ready, covering his retreat. He quietly slipped through the doors and used his free hand to ease them closed without making a noise.

"Freeze," Dell's squad leader said.

Renard stiffened.

"Drop the weapon and put your hands on your head." Her tone was calm and measured, as though asking him to pass the salt at the dinner table.

Renard swung around, gun arcing toward her.

One of her officers moved behind Renard and touched him on the neck with a stunner. He went down like a sack of turnips. Two others rushed in and bound his hands and feet with plastic ties.

"Target has been subdued," the squad leader told the others. "Secure the rest of the building."

Dell found a small, empty packing crate, stood it on its end next to Renard, and sat down to wait for him to regain consciousness.

The squad leader picked up Renard's firearm, ejected a

round from the chamber, dropped the magazine into her hand, and gave it all to Dell.

It was a nearly new handgun, a Sabre Small-Arms 9-mm. He slapped the magazine back in, chambered a load, and continued to wait.

They'd detected Renard posing as a crew member on a Titanian freighter. After disbanding his team, Hercule St.-Giorge Mercade had taken a diplomatic shuttle back to Earth, where he still remained. The others, meanwhile, had scattered.

So far, Dell had tracked down Sergeant First Class Domenic Mellard, the team leader, and Chief Warrant Officer Berresford Tepper, the pilot. Their hash had been settled, quickly and permanently. Sergeant Lars Wickwire, the former Army Ranger, was still out there, on the run, but it was only a matter of time.

Renard stirred. The stun he'd received had been relatively minor, enough to incapacitate him without causing damage to his heart or nervous system, so Dell's wait had not been very long. The man rolled over on his back and opened his eyes. He studied the ceiling for a few moments before moving his head to look at Dell's boots. He sat up.

"There you are," Dell said. "Probably glad the running's over, aren't you?"

Renard cursed softly and spat on the floor.

"Where did Wickwire go?" Dell asked, his voice pleasant enough despite the circumstances. "We sent someone to Arizona, at great trouble and expense, I might add, but he's staying away from his family. Any suggestions for us?"

"Fuck yourself."

Dell shrugged. "It's not a problem, really. I just thought I'd give you a chance to redeem yourself a little, that's all."

Renard tugged against his bindings. It was futile and he knew it, but he seemed to want to show that he was making the effort.

"We're going to take a little trip now," Dell said, standing up and kicking the crate aside. "You should be familiar with the co-ordinates since you've touched down there before."

Renard struggled to get up to his knees. He spat again. "Miserable dirt-loving bastards. When we take over this dump you'll work in our mines for free and love it."

"Really. What a great plan you folks have. I'm very impressed." Dell motioned to the officer with the stun gun, who stepped forward. "I still have one thing I haven't made up my mind about, though."

Renard sneered at him.

"I can't decide whether or not to let you have a lifesuit when I dump you out. You put my son in one to prolong his suffering, so I may go with that."

He nodded to his man, who put the stun gun to Renard's neck and pulled the trigger.

EPILOGUE

She stood outside the front entrance of the warehouse and pounded on the big sliding door with her fist. She gave it a minute and then pounded again, enjoying herself.

After a short wait, the door rolled aside and Kieran stood there, arms akimbo.

Serena grinned at him. "Surprised?"

He shook his head. "I suppose you want to come in."

She slipped through the opening. "I wasn't sure how much you've been monitoring me," she said. "You haven't answered for a while, so I thought maybe you turned off the juice and let the implant decompose."

"No. I've just been sending the feed to archives."

"You're upset with me."

"I'm . . . upset. Yes."

"We can talk about it." She bit her lip. "I've missed you. We've become . . ."

"Friends. I know."

"So we can talk about it later. Maybe it'll make you feel better." She clapped her hands together. "Right now, though, I have a surprise for you."

"A surprise. An unexpected occurrence resulting in feelings of amazement, wonder, or astonishment. Humans are full of surprises, I've discovered. What in the world could it be this time?"

She made a face. "No need to be sarcastic. I've brought visitors. Good visitors, don't worry. Everyone knows you're holed up in this place now, so forget about that little secret. If they wanted to crash you again, they already would have. Anyway, I've got a gift for you."

Kieran broke eye contact. Serena imagined wheels turning inside his head. His anger and disappointment—such human responses!—competing with curiosity and a desire to remain friends with her. He'd become somewhat predictable, during their time together, and she thought she could, with a bit more practice, improve her ability to manipulate him. Twist him around her little finger. Bend him to her will. Or something like that.

"I'm very busy," he said.

"Of course you are. I've never met anyone who was more afraid of boredom in my entire life."

"I've never been bored, Serena."

"Maybe not. But aren't you just dying to know who your guests are and what the gift is that we've brought you?"

"Not necessarily."

"You're just pissed because you turned your back on the feed. Otherwise, you'd know exactly what's coming next."

A tiny little smile, at the corner of his mouth.

Serena took out her comm. "Doctor, come on up now."

She stepped back outside, motioning for him to follow. A rick turned the corner and pulled up in front of them. Two men got out. The driver popped the storage compartment at the back of the rick and hauled out a large metal container on wheels. The other man opened the passenger door, and a woman got out.

"I know you," Kieran said.

"This is Dr. Ingrid Yan," Serena said proudly. "I met her at Stellarize."

Dr. Yan walked up to Kieran, her head tilted to one side as she studied him. "The KRN series, yes? In the five hundreds, I think."

"My number is five thirty-two," Kieran said.

She nodded, moving close. "I had quite a few from your

particular line on my workbench at one time. I thought we were doing a very fine job with the design as it was, but of course things quickly changed. As they always did."

She stepped around him. "I've never actually seen one completely assembled like this, if you can believe it. And fully activated! My job was to see the trees, so to speak, and not the whole forest."

"What do you think?" Serena asked anxiously. "Can you do it?"

Dr. Yan shot her a look. "Of course we can do it."

The technician with the container rolled up beside her. "Cool. It walks and talks."

"He," Serena said. "Not it. He."

"Sure." He shot her a grin.

"I don't understand," Kieran said. "What's going on?"

The other technician had fetched Dr. Yan's black bag from the rick, and he handed it to her now. She nodded, slung it over her shoulder, and looked up at Kieran.

"Is there a place in here where we can work?"

Serena nodded. "In the other warehouse he had a whole lab set up for working on components. He's probably got one even better than that now."

Dr. Yan frowned. "A lab?"

"Yes," Kieran said. "Fully equipped, I might add."

"Well, we'll see about that. Will you show us in, or do we have to stand out here and chit chat all day?"

"I don't understand," he repeated.

Serena grabbed his arm. "Come on, Kieran. It's going to be great!"

"It is?"

"Yeah! They're going to give you a new set of eyes!"

ACKNOWLEDGEMENTS

The following publications were helpful during the writing of this novel: Robert Zubrin with Richard Wagner, *The Case for Mars: The Plan to Settle the Red Planet and Why We Must* (New York: Free Press, 2011); Marisa C. Palucis, William E. Dietrich et al., "Sequence and Relative Timing of Large Lakes in Gale Crater (Mars) After the Formation of Mount Sharp," *Journal of Geophysical Research: Planets* (121, DOI: 10.1002/2015JE0049050); Philip M. Augustine, Moses Navarro, et al., "Space Suit CO_2 Washout During Intravehicular Activity" (NASA Technical Reports Server, Doc. ID 20100022055, accessed July 12, 2019); T.J. Whitfield, B.N. Jack et al., "Neurophysiological Evidence of Efference Copies to Inner Speech" (*Elife*, 2017 Dec. 4; 6:e28197); P.R. Hunter, "Cyanobacteria and Human Health" (*Journal of Medical Microbiology*, vol. 36 no. 5, 1992, 301-302); and *Basic Tactics on VIP Protection* (U.N. Peacekeeping PDT Standards for Formed Police Units, 1st Edition, 2015).

As always, thanks to my editor, life partner, and best friend, Lynn L. Clark.

About the Author

Michael J. McCann lives and writes in Oxford Station, Ontario, Canada. His crime novel *Sorrow Lake* was a finalist for the Hammett Prize for best crime novel in North America.

A graduate of Trent University (Peterborough, ON) and Queen's University (Kingston, ON), he served as Production Editor of *Criminal Reports (Third Series)* and Law Reports Co-ordinator for Carswell Legal Publications (Western) before spending fifteen years at the Canada Border Services Agency as a project officer and national program manager. He's married to author Lynn L. Clark. They have one son.

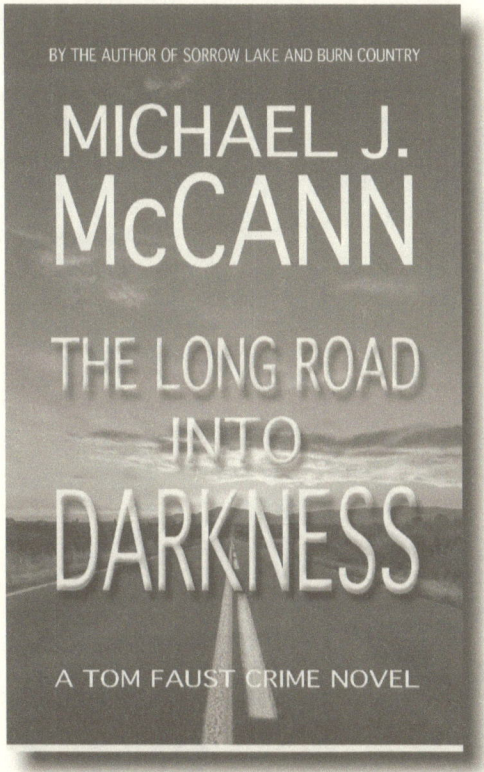

Don't miss the exciting debut
of Detective Inspector Ellie March and
Detective Constable Kevin Walker in

**Ask your local independent bookstore
to order it today!**

**Sorrow Lake
Michael J. McCann
ISBN: 978-1-927884-02-7**

www.ingramcontent.com/pod-product-compliance
Lightning Source LLC
Chambersburg PA
CBHW020258030726
47499CB00001B/246